STAR
in the
MIDDLE

*It is with sincere gratitude and devotion
that I dedicate this book—*

In memory of my mother, Frances Larese

—my first, and best, teacher.

STAR
in the
MIDDLE

Carol Larese Millward

WestSide Books
Lodi, New Jersey

Published by WestSide Books
60 Industrial Road
Lodi, NJ 07644
973-458-0485
Fax: 973-458-5289

Library of Congress Control Number: 2009930789

International Standard Book Number: 978-1-934813-13-3
School ISBN: 978-1-934813-29-4
Cover design by Chinedum Chukwu & Amy Kolenut
Interior design by David Lemanowicz

Printed in the United States of America
10 9 8 7 6 5 4 3 2 1

First Edition

STAR
in the
MIDDLE

1
Star

Grandma was really mad about the baby. Okay, so I screwed up, but I didn't do it to mess with her. I was prepared for hollering, not crying. I could barely look at her snotty nose and her red eyes. Why'd she go and act like that anyway?

She said to me, "Star, how could you do this to me?" Like I didn't feel bad enough.

I hid it from her as long as I could. I wanted to wait until my sixteenth birthday to tell her, but you can't hide a baby forever. It's, like, sticking out all over the place before you know it. Anyway, the baby didn't wait around for my sixteenth birthday. What did he care how old I was when he came into the world?

Wilson lied to me. He said it took a long time to get pregnant. He said even if I did manage to get myself pregnant, he'd stick by me. I didn't get myself pregnant; I had some help. And yeah, he's around all right, when it's convenient for him. He's still this big jock at school, and I'm a high school dropout. Dropout loser, that's me.

He's just like my parents. My father ran out on my

mother when she was pregnant with me, then she dumped me on my grandmother and disappeared. Grandma tried to find her. She said she raised her own kids, so why should she get stuck with me? Good question.

Here's another good question: *Where do you look for a mother?*

I wasted a lot of years searching for her in my dreams. I found her, too. She was the best mother ever. Sometimes we'd be cruising in a car with a heater that worked. Sometimes we'd be in the grocery store—with enough money to buy milk and eggs at the same time. Trouble was, by morning she was gone, gone, gone. Gone with my dreams of reliable transportation and groceries.

I guess now the prom has the same chance of happening for me as finding my mother.

Baby Wil isn't going to spend his life wondering whether his mother's dead or alive. I'm going to stick to him like glue. And Wilson, I told him to make up his mind—either he's here for us, or he's not. I told him I wanted his answer tonight.

Now, if this baby would just cooperate and go to sleep, I could think about what I want to say. What do you say to convince a guy that he has to change to keep a baby he never wanted in the first place?

Maybe if the baby looked more like Wilson....Wilson would probably like that. But you know, babies don't really look like anybody. People say they do, but they don't. Wil has a round bald head and sleepy blue eyes. He smells good, too—thanks to me. I keep my baby real clean. Grandma says that no matter how little you have, you can afford to keep your baby clean.

Star in the Middle

I like the way Wilson looks. He has thick, sandy brown hair and wild dark eyes. I liked the way he smelled, too. In school that is, when he leaned against my locker and told me how pretty I looked. He smelled clean then, like soap. He doesn't smell that great now. Mostly, he smells like beer. It's an off-season thing, he says. I guess he can abuse his body when he's not playing sports.

A baby needs so many things: formula, clothes, and diapers. Miss Marcie hooked me up with some programs that help teen mothers, like WIC, or Women, Infants, and Children, which provides formula. But Grandma said she didn't want any handouts. She says she hates handouts. But babies cost a fortune. And what teenager has a fortune? I sure don't. Grandma doesn't either. She already works two jobs.

At least Wilson lives in a decent house with his parents and his sister. At least Wilson has his own car and his own room, and his own spending money. I thought maybe Wilson's parents would want to help with his baby, their grandson. But Wilson said they don't even want to hear about it. It? I remind him that Wil's not an 'it'—he's his child.

Grandma's furious with Wilson for not helping with the baby. She said there is no excuse for him not to step up and be a man.

Wil is not easy. He needs me for everything. When he's hungry, he wants food now. And when he's not sleepy, forget making him sleep. I used to beg. Crazy, huh? Begging a baby to go to sleep is like begging your body to produce a period when it's intent on producing a baby instead. Wil doesn't care that I'm sleepy—he wants to be held and cuddled.

Right now, for instance, I should be getting ready for Wilson. I mean, I'm still wearing yesterday's clothes and I have spit-up in my hair. How attractive is that?

"Please go to sleep, Wil. Please, please, PLEASE." See how easy it is to fall into begging a baby? "Really, Wil, your father will be here any minute. I told him Grandma's out for the night. That got his attention. I see I have your attention, too. Look at your smile. Maybe you do have your daddy's dimples. Your crib's nice, huh? Mommy will be right back. Okay? Please, Wil, just ten minutes—that's all I need."

I reach for the mobile, set it in motion. Farm animals dance to the tune of 'Old MacDonald Had a Farm.'

I spend my life backing out of this bedroom I share with my baby. The room's so tiny, the crib touches my bed. And we had to move the dresser into the hall.

I like to just stand in the doorway and watch Wil when he doesn't know I'm there. He looks around, kicking his feet. Sometimes I lean against the doorframe, grateful that it holds me up. I'm always exhausted. *Awesome cooing, Wil—good job! Sing yourself a lullaby: Such a good baby. I can almost feel the shower's hot water now.*

Arms wrap around my waist from behind, like a trap snapping shut. I can't move. "WILSON! Stop it! I mean it. Get off me. You scared me half to death." Wilson laughs into my ear and holds me tighter. I'm trapped. I can't fight. I can barely breathe.

"Got someplace else to be, baby girl?" he asks, burying his lips against my neck. I feel his hands, warm and strong, as they turn me around to face him. I go limp, feel my exhausted body come alive. Wilson knows. He presses his open mouth against my lips until they part, then he presses even harder.

I try to remember where I put the condoms Miss Marcie gave me yesterday. I told her I wouldn't need them—I was done with sex for a while. She said she hoped that was true, but she pressed them into my hand anyway.

It's hard not to want sex when you miss someone the way I miss Wilson. I want him to hold me. I want to feel his body as it bends into mine. I want to look into his eyes as he calls me 'baby girl.' I want to hear him say he loves me.

I hear the baby stirring, crying—and something else comes alive in me. It's sense against senses. Wilson doesn't say he loves me, not ever, and all I can hear right now is his need. And all I taste is the booze on his breath.

I break free, looking back at the baby we made: The baby that floated in my body, kicking at first like a tiny frog in a pond, and then rolling over slowly like a beached whale longing for the ocean. I search my mind for some clue about how to make my life different than it is at this moment—how to erase this desire I have for Wilson, and focus on what I want from him for Wil.

The baby's quiet now and Wilson reaches for me, but I'm ready. I move away from him.

"How'd you get in here anyway?" I close my eyes so I don't see how his face breaks into little-boy dimples.

"Credit card, baby girl. It opens doors."

"Very funny. How'd you get a credit card?"

"Baby girl, getting a credit card is not the problem. Come here and tell me what you need. I'll make all your dreams come true."

"Stop being goofy, Wilson. I need you to listen for your son while I take a shower. We can talk about my other dreams later."

"The warden's gone. We're gonna do more than talk. I miss you. You miss me, too. Right? We both need this." He purrs in my ear. "We're good together, baby girl." Wilson pulls me into his arms, kisses my mouth, then slides his lips down my neck.

My body falls into his. I close my eyes and force myself to hear my baby cry. My body stiffens, my jaw clamps shut. The best defense is moving away from this—this seduction trap he does so well. "I'll be back in ten minutes and we'll talk. Listen for Wil, please."

"Come on, baby girl. We're finally alone."

"Don't whine, Wilson. We're not alone. We have a son. Listen for Wil, please," I repeat. I leave him standing there in the hall.

I go to the bathroom and turn on the light. My image jumps out at me from the medicine cabinet mirror. My flushed face gives me away. I want Wilson.

Is this why I called him? I told him I wanted to talk to him. But is that really what I want? To talk to him: give him ultimatums? It's what I have to do, for Wil's sake. I know that, but part of me still wonders what I really want.

I strip off my clothes, ball them up and throw them into the hamper. I hear footsteps in the hall and lock the door.

I've locked him out, but he's still there, kissing me. It's what I want, the kisses, closeness—not the rest.

I turn on the water and let it warm up before I get in. The water beats down on me, and I open the shampoo bottle—the smell of coconuts mingles with the steam. I'm happy. I'm warm. I take my time: lather up, wash myself clean—willing myself to be strong and not give in to Wilson's lust.

I get out of the tub and dry off. Too late I remember my clothes sitting on my bed. I wrap myself in the towel and comb my fingers through my red hair. I wipe steam from the mirror and see a sprinkle of freckles across my nose and cheeks. I examine my lime green eyes. My neighbor's a hair stylist and she gave me a great cut just for babysitting her bratty toddler.

She also gave me samples of body spray—I spritz the burnt vanilla over myself. The basketball I held in my body for thirty-four weeks left a flabby pouch where tight muscles used to be. My body will never be the same.

Wilson's waiting when I open the door. He lifts me up and carries me to my grandmother's bed. "No, we can't, not here," I whisper, as he lowers me onto the sheets, pulling at the towel until it falls away. His eyes are on me as he tears off his clothes. I feel myself slipping under, and my eyes close. He brushes my lips with his so lightly that it's almost not real. His lips are like a breath, a flutter of dragonfly wings.

I twist away, and then back to him, like he's a magnet and I'm made of metal. He holds tight to my hands and I know that it's over. It's done. This boy is the father of my baby; this boy is the man that I love.

The tears escape before it's even over. All that passion we feel passes swiftly through us like a train's whistle in the night. It drifts away to unknown places; steam evaporating into nothingness, leaving us both spent, and me feeling even more powerless than before. My tears stir up Wilson's anger; his cheeks are so full, I think they'll explode.

"Don't even start, Star," Wilson hisses the name he knows I hate. He hates it, too. *Star*. Why not Moonbeam or Comet? My mother left me with nothing but a name I hate.

"DON'T!" he spits out again as I continue to cry, turning away from him, curling into a ball.

Wilson stumbles out of bed and pulls on his boxers and jeans. He works at the zipper, fumbles with the snap—tugs his shirt over his head.

"You called me, Star, remember that. You wanted this. Talk?" He kicks at the bed frame. "What a joke. What do we have to talk about? What? I have nothing to say to you. And that kid—he's not mine and you know it. There must have been ten guys hanging out on the corner whenever I came up here. How many of those guys did you do, Star?"

How many of those guys did you do, Star? It's the last thing I hear. He's gone. Soundlessly gone. I will myself to sleep and dream about visiting my great-grandmother in Pennsylvania. She's been dead for years, so I'm surprised when I find her putting my great-grandfather's coal-mining clothes through the old ringer washer in her basement. The clothes swish and twist in dirty gray wash water laced with sparse suds, and then she feeds them through the ringer. I feel the air go out of me as I watch the clothes flatten and drop into the rinse tub. I feel flat and lifeless, too; dirty, and drowning in ice cold water.

I hear that baby crying. The baby that Wilson claims isn't his. I force myself to wake up for just a minute, until I realize that I'm naked in my grandmother's bed. I smell sex on her sheets and my skin feels like it's rotting with guilt. I sink into my misery and sleep. I'm hovering on a high windowsill, naked. I close my eyes and lean forward, taking flight. The air is cold as I tumble fast to the street below.

I'm lying face up, eyes wide open, red hair plastered to the ground. The guys who hang on the corner stand in a circle above me. They are black and white and brown boys, with pants hung low on their hips, boxers showing, cigarettes hanging from their lips. They nudge each other and shrug their shoulders, asking what they should do with me. I want to tell them to call 911, but I know I'm already dead and decaying. Wilson comes by and covers my naked body with his jacket.

I hear the baby cry. The baby's father hears it, too. He walks away from the sound. I lie there rotting: unable to tend to that baby, the one that Wilson claims isn't his.

2

Wilson

I'm seething as I run down the steps and out of that crummy house Star lives in with her self-righteous grandmother. Some wise guy is sitting on the hood of my Jeep. I get in and gun the engine. He stares at me through the windshield and gives me the finger. I put the car in drive, pumping the brakes hard as the car lurches forward. Some punk pulls the freak off my car and drags him into the mob of freaks hanging on the corner. I salute as I drive away, squealing the tires.

I don't need this. I hate this part of town. I won't be coming back.

I turn on the radio, loud. Some stupid song about falling in love blasts me. What does love have to do with anything? Star makes my skin crawl. Why'd I ever let myself get involved with her? I shout this question over the music. I take a deep breath and grip the wheel. I slam on the brakes as the light turns red. Too late. I slide into the intersection and a siren screams as blue and red lights flash. I pull slowly to the curb and shove a piece of gum in my mouth, chewing frantically. How long ago did I drink that last beer? I roll down my window, spinning a story in my brain. It better be a good one.

"Good evening, Officer," I gulp, "sorry about that."

"Is there a fire, son?"

"Excuse me, sir?" My voice cracks. I swallow hard, but my fear won't go down that easily. Too late I remember the gum, which is now wadded at the back of my throat. Somehow the thought of choking to death leads me to understand his attempt to joke about a fire.

"No fire, sir," the words find their way out past the gum.

The officer shrugs his shoulders. "License and registration?" I twist and turn in my seat belt, trying to dig in my pocket for my wallet. "Take your time, son," the officer says in a monotone voice. It is hard to tell if he means it, or is being sarcastic. I clear my throat as I fumble through my wallet, then hand him my license. I lunge for the registration in the glove box and get snapped back into place by my seat belt.

"Wilson Fletcher?" the officer asks.

"Yes, sir." I unhook my seat belt and go for the glove box again.

"First time?"

"Excuse me?" I can feel my face go red.

The officer appears to study my license, and then looks me in the eye. "Is this the first time you've been pulled over?" I hand him the registration, trying to keep my hands from shaking.

"Yes, sir," I say, wondering, *How stupid am I?*

I shiver as he goes back to his cruiser. I unwrap

another piece of gum and ram it in my mouth. If I can't taste the booze, can he smell it? My mother'll freak out if I get a DUI. I can kiss this ride goodbye. Meanwhile, he's taking forever. I mean, what's the man doing, having his car serviced? How long can it possibly take for him to radio in to find out if I'm telling the truth about no priors? I'm sweating and this Jeep feels like a stew pot. I turn to the sound of approaching footsteps.

"Mr. Fletcher," the officer says, standing over me. I squirm in my seat and look up at him. "How many sacks did you have last year?" I try to hide the smile that creeps across my face. I fold my arms over my chest.

"Seven, sir."

"Another big football season's coming up, son. So I've written you a warning. You need to slow down. And I'll be watching."

"Yes, sir."

Man, I hope he didn't hear me sigh, sucking air like a scared little kid. The flashing lights stop and I just sit there for a while, huddled over the steering wheel.

Could this night get any worse? I stretch out my legs, rub my cramping calves and try not to think about Star. I tell myself she deserved what I said to her. Her crying like that makes me feel like a freak. Did she, or did she not, invite me over there? If sex is that bad with me, then why'd she call? Her kid's not my problem. So what's there to talk about?

I put the car in gear and pull out slowly. The night's a total bust. Hobbs and Boland are halfway to Baltimore by now, on the way to the game. Hell, they probably gave Cushman my ticket.

How stupid am I? She calls and I go running over there, like I have nothing else to do but have sex with her. Girls from that part of town are easy. A guy doesn't even have to spend a penny on them.

Not that I needed her. Girls are always hitting on me, popular girls: soccer players, track stars, cheerleaders, even. The trouble was, as in past tense, I had no game. I needed someone to practice on. Enter Star.

I'd seen her around school when she was a freshman, and then at the pool last summer.

She has this hot body, and that amazing hair. She was lying in the only foot of shade on the entire pool grounds. It looked like a good opening. I sat on the grass beside her and asked if she'd share her shade with me. She kept her eyes closed, "Not a chance," she said, rolling onto her stomach without looking at me. "This piece of real estate is seriously valuable to freckled people who want to control a summertime outbreak. So, unless you have freckles, you are out of luck."

I scanned my body and found a freckle on my arm. "Found one," I told her.

"I said freckles," she said, into the towel under her head. "As in plural." I scanned again, finding a freckle on my leg.

"Hey, I found another one! But how're you going to know unless you actually look at me?" Star sat up and brushed the hair out of her startling green eyes. "See," I told her, pointing to the two brown spots I'd found.

"Those are birthmarks, Mr. Fletcher," she said, rolling those eyes at me.

I tried to act surprised, cool, "You know my name?"

Star wasn't having it. She coolly reminded me that it was no big deal that she knew my name, since we go to the same school. Five minutes into the conversation, I knew this was the girl I wanted to score.

It's scary not to remember driving home, but somehow I'm sitting in my driveway. I slide out of the Jeep, go to the back deck and drop into a chair. The moon's carved very thin tonight and the North Star shines bright. I remember the night Star wanted me to admit I hated her name as much as she did. I was still trying to score with her—after weeks of trying—so I told her I hated her name, too. But I lied. Saying you hate the name *Star* is like saying you hate the Milky Way.

3
Star

Sunshine glares through the window blinds, assaulting my eyes as I strain to keep them open. It takes several minutes to remember that I'm a mother who hasn't heard her baby once the whole night long. Then I realize, too, that I'm still in my grandmother's bed, and yes, I'm still naked.

I find my only available clothing, a bath towel in a heap on the floor where Wilson discarded it. I know not to wear my grandmother's bathrobe, and there are other boundaries not to be crossed, like having sex in her bed.

I bury my head in the towel and pull back from the smell of the cheap fabric softener we buy to save money. I fall back into bed, grabbing a pillow and hugging it to me, hoping to catch Wilson's scent. But instead there's that same sour laundry smell, clinging to the towel.

I'm in no hurry to get up and face my grandmother. It's easy to picture Wil safe in her arms. This isn't the first time I've slept through his needing me. She'll have many recriminations for me—they can wait. But the taste of bile in my mouth reminds me that though Grandma's tirade can wait, Wil, my baby, can't.

I get up and wrap the towel around me. I remember Wilson waiting as I opened the bathroom door, still warm from my shower and smelling like burnt vanilla. I remember, too, that although Wilson was not the first, he was the first one I *chose*.

I know there's little chance of stepping into the hallway without Grandma seeing me dressed in terrycloth. This house is a matchbox: tiny and combustible. Covering my face with my hand, I step cautiously over the threshold and wait for the shrieking to begin. *Silence*.

I peek through my fingers and race up the few steps to my bedroom, go in, and freeze. Grandma's asleep on my bed, with Wil wedged against the wall. Miss Marcie would die if she saw this.

How many times have we been told in parenting class about the dangers of babies being trapped between the wall and the mattress, and suffocating to death? How many times have we been given SIDS statistics? Sudden Infant Death Syndrome: I shake the thought from my head.

Right now doesn't seem like a good time to lecture my grandmother about the 'best parenting practices.' Anyway, she never likes one bit of information I bring home from parenting class, and tells me that when Miss Marcie's raised three children and a grandchild, then she can talk.

My clothes that were on the bed last night are nowhere to be seen, so I step back into the hall and find them on top of my dresser. I go into the bathroom and dress quickly in jeans and a faded green, oversized t-shirt. I brush the horrible taste of regret out of my mouth, and rake a brush through my hair.

Star in the Middle

If not for Wil, I'd be in my running gear and out on the streets, training for cross-country. If not for Wil, I'd be going to the pool today. If not for Wil, I'd be starting eleventh grade in a few weeks. And if not for Wil, I'd still have Wilson.

I wish I could get these thoughts out of my head. The reality of Wil is bigger and wider than my life—it spills so far out on all sides of me that there's no getting around it in the foreseeable future. *And I know I'll pay for sleeping through the night.*

Angela—she goes to the center—said in support group that she got pregnant because she thought it would keep her boyfriend in her life. Nikia didn't say that out loud, but I know she thinks the same thing. I didn't get pregnant to keep Wilson. I got pregnant because I was too tangled up in my past garbage to prevent it.

My throat closes and I swallow hard. It's amazing to me that somehow I've forgotten how to swallow. It takes several tries to make the lump go down instead of strangling me to death.

The baby's crying. I want to get him, but I'm afraid to face my grandmother. I'm also afraid not to. I lower myself onto the edge of the tub and try to find the courage. *I am so dead.* I know she must have been a nun in a previous life because her ability to heap on guilt is divinely inspired. *How many commandments have I broken? I not only failed to avoid the near occasion of sin, I let sin into her bed.*

She's threatened to throw me out of here before. I wonder if this'll be the day.

The crying moves closer and the bathroom door opens.

23

"Star, do you not hear YOUR baby crying?" My grand-mother's eyes are locked on mine. "Were you drinking with that worthless boy last night, Star Peters?" Wil turns up the volume and now cries louder than my grandmother's yelling: "How low will you go with that sorry excuse for a man?"

I hold back the words I want to shout—*You don't even know Wilson.*

"I was not drinking," I say; my voice is rusty with un-spoken thoughts. I reach for Wil, but she spins him away from me.

"You were passed out. Did you not hear this baby cry-ing all night?"

"He didn't cry all night."

"How would you know that, Star? Do you know what it was like for me to come into MY OWN home, into MY OWN bedroom, and find my beautiful granddaughter sprawled across MY BED like a drunken SLUT? Where's that boy in the light of day, Star? Hell, where was he when his baby was screaming his lungs out all night, while I was trying to sleep?"

I want to tell Grandma it's not good for a baby to cry for long periods of time. Miss Marcie said so. I want to tell her that you can't spoil a baby under six months old by picking him up, like Grandma tells me. Babies have to get their needs met to feel safe, and crying's their way of com-municating that they need to be fed or changed or com-forted. Miss Marcie said that, too.

I want to ask Grandma why she didn't pick him up and

comfort him, but I already know the answer: she'd worked two jobs yesterday and she'll be damned if she's going to come home and take care of my kid for me. What I really want to ask Grandma is why she didn't wake me, but I'm afraid to hear her answer.

Grandma refuses to hand Wil over, so I go to the kitchen to make him a bottle. My hands are shaking and I spill powdered formula all over the counter. I run hot water into a pan and put the bottle in to warm.

The rocker in the living room's working overtime—set on the anger speed. Wil is still screaming and I'm sick, not knowing when he last ate or when he last had a diaper change. *I'm a terrible mother*. My head is bowed as I walk into the living room.

"Please let me hold Wil," I plead, shifting my weight from one foot to the other, and shaking the warmed bottle in my hand. Grandma gets out of the rocker and hands me the baby.

Wil stops crying and his body heaves as he tries to catch his breath. I put the bottle on the end table and put him over my shoulder. I pat his back and tell him how sorry I am.

I tell my grandmother, too, but she shakes her head and hisses, "Tsk, tsk, tsk."

I close my eyes and picture the peddler from the *Caps for Sale* book, and the monkeys sitting in the tree, mocking him. I try to remember the colors of the caps, but all I can see is the checkered one. Miss Marcie said that it's never too early to start reading to babies, and I decide to go to the library and sign that book out.

Wil's quiet now. Accustomed to the guilt speed at which I rock the rocker, he's comforted and calm. When I cradle him in my arms, I'm afraid that he's fallen asleep without taking his bottle. But he looks up and smiles at me. I try to hide the tears that slip down my cheeks and rain on his sleeper. I put the bottle to Wil's lips and his little bird mouth opens and greedily accepts my offering. He's so beautiful that I can't take my eyes off him.

"How could I not wake up?" I've spoken the words out loud, and search my grandmother's face. She shifts her eyes away from mine.

"You didn't hear him," the words slip through her teeth. "Maybe because you're so used to sleeping in the same room with him. I changed him and gave him his bottle, but he didn't want to go back to sleep in his crib. I put him in bed with me. I know your Miss Marcie would not approve, but I worked two jobs yesterday, Star."

"I'm sorry, Grandma."

"This happens every time you're around that boy, Star," her words are sharp now, and unforgiving. "He knocks you into the middle of the next day every time. Your reaction to him is no different than..." she stops, mid sentence, her thoughts catching up with her words.

We're quiet now, both still lost in Grandma's unfinished sentence. I feel my pores open to expose festering wounds.

She continues in a calm voice. "Star, I don't think I can do this anymore, watch you destroy your life. I'll give you a couple of weeks to find someplace else to live."

And there it is—this foreboding has now come to pass.

"Grandma, you can't."

"I'm out of options here, Star. I can't be here every minute with you, and you can't be trusted to protect yourself."

"But, Grandma, I have nowhere else to go."

"Your Miss Marcie can find you a foster home, with people who can give you the supervision you need."

"What about Wil?"

"You obviously can't take care of him. Let's revisit adoption." Her words sting, driving a splinter in so deep that no amount of prodding would extricate it. I picture it there, under my skin, but know that trying to remove it will only make it worse.

I failed to get up and care for my baby one night. Okay, well, big fat deal, how many nights have I gotten up? I've changed millions of diapers. Made millions of bottles. How about that, Grandma? Give me a break here.

I know the splinter has broken free—it's moving through my system now. When will it penetrate my heart?

"Star, I'm not trying to hurt you. I'm trying to help you make good decisions for yourself, Star, and for Wil."

Grandma's words rise in the air as she speaks, appear in a bubble above her head—imprinted there on the airwaves, quivering. I see those words as the title of the book of my life: *People Who Said They Wouldn't Hurt Me But Did*. Chapter 1—Everyone.

Chapter 2—How Many Good Decisions Does It Take to Erase What Someone Else Has Done to Me?

I close my eyes. Bits of my dreams swim through my consciousness: I'm falling from the window ledge, through the darkness to the street below. The air whizzes by my ears, takes my breath away. I will not fall: I will not fail. I will not leave Wil the way my mother left me. Nothing—no one—will convince me that adoption is the best decision for my baby. I don't want him growing up in constant search of me, expecting to find me around the corner, or two streets over, or in his dreams.

When I open my eyes, Grandma is gone. It's Sunday. She's getting ready for church.

I pack Wil's half-finished bottle into the diaper bag and ram it under the seat of the stroller Miss Marcie said I could borrow over the weekend. I gently lift him, still asleep, from my shoulder and put him in the reclined seat, securing the straps. A smile crosses his lips and dimples his mouth. The tears flood my eyes, rinsing away the sleep and despair that I felt when Wilson walked out on me last night.

I push the stroller to the door of the mudroom and through the back door, lifting it down the steps. The morning air is already thick with summer heat. The wheels of the stroller complain as I force them through the overgrown grass, around to the front of the house and onto the street, where I pick up speed.

"Hey, Star power, what's the hurry?" Rodney Dobson, a boy my age who lives next door, stands in front of the stroller, blocking me. I try to move around him, but he moves with the stroller.

"Star, babe, answer me one question," his voice is loud and cocky like he's playing to an audience of his hoodlum friends. I glance around quickly; he's alone. His eyes travel up and down my body.

"Why'd you go get yourself knocked up by that phony jock when you have 'the man' right next door?" In one swift movement he grabs my arm.

"LET GO OF ME." My angry voice appears to amuse him. He laughs, tightening his grip as I swing at him.

I hear her before I see her. She comes thundering down the steps of her house and grabs Rodney by the ear.

"Maybe Miss Star wants a man who can pass the ninth grade," Mrs. Dodson says, twisting Rodney's ear. "Get in that house 'fore I knock you upside your head. Where've you been? Where've you been all night?"

Mrs. Dodson swats at Rodney as he runs up the steps in front of her. She berates him all the way into the house. Their angry voices drift back at me through their open window.

I bend down and look at Wil, still asleep in the stroller. My hands shake as I grab the handle and push, willing my feet to move.

Rodney used to be my friend back in elementary school. Back when he didn't hang out with the freaks on the street corner. Back when he wasn't one of them, sneering at me and pawing at my body, and not letting me pass. Now he runs up and down my front steps at night, scaring me into believing someone's breaking in. Rodney used to be my friend. Now he's just another casualty of my childhood.

I push on past the houses that used to look and feel safe. My grandmother keeps telling me the neighborhood has changed, like I'm blind. Like I can't see what's happening. Like I don't see the broken glass and beer cans rotting the landscape of my childhood. Like I don't know that good people are double locking their doors to keep out the change that rolls down their street, stealing their children to waste away, sniffing stuff up their noses.

I know it's bad. I don't care what they say it does *for* them—I see what it does *to* them, like what it's done to Rodney.

The heat cooks my legs under my jeans. My feet hurt and I look down to find flimsy flip-flops on my feet where my running shoes should be. So far today, I've run away from my grandmother, outrun Rodney with some help from his mother, and made my way into a neighborhood where windows aren't boarded over and the lawns are mowed to perfection.

You can still hear sirens in this part of town, but they aren't so loud that they drown out birds singing or children playing.

I think about TV mothers telling their children to not stray too far from the house, to stay in the neighborhood. I wonder if I'll ever be able to say those words to Wil, or if I'll ever be able to give him a safe place to live.

Maybe my grandmother's right. Maybe he would be better off with another mother, and with a father who actually wants him.

Wil's still quiet as I guide the stroller past geese and ducks swimming on the lake toward my favorite bench in City Park when I notice a Goth inhabiting it. A long black coat drapes his shoulders and hangs over the bench to the ground. I hear my name as I turn and attempt to flee.

"Star Peters, Star, come sit with me."

It's Todd Ryan, or is it Ryan Todd? It's been awhile. He used to be my friend in middle school, before he started chasing dragons and piercing body parts that made me wince just thinking about them.

"Come on, Star, the babies can be our chaperones."

When I turn, I see Todd slouched down on the bench, arms crossed, baby stroller at his side. My curiosity surpasses my need to disappear.

Todd keeps his eyes on mine as I make my way back and sit down as far away from him as the bench will allow.

"I don't think I'm contagious, Star," he says with a wink. "At least I hope you won't feel the need to run off and leave me sitting here, all alone with the baby."

I read the amusement in his eyes. What's that about, anyway? I thought Goth people were all depressed. I can't stop staring at the multiple hoops that decorate his brow, the gold ring through his nose, the studs marching up his earlobe. My mind imagines what other body parts he's had pierced or tattooed, and with what? Dragons? Skulls? Chains?

"I'm sorry, Ryan, I mean, Todd," I stumble over the words that shoot out of my mouth like balls from a popgun. I close my eyes and take a deep breath. "I'm sorry, Todd."

"What bothers you most? That you can't remember my name, or that I'm not as uncomfortable with the way I look as you think I should be?"

"I *do* remember your name, and how you look is your

business." I trap my hands between my knees and sit back on the bench, trying to take an inconspicuous sideways peek at Todd. He winks at me again and I bury my head in my hands.

"Come on, Star, relax. We're just two people parked on a bench passing time."

I keep my eyes covered, trying to remember if I've talked to him since his voice changed, since stubble started sprouting on his face. I search for something to say.

"Boy or girl?" My voice comes out in a whisper now.

"Girl."

"Ahh! Name?"

"Her mother named her Nevaeh."

I drop my hands, and look at Todd. "Pretty."

"It's heaven spelled backwards."

"Clever. Wish my mother had thought of that." I'm mortified as *Star* spelled backwards twinkles through my brain. Todd's laughing uncontrollably beside me.

"I know you've always hated Star, but Rats? Give your mother a break. Let's see, rodents or a celestial body? So you're still so sensitive about your name, huh? Why, Star?"

"No fair. I asked you an easy question."

"Okay. Well, boy or girl?"

"Boy."

"How nice. I bet you were thrilled. Bet you wanted a boy so you could name him after his father."

"Those are bets you would lose. I wanted a girl so I could name her anything but Star."

4
Wilson

I hate this Mass. I mean, okay, I'll go to a later Mass, no problem. But, every time my parents drag me to *this* service, Star's grandmother shoots poison dagger looks my way. I know she thinks she knows me—even though I haven't really talked to her in months. She also thinks I knocked-up her granddaughter. But just because I hung out with Star, doesn't mean I was the one.

It doesn't help that I'm sitting here, listening to a sermon on the evils of abortion again. How many Sundays a year are they going to devote to this topic?

There are 911 tiles on the floor of the waiting room at the abortion clinic. I couldn't believe it, so I counted them again. I know this because I took Star there when she came to me, all freaked about a pregnancy test she failed, or passed, depending on how you look at it. What was I supposed to do?

Like I said, Star was hysterical. So she missed a period; so the stupid stick turned blue. She still looked the same to me—same flat stomach, same great body. How could she be carrying a baby? It was the only thing I could think of to do—take her to the clinic. She was in there a very long time.

Afterwards, the counselor pulls me aside and asks me if the sex was consensual. "Of course it was consensual," I tell her. What the crap did Star tell her, anyway?

"Well, if she's pregnant, she must have been messing with someone else." I didn't mean to blurt it out; I just couldn't hold it back.

"*If* Star's pregnant?" the woman says to me. "Star *told* you she's pregnant."

I think that maybe Star was as hysterical with the counselor as she'd been with me, so I tell her that Star's the emotional type. She raised her eyebrows at me, like I was some kind of a creep. She said being pregnant is a very emotional time for a young woman, and that I should be more understanding. I couldn't believe what I was hearing. And anyway, how am *I* responsible for Star's mental state?

Then she asks if we had unprotected sex.

"Well, yeah, but just a couple of times, and it wasn't my fault. I always had a condom with me." My mother's a public health nurse for god's sake.

And that's another thing: my mother. She preaches abstinence, and then leaves condoms in my room. What the crap is that? Anyway, the condom: it's just that Star would get upset when I stopped long enough to put one on, and then she'd want to stop. So it was just easier not to use it, which is what I told the counselor.

That must have not sounded right either, because this time, that up-tight counselor's eyebrows went into overdrive. She said perhaps I should look up the word *consensual*.

How dare she say that! I never forced Star to have sex with me. I got heated, as in extremely angry, and said to tell Star I'd wait in the Jeep.

I leave the church when people start getting up to go to communion. My parents will ask me a million questions when I get home about why I didn't go to communion. I'll hear the lecture about it being disrespectful to leave before the end of Mass.

Well, isn't it disrespectful for Mrs. Peters to sit there glaring at me? And for me to be thinking about the significance of the number of tiles on the floor at the abortion clinic? I had to get out of that church.

Star doesn't even come to Mass anymore. It's probably better; I mean, she'd have to bring her kid. *What if my mother saw and recognized her?* Star'd been at my house once when my parents came home before they were supposed to. I don't need the hassle of being asked questions I don't have answers for.

Star dropped out of school when she started showing. Which was better for both of us, I guess. It felt right. I mean, I felt for her and everything, but what else could she do?

You know how sometimes you think you want to do something, and then, once you've done it, you wish you could go back and not do it? Well, lately my life's been a series of 'wish I had waited events.' Like just now, walking out of the cool church, out into the breath-stealing heat. Maybe Mom was right about leaving church early. Maybe God has limited the amount of air I can breathe because I've been disrespectful. Nah, God has better things to do than mess with me like that. This is just another hot, stinkin' day.

Back when I was a little kid, I liked going to Mass. It felt so safe, being in church with the statues and stained-glass windows. I remember once my mother asked me if I had a favorite artist, since she'd always point out the illustrations in the books we read together. I said I thought the sun was the best artist ever.

I could see her surprise and the confusion on her face, and I thought maybe I'd done something wrong. Then she said, "Wil, what kinds of art does the sun do?" I told her that the sun shone through the stained-glass windows at church, spreading art all over the place: altar, pews, and people. I told her that once, when I looked at my arm, I found that the sun had painted a star there—a star that I could touch.

Sometimes, as a kid, you get to have magic moments with your mom. That was one of ours.

Star in the Middle

The streets are quiet today. There are patches of traffic in certain areas, where people are spilling in and out of churches. The rest of the town is asleep, trying to avoid that Sunday morning, leftover-meatloaf feeling they have after whatever crap they got into on Saturday night. In this town, Sunday mornings are to churches what Friday and Saturday nights are to bars. There're probably an equal number of each. Maybe that's why I resent church these days, having to wake up and stare at myself in the mirror, when I could be shielding myself from reality under my pillow.

I pull into the parking lot at City Park. A million ducks, geese, and swans float on the lake, and only two other cars sit in the parking lot. Last summer I used to hang out here all the time with Star. We were either here or at the pool. That was before I had my license. I had to be really creative about getting Star into situations where we were alone, where I had opportunities to score.

And I soon found out that she didn't fit the mold of a girl that guys busted on, a girl from that part of town. It didn't stop me from trying, though. Maybe it was even the reason I fell in love with her.

The sun is hot through the windshield. I look at my arm, half expecting to see a star imprinted there. But I'm almost a man now, and know that the sun needs help to form those kinds of illusions. Then why am I so disappointed not to find it?

I open the car door. The air-conditioning inside slams the hot air outside in the space of the open door. I'm caught up in yet another dilemma: whether to sit in a cool vehicle with nowhere to go, or walk onto a hot landscape in search of solace.

I start walking a familiar path, knowing where it'll lead me. The smell of breakfast drifts over from a cafe across the street. Strong, tempting smells drift my way: bacon, pancakes, coffee—and the empty pit in my stomach growls for food, but the rest of me wants something else.

As I grow closer to Star's favorite bench, I sense that she's there, even before I see her. Her red hair is alive with sunlight that darts through the leaves of the oak tree shading the area. I feel a warmth flood my body and start walking toward her. I want to tell her how sorry I am about last night. I want to tell her that I'd missed her so much, I just couldn't keep my hands off her.

She sees me at the same time I see him—that Goth freak. The one that knocked up his dog-collared, black-lip-stick-wearing girlfriend, only to have the kid dumped on him when she blew out of town with some other freak.

I try to move toward Star, but my legs are locked in place. As he and Star walk toward me, I try not to stare at the Goth and the hardware that decorates his face. Star's holding her kid. The Goth is holding his kid, too: a baby dressed in so much pink it's hard to tell where the clothes end and the kid's pink skin begins. Maybe he just hasn't found a line of Goth baby clothes yet.

"Can you get lost? I'd like to speak to Star," I say, keeping my eyes on the loser so I won't have to deal with whatever emotional crap Star has written all over her face. I don't need this today. None of it.

"Wilson, knock it off." I love Star's voice, but hate the attitude.

First of all, Star, just because you decided to name your kid Wil, doesn't mean that I'm automatically Wilson. Wilson is my father, not me. So, call the kid Wilson and go back to calling me Wil, like you used to.

"Come on, baby girl, I'll drive you home." The words slip out before I realize that I've put myself out there to be shot down in front of the freak.

"Are you talking to my daughter? Don't you think she's just a tad young for you? What's that, baby girl? Oh, I agree....Fletcher, Nevaeh says you're definitely not her type."

I feel my fists balling up and I want to jump the big brave guy hiding behind the kid. I could take him down with one punch. And what's he doing here with Star anyway, or what's she doing with him? I try to block the image of him on her, all over her, but I can't. I rub my eyes with the palms of my hands and take a deep breath.

"What are you doing here with him, Star? Is he your kid's father?" I growl. Star's face crumbles instantly, but it takes the freak a minute to react. His laughter is the most irritating thing about him, even more irritating than the way he looks.

"My sperm's that good, Fletcher? I've never had sex with her, but she had my baby and named him after you. I can see why you're upset, loser."

"Who are you calling a loser?" I move on him, but Star steps between us.

"Todd, would you excuse us, please? I'd like to talk to Wilson."

"Star, are you sure?"

"I'm sure. I'll see you around, okay, Todd?"

"Who's the loser now, freak?" I move to the bench and watch them strap their kids into strollers. I think back to one night last September. I had just gotten my license and wanted to take Star out to Gap Run, where we could really be alone.

I wanted to park the Jeep and pull her into the back seat. I thought I'd waited long enough, paid my dues. We got halfway there and Star made me turn around. We came here instead. The night fell over us and the stars rose above us as we sat on this bench and kissed until I was almost crazy.

Maybe I would have been better off with one of those girls who knew how to hit on me. One of those girls who had all the moves. One of those girls who scared me to death because I was afraid I couldn't keep up, afraid I'd get laughed at. Maybe I'd have been better off with one of them, but I was already in love with Star.

Star's finished messing with her baby and is sitting on this bench—her bench, our bench. I expect tears when I look at her, but she's dry-eyed. I slide close to her and close my eyes, put my lips on hers. She kisses me back for one brief second and is gone.

I open my eyes to find her standing above me, clutching the handle of the stroller. "Goodbye, Wilson."

I try to speak, but Star's goodbye kiss has left a sour taste in my mouth. I swallow, as Star fades away, pushing the stroller.

Some goose on steroids walks up to the bench and honks at me. I shoo him, but he keeps coming back: He,

40

she, whatever it is, how can you tell on a goose? I read somewhere that they mate for life, and I wonder if this creature lost its mate and relates to me in some pathetic way. I just want to get away from it so I start walking toward the car, but it's not finished with me yet. I walk faster and the goose keeps up. Its honking invites other geese to join the chase, and soon I'm the leader of a goose parade.

I'm sure that hell's twenty degrees cooler than inside the Jeep as I slide into the driver's seat, leaving the geese to bump into each other and looking for another leader. As I drive away slowly, one goose remembers it can fly. The rest follow as they wing their way to the lake. I'm envious of their ability to fly, then land on the cool water and glide away.

The air-conditioning finally cools the Jeep just as I pull into my driveway. I jump out and slam the door, then enter the house. The kitchen smells like bacon. I missed brunch, but find a plate of food in the microwave. I'm too hungry to wait two minutes for the food to warm, so I slop syrup onto my pancakes from the bottle on the kitchen counter and stand there, hunched over, eating.

My mother sneaks up behind me, taking my plate to the table, then directs me to sit. She goes to the refrigerator and pours me a glass of milk. I settle in and attack my food, hoping to finish before the lecture begins.

"How are you, Mom?" She barely has time to slide into the chair across from me. I know I have to start the conversation if I'm going to have any edge at all. I flash her my dimples, a trick my father says has worked pretty well since birth.

"I'm fine, Wil. How are you?"

"Couldn't be better."

"How was church?" Okay, well, she was there. Is this a trick question, or her way of asking why I left early? This may be easier than I thought.

"It was good, but the church was so hot. I had to get out of there."

"Oh." My mother is in quiet-stare mode and I'm afraid to move, afraid to trip the on-switch. Too late, I blinked. "Wil, do you know Mrs. Peters?"

"Mrs. Peters?"

"From church. I noticed she kept looking over at you like she knows you. Is that where I remembered Star? From church?"

"Star?"

"Wil, please, that pretty little girl you brought over here that day."

"Ohhh! Star. Yeah. Mrs. Peters is Star's grandmother, so I've met her a couple of times."

"Really. What ever happened to Star?"

My stare-mode doesn't work as well as my mother's, so I try my bruised look. I don't have to try too hard, since I suddenly realize I've been hiding it from her for months. "She's around, Mom," I tell her.

"I guess if you know Star, you also know that her grandmother used to live in this neighborhood. She lost her husband to cancer, and then her son—the middle child, I think—got sick and died after a lengthy illness. Mrs. Peters sold the house and moved into a smaller place elsewhere. We pray for her oldest son at our prayer group—he's a career military man and stationed in Iraq. I don't know whatever became of her daughter, who I guess is Star's mother."

The question I want to ask is glued to the roof of my mouth. I rub my tongue over it to break the words free. "Mrs. Peters is in your prayer group?"

"Oh, no, she's at work when we meet. We have a prayer petition basket at church."

Her words spell relief in capital letters. Time to change the subject. "Where's Dad?"

"Outside, cooling Stu off with the sprinkler. That dog will not stay out of the pool, and it's driving Dad crazy. I wish you'd stay and swim with us, instead of going off to the town pool."

"You know what, Mom, I think I will. I'll go change."

I take the thirteen steps upstairs two at a time. From my room I look out my window and see Stu, our dog, lying on his back under the sprinkler. His mouth is wide open and he looks like he's smiling.

Dad's floating on a raft in the pool. My sister's probably off with her boyfriend somewhere, lamenting about them going off to different colleges this fall.

I think about my conversation with Mom, about Star's grandmother and the others, and realize that, in all the time I spent with her, I never once asked Star about her family.

5
Star

The honking horn makes me move even faster than I have since the phone rang and woke me. Thank god for telemarketers, or I'd have missed our van ride to the parent center.

Wil was up half the night crying, so I slept through the alarm, then went back to sleep after Grandma woke me before she went to work.

Will I ever get this right? I race toward the door while I juggle Wil over one shoulder, the diaper bag over the other, and push the stroller across the living room. The knock comes just as I reach the door and fiddle with the locks.

"I'm sorry, Miss Patty, I'm sorry, sorry, sorry!" the words come in a stutter, like a soundtrack for the damaged record of my life. Reminds me of my grandmother's old phonograph records that she refuses to part with, even though they skip and repeat the same thing over and over. Grandma says they get stuck in her favorite places for a reason. I wonder about the benefits of just breaking them in half and throwing them in the trash. Then I start to wonder

44

how long I can stay damaged before I break into pieces, too.

"It's okay, Star honey," Miss Patty says, with what little breath she has left after racing across the street and climbing the steps. She smiles at me, but I know that she's worried about getting us to the center late. Miss Patty never complains to us, but we all know she didn't worry so much about being a few minutes late when the old director was still there.

"How's Wil this morning?" Miss Patty asks as she collapses the stroller, picks it up, and ushers me out the door and down the steps.

"Miss Patty, I didn't hear the stupid alarm because Wil was up half the night and he spit up all over the crib sheet, and then he pooped a bucket-load in his diaper after he was already dressed for school and it got all over his clothes, and I had to dress him again. Oh no! His socks don't match. What should I do?" I am out of breath, and totally embarrassed.

Miss Patty smiles at me. "Shhh! We just won't tell him." I follow Miss Patty across the street. She goes to the back of the van to put the stroller in. I buckle Wil into the car seat and pull the seat belt across my chest. I look up just in time to be treated to another one of Miss Patty's smiles.

"Thank you for moving back, Nikia," she says, puffing herself up to sit tall in her driver's seat. She starts the van, and we're off.

"Just don't tell Rosa Parks," Nikia grumbles, from the back seat of the van.

"Now, Nikia, I think Rosa Parks would be the first person to give up her seat for a good reason, and for the good of everyone else in the van." Miss Patty's voice is confident, and she backs up what she says with another warm smile.

I'm always the last one on the van in the morning, but I've heard that Miss Patty encourages everyone to fill in the seats from the back forward to save time for everyone. No one wants to sit way in back, and sometimes, I have to step over people and trample diaper bags with this baby in my arms to get to the only seat left open in the back. Miss Patty says that she's not going to force us, but we should know the right thing to do.

I don't know why she gives us so much credit. I look back at this collection of other travelers. I know they haven't been so great at choosing the right thing to do any more than I have. It's not that I'm sorry about the choices I've made; disappointed maybe, but not sorry. It's the stuff that was forced on me that grays out everything else in my life, robbing my days of color.

Miss Patty pulls the van into the reserved space at the front door. Another one of her bright smiles prompts me to look at the clock on the dashboard, which says we're four minutes early. I wait as everyone shuffles out, negotiating pregnant bellies, babies, and diaper bags. I want to tell Miss Patty again that I'm sorry, but she holds up her hand to stop me, saying she's glad I'm here and not just stuck at home all day.

"You know, Star, I've been driving these vans and school buses for a long time. I've waited on elementary school children because they couldn't find their shoes, and

I've walked kindergarten children to the door when their parents lost track of time and weren't at the bus stop to meet them.

"You can choose to look at that time as minutes lost, or beads on a rosary, or pearls around your neck. The truth is, very seldom did my passengers make me late. What makes me late is heavy traffic, car accidents, and poor road conditions—things that can't be fixed by you standing outside on the street corner with your baby, waiting for me. So stop apologizing. Now, go on in and get yourself some breakfast."

My mind is numb as I drag through the building toward the child development area. "Star, good morning," Miss Ann says, reaching for Wil. I hang up the diaper bag and put Wil's bottles in the refrigerator, keeping one aside to give him now. "How was your weekend?"

"You don't want to know," I say as she hands Wil back. I change his diaper, pass him off to her as I wash my hands, and then settle in the rocker to give him his bottle. Wil sucks lazily at the nipple. He had his fill of formula during the night, when we both should have been sleeping. That's my opinion, and obviously Wil doesn't agree.

I wonder what the big rush is to get us here in the morning, since we have down time before breakfast and before classes. Most of the girls are going off to GED class after breakfast.

I finished my sophomore year here at the Parent and Child Center, through a high school credit program. Miss Marcie and my school counselor are trying to talk me into going back to the high school in the fall for my junior year.

They just don't get it. I want to get a GED and move

on with my life. What's left for me at school? I don't have the time or energy to train for cross-country, and what would I do with Wil, anyway? Should I take him to football games and embarrass his father? Maybe Wil can help me get ready to go solo to the prom. Forget it.

Wil falls asleep. I watch his face: eyelashes that flutter like butterfly wings, skin so soft and new, a smile so full of trust that it makes me want to cry. But not here, not in front of everyone, these girls who go through the motions of being tough women all the time.

Miss Ann tells me I can put the baby in his crib and let him sleep. Technically, I'm supposed to take him to breakfast with me, even though he's too young to eat solid food.

Breakfast is scrambled eggs with muffins, fruit, and cereal. Mae, Jessica's baby, is throwing her eggs off the high chair tray and onto the floor. Miss Marcie tells us in parenting class that babies don't throw food to irritate us—they're experimenting. She talks about cause and effect. Mae leans over the side of the high chair and throws another handful, squealing with delight, her dark eyes shining.

"Knock it off, Mae." Jessica's voice is raspy. Apparently, she's irritated, no matter Mae's intention. "You don't see Miss Marcie in here cleaning this up, do you?" And she's echoing our collective thinking on the topic.

My need for sleep far outweighs my need for food. I slip out of the dining room and go to the lounge. The couches and chairs are not just uncomfortable, they are ridiculously uncomfortable. They're chosen, I'm sure, specifically to prevent us from sneaking in here and falling asleep. No matter. All I have to do is close my eyes and I'm out of my misery in seconds flat.

When I awaken, drool on the hand I've used as a pillow, Mr. Sullivan is sitting in a chair across the room, flipping through pages in his planner. Looks like they've brought in the big guns. I clear my throat and sit up.

"Well, good morning, Ms. Drooling Beauty," Mr. Sullivan says, chuckling. "Sorry, it was just too good to pass up." He puts his planner on the table beside him.

"Good morning, sir" I reply, mortified. "How are things in Student Services?"

"They'd be better if I could talk you into coming back to school," he tells me. "Mr. Clayton and Miss Marcie tell me you plan to drop out and become a statistic, one I'm not ready to live with."

"I'm already a statistic you're not ready to live with."

"Let me be the judge of that. Miss Marcie tells me that she can help you figure out the logistics of childcare. Your grandmother said she's willing to do whatever it takes to keep you in school."

"Really? Because, she's just given me two weeks to find a foster home for myself and adoptive parents for Wil." The words come tumbling out before I remember that I'm too embarrassed to have anyone, least of all Mr. Sullivan, hear them.

"What? No! I just talked with her on Friday. What possibly could have happened over the weekend to make that sweet lady say something like that?" I feel my face go crimson with heat.

Mr. Sullivan is stoic, his face unreadable. But I know he knows, and he sees that I know he knows.

"Star, is there something we should talk about?" I bite my lip, and miraculously hold back the tears that are threatening.

He's quiet: waiting, searching. "Excuse me, Star," he says. "I just need to get a drink of water."

I lie back down and study the poster on the wall above the chair Mr. Sullivan vacated while I wait for Miss Marcie to come steamrolling through the door. Mr. Sullivan doesn't need a drink of water. He needs someone else to ask me the questions whose answers he doesn't want to hear.

The poster spells out ABSTINENCE in red, with the words PARENTHOOD CAN WAIT in rainbow colors below it. There's a gorgeous looking couple on the poster, beaming with happiness. They must not live around here. I close my eyes, but the rainbow-colored words pop out of the darkness: PARENTHOOD CAN WAIT. Too late now. I am so tired.

Footsteps...Five, four, three, two, one: There it is. Miss Marcie pokes her head around the doorframe. "Star, may I speak with you?"

"No," I say, trying to smile. "I need my sleep." She walks into the room and taps my leg. I swing my feet to the floor so she can sit down.

"Is there something we need to talk about?" There's a note of caution in her voice that I've never heard before. Miss Marcie already knows how I hate her asking me fifty well-thought-out questions to get the one stupid answer she's beating around the bush to hear.

"Yes, I had sex in my grandmother's house, and yes, she knows, and yes, I know it was incredibly stupid and selfish of me."

"Well then, is there something else we need to talk about, like, say, aren't you glad you had those condoms you told me you didn't need?" It's the 'did you use a condom' question in disguise. Very clever, Miss Marcie. *Does a backhanded question deserve a backhanded answer?*

"It's not like I'm pregnant." Why does my voice sound so defiant? And why can't I stop bouncing my leg and staring at Cinderella and Prince Charming, abstaining there in Wonderland?

"Do you know that for sure?" she asks so gently that it infuriates me.

"I have to go grab Wil, it's lunchtime already."

"If you need to talk, Star, I'll be in my office," Miss Marcie says with a sigh. She gets up and leaves the room, only to return again as I'm dragging myself off the sofa. "Be sure you attend the full afternoon program," she says, her voice now packed with volume.

I go out in the hall and check the bulletin board to find out what the big deal is about afternoon programming. 'Questions for Miss Eve: Everything you ever wanted to know about birth control!' I yawn, thinking about curling back up in the lounge.

I find Miss Ann sitting in the rocker, feeding Wil his bottle. "Sorry, Star, he couldn't wait," she says. She stands up and hands me my baby, and a bottle with half an inch of formula at the bottom.

"Do you have the book *Caps for Sale* here?" I ask, dropping into a rocker.

"Maybe in the toddler room." She goes to the bookshelf and brings back the book *Brown Bear, Brown Bear, What Do You See?* "Here," she says. "Read."

I balance Wil in the crook of my arm and read the title on the cover, *"Brown Bear, Brown Bear, What Do You See?"* I open the book and read to Wil about a brown bear, red bird, yellow duck, blue horse, green frog, and the other creatures in the book, showing him the illustrations as I go. When I look at Wil, he's staring intently at the purple cat in the book. How can this be? He's only two months old.

I look down to find that two other infants have crawled over, and they're sitting at my feet, listening. I slide off the chair, and Wil and I sit with the babies on the floor as I continue to read. By the time I ask the babies what they see, their moms have arrived from GED class and have joined them on the floor. They read along with me, and help their babies clap their hands at the end of the story. I close the book and pull Wil close. "I love you, baby boy," I tell him, kissing the top of his head.

Then I strap Wil into a bouncy seat and carry him to the dining room. I can't get the words in the book out of my head. I guess that's the point. Miss Marcie says repetition is good for babies' developing brains. I wish it were as easy to memorize math equations.

Mae is gobbling up her food at a surprising rate, and her face, hands, and bib are covered in sauce. Apparently, eating food wins hands down over throwing it when a baby's hungry enough. Or maybe the spaghetti's just too good to pitch over the side.

I move food around my plate. I remember when I first found out I was pregnant. I thought that if I didn't eat much, I'd lose the baby, or, at the very least, hide its existence longer. Then, when I had him early, I blamed myself and worried about him being so tiny. I'm not hungry, but I finish the meal.

I hang out in the nursery with Wil, trying to avoid the inevitable class until the very last minute. By the time I get to class, the nurse is writing ABSTINENCE: THE ULTIMATE BIRTH CONTROL on the board in big bold letters. I hear several snickers around me. There's something so familiar about Miss Eve that my hands start to shake and I don't know why.

"Who's joined us?" Miss Eve can't hide her surprise when she spots me. "Star," she says, looking me over. "Well, honey, you're so tiny. You can't be very far along." I look down at my oversized t-shirt and back up at Miss Eve—*a.k.a. Mrs. Fletcher—Wilson's mother!*

OhmigodOhmigodOhmigodWilsonnevertoldher! Thoughts in my brain ram together, jamming tight. My mouth is frozen and all eyes are on me, waiting for me to speak. I shake my head no so they won't give me away.

"It's nice to see you," I manage, as my insides churn.

"It's nice to see you, too."

Nikia asks, "Do you know Star?" Everyone else has printed their names on construction paper tents in front of them. For Miss Eve to call me by name without the tag, she'd have to already know my name.

"We've met, haven't we, Star?" Miss Eve says to the group while looking at me. I nod.

"While I was writing on the board, I heard some reactions to the message printed there. Anyone care to comment?" Her eyes travel around the table.

"You're Wil Fletcher's mother, right?" Everyone

knows Wil from sports, and they've seen his parents in the bleachers at all his games.

"Yes, Nikia. Wil's the younger of my two children. His sister will be a junior at Syracuse this fall."

"Well, we have a poster in the lounge with a guy on it almost as fine as your son. The poster advertises abstinence, but that guy's too hot to be feelin' it."

"Do you think you have to look a certain way to abstain from having sex?" Miss Eve asks. I swallow hard and look down at the table in front of me.

"I really think you're asking the wrong crowd," Shannon tells her. "That horse already has left this stable." Nervous giggles mingle with sighs around the table.

Miss Eve raises her eyebrows. "Do you think that you can't make the choice to abstain from sex, just because you are pregnant or already have had a baby?"

"Why would we want to? I mean we're already...I mean...." Shannon takes a deep breath, "Just why would we want to?"

"I can think of a couple of really good reasons. Can any of you?"

"Future unwanted pregnancies, STDs," I tell her.

"That's right, Star. Those are two very big reasons."

"I learned my lesson," Shannon tells her. "I can't trust my boyfriend to use a condom even when I have one, so I'm on the pill."

"Will the pill protect you from getting a sexually transmitted disease? Will an IUD, the patch, a diaphragm?"

"He doesn't have any sexual diseases," Shannon boasts.

"How do you know?" Miss Eve asks. "Are you taking his word? Has he been tested?

"Every time you have sex, you put yourself at risk. You don't know how many other sexual encounters the person you're having sex with has had, or with whom. If you're pregnant, it's even more important that you abstain—unless you are in a committed relationship with someone who's been tested, someone you can trust. Otherwise, you're putting your baby's health at risk, as well as your own."

"Just because I made a bad choice with one guy," Jessica says, "doesn't mean I have to continue making bad choices. Mae's father said he loved me. We used condoms, but I got pregnant anyway. But Tyler's gone. Doesn't even want to meet his daughter."

I slip my shaking hands between my knees and swallow hard. What'll I do if I'm pregnant again? Why couldn't I say no to Wilson? I know the risks. I live with the result of unprotected sex every single day.

"Miss Eve, what do you tell *your* kids about sex?" Shannon asks.

"I tell them that I hope they'll wait until they're in a committed relationship to have sex. I also make sure they have protection available to them, should they choose to have sex. My children's physical health and emotional well-being are very important to me," she replies.

"Are there any more questions?" Miss Eve asks, as she scans the room for hands.

Then she continues. "During our class sessions, we'll talk about different kinds of birth control, and how you can best protect yourself. For instance, if you're on the pill to prevent pregnancy, using a condom further decreases the chance of your becoming pregnant—and it helps protect you against sexually transmitted diseases as well. I'll also be available to talk to you individually, to answer any questions you may have. Please call me anytime. My work number is on the information sheets I'll hand out today."

Miss Eve looks down at her beeper. "Excuse me, I have to take this. Let's take a ten-minute break. Miss Marcie said there's a snack of fruit and muffins waiting for you in the kitchen."

The smokers in the group usually make a dash for the door as soon as the presenter leaves the room. But today, everyone is quiet, and they're all looking at me.

"Girl, why'd you let Miss Eve think you're pregnant?" Nikia finally asks.

"Just don't tell her, please."

I know they've all heard the rumors. I'll plead with them, if I have to, to not tip her off: to let her continue to believe I'm pregnant, so she doesn't start adding things up. I was stupid enough to name the baby Wil, even though I've never admitted to anyone who Wil's father is.

"Let's go get a muffin," I suggest. I don't really want to get off my chair, but I need to get away from their curious stares.

"Star, you don't look pregnant, girl," Nikia says, shaking her head. Nikia pushes away from the table and follows me out the door. She heads outside with Shannon for a cigarette. Jessica, Tasha, Destiny, Angela, and I go to the kitchen, where Tasha takes the fruit out of the refrigerator.

I get bowls and spoons. Jessica rips the wrap off the plate of muffins. Destiny grabs a muffin, and stands there eating it while staring out the window at Shannon and Nikia as they puff away.

"I quit smoking! Nikia could do it, too," Tasha says, standing at the window with Destiny, rubbing her pregnant belly. "It's so bad for the baby. Really. Nikia laughs off the stuff Miss Marcie tells us about smoking and low birth weight. But just think about it. She's inhaling all that crap, and then standing out there breathing in all the smoke that her and Shannon are polluting the air with. It's disgusting. Her baby has nowhere to hide from it."

I suddenly have a need to see Wil. I throw my half-eaten muffin into the garbage and go to the nursery. Wil is doing tummy time on the floor. He raises his head off the blue flannel blanket while Miss Ann encourages him by shaking a rattle and calling his name. "What a great job, Wil. I like the way you're working hard to lift your head." Wil plops facedown on the blanket after a few seconds, and Miss Ann rolls him onto his back. I tell Wil good job and scoop him up.

"Star, you are supposed to be in class," Miss Ann tells me, taking Wil from me.

"Yes, our break's about over, Star," Miss Eve says from the nursery room doorway. "I'm gathering up my troops. Who have you got there, Miss Ann?"

"This is Wil, Star's baby. He's a star at tummy time." I try not to look at Miss Eve as she steps into the room and takes Wil's hand.

"It's nice to meet you, Wil," she tells him, in a cheerful voice. Then she looks at me—her head cocked to one side, arms crossed. Okay, well, there are at least a million babies named Wil in this town alone. I will not give away Wilson's secret.

"We better go, Miss Eve." I give Wil a kiss and stumble toward the door, trying to get a head start, trying to lead her away from my baby.

"Star?" Her voice is so soft as she falls in step with me. "Is a baby's health care nurse coming to see you and Wil at home?" Miss Eve, *Wilson's mother,* asks me.

"Yes." One word. I feel rude, but it's all I can manage.

"Excellent," she says. "Who?"

"Miss Grace." Two words. A small improvement.

"Excellent." Please, please, please don't ask me any more questions.

"Would you mind if I tag along with Miss Grace the next time she comes to see you?"

"It's okay with me, but Miss Grace probably wouldn't like it. You know, that's just how she is," I lie. It's easy to lie when I'm trying to protect Wilson.

"Oh, I think I can square it with Miss Grace," Miss Eve says. "I'm glad it's okay with you, Star. I'll look forward to the visit."

She's a master at traps, just like her son.

6
Wilson

The lock gives and I am in. I slip the credit card in my back pocket and walk through the mudroom. *Who calls a room in their house a mudroom? Isn't that like asking for trouble?*

The kitchen is painted yellow, but the shades are pulled down and it's dark. I squint to see the contents of the first drawer I open, which is full of knives. I close the drawer and open another—rolling pin, measuring spoons, and a million cookie cutters. *Who could possibly use this many cookie cutters?* The third drawer has dish towels.

The phone rings and I jump. I wait as the machine picks up. "Hi, Star. It's Todd. I couldn't believe it was you yesterday. Nevaeh and I will be at the park around 4:30. Hope we'll see you and Wil there. Bye." I trip over a stool going to the phone, and my finger hovers over the button for just a second before I erase the message. Star has enough stuff going on without Todd bugging her.

I dump the contents of a mug on the counter and the key jumps out at me. I pick it up and feel its cool smoothness before shoving it in my pocket. I hold the mug level with the counter and push paper clips, pushpins, and tacks across the counter and back into the mug.

I go out the back door, careful to leave it unlocked. A swarm of bugs rises out of the tall grass as I walk by, returning to their hiding place after I pass.

There's this guy in the alley behind the shed. He stares at me with this stupid grin, but when I walk toward him, he takes off. I close my eyes and try to picture his face. I know I've seen him around here before.

I open the shed with the key, all the while trying to figure out what exactly I'm doing here—besides mowing the lawn. I had to trample down ankle high grass when I was here Saturday night and it needs to be cut. I check my watch. Star's at that center place where she's been going since she left school. Her grandmother's at work. *It'll be awhile before they get home.*

The gas cap does not want to come off the mower and I grit my teeth. It finally gives: the tank is full. Star told me that she only gets to mow on Sundays when her grandmother's home to watch the baby. Last Sunday it rained, and yesterday she probably fought with her grandmother because of what happened between us on Saturday. *That woman always knows everything.* It's like she's tapped into Star's psyche. Either that, or Star's just not sneaky enough to hide things that are none of her grandmother's business.

The mower doesn't want to start any more than it wanted to give up its gas cap. I finally get it going after the tenth try, but who's counting? The front yard's small and it's done in no time. That kid, Rodney, comes out on his porch and watches me like a hawk looking for prey. He's part criminal but a bigger part dork. It's like the freaks on the street pulled this dork in and dressed him up as a gangster. It's really a dangerous combination, and this Rodney dude is destined to get himself killed playing dress-up.

The lawn mower complains more about the high grass in the backyard than it had out front. I wonder when Star last mowed it. Maybe it's just tired. It *is* hot today. Sweat rolls off my forehead, down my back—*I need a beer*.

I think about the stuff my mother told me. About Mrs. Peters watching her husband die of cancer, and then her son. I think about Star's uncle in Iraq. I guess the daughter my mother talked about that went missing is Star's mother. *How hard would that be, to grow up without a mother? No wonder Star gets so hysterical over everything.*

I don't know why I can't stop thinking about any of this. I guess it's just easier to understand Star, knowing what I know. It's not my fault Star went looking for something and cheated on me. I mean, I'm sorrier than anybody that she got herself pregnant. Maybe no one can give Star what she's looking for. But, what I still don't get is why she's trying to pin it on me. I thought we were friends. We didn't even have sex until it was practically October, and that kid shows up in May. Does she think I'm stupid? Most of all, I'm sorry about Saturday—no matter what, I can't treat Star like that.

I hit a patch of dirt behind the shed and the mower throws a rock and stalls. *Now I really need a beer. The skin on my face is fried. My mother'll lecture me about not wearing sunscreen.* I sit on the grass and stare at the dirt rising up out of the ground. *Did they bury a pet here? Plant a tree that died?*

There's a tiny dogwood tree growing in the alley just outside the fence. I go to the shed and grab a shovel and dig a hole. I find a bucket in the shed and fill it with water from the outside faucet. The dirt is thirsty and soaks up the water. I fill it again. The soil around the seedling gives easily and I move it from a place where it'll eventually be destroyed to the hole I've dug in Star's yard. The lawn mower groans, starts, and I finish mowing.

The shed is all neat and orderly—like the house. I put the shovel and bucket back where I found them. I ram my thumb with a nail in the toolbox, looking for something to clean the lawnmower. The only thing I can find is a screwdriver. *It'll have to do.* I scrape the crud off the bottom of the mower and throw it in the trashcan outside the back door.

The crud on my good running shoes is a little harder to deal with. What was I thinking, wearing them here in the first place? The grass clippings are too long to just leave all over the lawn, so I pull out the rake and rake them around the trunks of a couple of trees. One's a maple whose leaves turned great colors last fall, and an oak that held on to its brown leaves most of the winter. I cover the dirt around the dogwood with a thick layer of clippings as mulch.

I wonder what Star does at the center. It's another thing I never asked her about. She had a tutor when she was stuck home for six weeks after the kid was born, so she finished her course credit stuff on time. *Maybe she just likes hanging out with other girls that have kids. Or maybe she's already working on a GED. Maybe Star'll graduate from high school before I do. That would be too weird. I guess a GED is the same as a diploma.*

The door is closed and locked before I remember to go over the checklist in my head. The shed is locked up tight. The key's back in the mug. A tug on the lock assures me that I've locked the door, but if I can get in with a credit card, so can any thug on the street.

I need to talk to Star about installing a chain lock. Maybe I'll just come over tomorrow and do it. Of course, that also means I'll be locking myself out. But, that's okay. I did this to make up for Saturday, I guess. I won't ever sneak up on Star again like I did Saturday night, not listen to what she's trying to tell me. And besides, I'm not in the habit of breaking into people's houses. I don't plan on making this a habit.

Rodney is still on dork patrol as I get in the Jeep and drive off.

Since the public pool is on my way home, I decide to stop there to cool off with a swim and to bug Boland, *the big-shot lifeguard*, at the same time. It's funny how chlorine smelled so different last summer, when I knew I'd be lying on a towel next to Star. The anticipation of being with her got to me every time I hit the locker-room door and smelled the chlorine.

This year it just smells like chlorine, a necessary part of summer, pools, swimming. Boland's being a lifeguard is laughable, because I wouldn't exactly put my life in his hands.

"Hey," he says, jumping down from his chair.

No doubt he wants to bust on me about missing the game to go to Star's place.

"You missed one hell of a game."

He's so predictable! "Just shut up. That's information I don't need to hear."

"Yeah, well, Cushman sends his thanks for the great seat." I thought as much, but I keep it to myself.

"I know why you're still hanging out with Peters, but it's not necessary, man. Cate Hobart's been hanging here all day, looking for you. She's hot, and she doesn't have baggage. Star's got baggage that's never going away, no matter how good she looks."

"I'm done with Star. Why even bring her up?"

"You didn't blow off an Orioles' game to hang with your mommy, Fletcher. Everyone else was accounted for, had to be Star." Bo has this mocking tone in his voice when he says this. His eyes dart around the pool before he goes on: "So, how was it?"

"Dude, shut up." I deck him and jump into the pool before he can hit me back. The water's not much cooler than the air, but it washes away the dirt and grass clippings—a bonus for the other swimmers, I'm sure. The pool's so crowded that it feels more like a bumper car ride than swimming.

After I crash into yet another unsuspecting swimmer, I decide enough with the laps. I use the ledge of the pool as a pillow, close my eyes and try to think of the time before Star became a mother. We talked—a lot. I don't remember what we talked about, but Star was fun to be around.

Star in the Middle

At first it ticked me off. I was looking for something else from her. And it wasn't only that I could *talk* to her— we swam, ran, played tennis together. She was so competitive. I usually hate that in girls, but Star wasn't in-your-face competitive. It wasn't like she was trying to clobber me. It was more like she was trying to prove something to herself.

"Wil." I open my eyes to find Cate Hobart hugging the side of the pool with me. How is it that a girl can look that good soaking wet?

"Cate."

"How are you?"

"Wet."

"Want to dry off?"

"Eventually."

Cate looks ticked off, offended. But I have no game to bring on. Apparently neither does Cate, or at least none that she wants to invest in me. Star would have said something like, "Okay, well, Fletcher, if *eventually* ever comes, I hope you can find your towel."

But Cate just hauls herself out of the pool wearing this black bikini that looks good coming and going, and this sight snaps me back to reality: Star is sixteen years old and has a baby she intends to keep.

Ninety-nine point five percent of me wants her to give up that baby and come back to school. The other point five percent is undecided. *I mean, why does she want to keep the baby? Is it for her? Or, is she in love with the father? Is he in her life? If he is, why does she look at me like that? Why does she call me? Why does she want me to believe that kid's mine?*

The shrill of a lifeguard's whistle stabs my eardrums and I look up at Boland. He gives me the thumbs down like he has been privy to my conversation with Cate. I guess Cate's reaction speaks for itself; she's now strutting toward the locker room like she's walking on fire. I want to chase her down, think of something clever to say. But nothing jumps into my mind so I stay put. Maybe it's all the hooting and hollering going on around me. Or maybe I couldn't be clever even if I had Cyrano de Bergerac feeding me lines.

Lifeguard whistles explode from all around me, and people start fleeing the water in all directions. It's break time for the lifeguards, who start diving into the pool the instant I, the last swimmer, exit the water.

The bench where I'd dropped my towel is hot as I settle on it. I slide my body down so my head is resting on the back of the bench and my feet are spread out in front of me. The towel feels warm as I cover my face. I daydream that Star pulls the towel off and kisses me. One imaginary kiss leads to more imaginary kissing, and I have to sit up with my elbows on my knees and take a mental cold shower before I embarrass myself.

Then a fudge bar drops from the sky onto the bench beside me. I look up to find Boland standing over me, sucking down what's left of his. We've both been addicted to these things since first grade, when we discovered we could dump our crummy lunches and instead buy treats from the cafeteria ice cream lady.

"Bombed with Hobart, didn't you, loser?"

"Hey, maybe I'm just not into Cate, dude."

"Fletcher, you're nuts."

"*You* go after her." The paper slips off the fudge bar with one good yank. I shovel the whole thing into my mouth—instant brain-freeze. I pull it back out and take a bite. The chocolate's sweet and I already want another before this one's even gone.

"I would, Fletch. I would go after Cate. But, for some stupid reason, she's hooked on you the same way you're hooked on Star."

I break the naked Popsicle stick into splinters. "Cate's not hooked on me, and I'm sure as hell not hooked on Star."

"You are so lying through your teeth," Bo hisses. Like it's any of his business anyway.

"Shut up and go buy me another fudge bar."

"Get a job and buy it yourself. That was just a pity gift anyway."

"I don't need a job to buy a fudge bar, you moron. And I don't need your pity. You're such a jerk sometimes."

The bench bounces as Bo plops down, practically in my lap. You just can't insult this guy, and he doesn't go away easily, either.

"Look, Wil, if you want to screw up your life, go for it. HEY! Where are you going?"

"Home. This bench is way too crowded for me."

"Jeez. Will you get back here?"

I sit back down, look up, and squint into the sun. "Don't you have to go save someone from drowning, Boland?"

"Yeah, you."

"Boland, where do you get this stuff? Do I look like I'm drowning?"

"You look like you're drowning in Star-lust."

"Shut up already, Bo."

"I'm trying to make a point here, Fletcher."

"Then cut the crap and make a point."

"The point is, football practice starts in a couple weeks. Are you playing or not?"

"What kind of idiot question is that?"

"Well, some of us're betting you'll marry Star and set up housekeeping with her and your kid."

"That's so screwed up. *Me* marry *Star*? Are you nuts? I'm in high school—remember that little detail? And, that's her kid, not mine." I bite down as hard as I can on part of the splintered stick. "I'm going to pretend I didn't see you roll your eyes, Boland."

Bo lowers his head into his hand and pinches his forehead between his thumb and fingers. This is a signature move he picked up from his uptight father.

"I'm betting Cushman's spreading rumors. He so wants my position on the team. Tell him to go..." I stop cold when I see the look on Boland's face. He's *so* not buying any of this. *What? Am I the talk of the town? Everyone thinks the kid's mine?*

"I have to get back to the chair. Call me later." I watch as Boland struts off, flexing his muscles. *Show off.*

I suppress the urge to chew my nails. Star actually got out a magnifying glass one day to show me how much dirt is under our fingernails, and I never forgot it. Not that dirt will kill me, but still, *gross*.

Star in the Middle

Boland's sitting at the edge of his lifeguard chair like he's some big deal celebrity. I want to punch him out, but it'd be pretty hard to take him down. He outweighs me by thirty pounds, and when he's not in the pool swimming his brains out, he's at the gym lifting weights. He'll be varsity quarterback again this year, a position he took away from a senior last year when he was still a junior. Hobbs is his go-to receiver. They don't get why I like playing defense so much, but that's my choice. The three of us have been best friends since first grade.

Cushman wants my position on the team. I know he does. He's a junior, so he can wait. He also wants to weasel his way in with Boland and Hobbs. He can take me or leave me. I don't have much use for him, either.

Boland's a big-shot because he's quarterback. He got the hottest girl in the senior class last year. She dumped him in June, said it wasn't fair to tie up his senior year when she's going off to college. Nice way to dump a guy, right? Very smooth. Boland didn't think much of it, though, and he's been bummed out all summer. I don't feel too sorry for him. Football season's coming and the quarterback'll have all the ladies lined up at his car.

Hobbs has been dating the same girl since he turned twelve—no kidding. Her name's Elizabeth Anderson. She's this little stick of a girl whose body hasn't quite caught up with her age. She's a runner, like Star, and she's pretty smart. Star and Elizabeth got to be pretty tight before Star left school. Star liked it when we hung out with Hobbs and Anderson. Anderson doesn't let people in too easily, but once she makes a friend, she's totally loyal forever.

I think Anderson still calls Star sometimes. In fact, I saw her on Star's front porch once, after the baby was born. It wasn't like I was stalking Star or anything. I'd just drive past her house sometimes. There was Elizabeth, dressed in running clothes, knocking on Star's door with a gift bag in her hand. Maybe that's where all the stuff Boland laid on me is coming from.

I don't give a crap where it comes from. I just want to know where it's going, and whether or not it'll flatten me. Hey, maybe I'll be flat like that boy in that kids' book *Flat Stanley*. I'm sure it wouldn't take much to talk Star into rolling me up and sending me off to some distant place where I can start over.

Come to think of it, some of my conversations with Star were pretty weird. Once, when we were in the family room at my house, Star started pulling out all these kids' books my parents used to read to me. Star said that she learned to read early because her grandmother didn't have much time to read to her and she loved books. I started teasing—making fun of 'Poor Star.' *It was the first time she cried in front of me.* I still feel pretty lousy sometimes, when I think about that day. Do all redheads' faces get that bright when they cry? I felt horrible, and thinking about it makes me sigh. *It feels good to sigh for some reason. Lame as that may sound.*

I should pick myself up off this bench and go home, but I have no motivation to go anywhere. I roll up my towel, use it as a pillow for the back of my head, and stretch out. The sun is burning holes through me at this point, but who cares? I cover my eyes with my hands.

Star in the Middle

I can't banish the image of Star's red face smeared with tears. I try to think about the noises around me: Water splashing, people laughing and shouting. Summer sounds. But Star and her tears are embedded in my brain.

Next week, I'm going to have my senior pictures done. The week after that, I'll throw myself into football. Two weeks after that, I'll start my senior year. I should be happy. But all I can think about are Star's fingers wrapped around the green cover of *The Giving Tree*. The black-and-white illustrations fast-forward through my head, until the shriveled-up old man is sitting alone on a stump.

What if the kid's mine?

7
Star

Have you ever scrubbed your hands so much that you're down to a new layer of skin? I've been cleaning house since Wil went down for a nap after his first bottle this morning. Grandma insists that I scrub the house thoroughly every Friday morning when the center's closed and I'm home, supposedly doing nothing. Okay, well fine. I clean the stupid house. But then my hands smell like bleach, and I can't have that strong odor around Wil, can I? It makes me gag, so how can it be good for him?

When you have a baby, days drag but the weeks fly by. How does that work, do you think? One minute I'm dragging myself out of bed on Monday morning, and then suddenly it's Friday and my hands are raw from cleaning. I feel gross.

The pain over my eyes intensifies with each knock at the door. "Stop knocking. You'll wake the baby." My words slip out through clenched teeth. That jerk Rodney better not be here to harass me this early in the morning. "Who is it?"

"It's Todd. Can I come in, Star? Rodney's leering at me from his front porch. Doesn't he ever sleep?"

I can feel my eyes dart across the porch as I open the door. "Don't freak because Nevaeh's not with me, Star. I just want to talk to you. I tried to call but the phone's been busy all morning."

"Todd, it's barely 9:00 A.M. I took the phone off the hook so it wouldn't wake Wil."

"It's 9:10. My mother taught me never to show up at anyone's house before 9:00." Todd's mother died in a car accident more than three years ago, so I guess that tip's been stuck in his mind for a while now.

"Come in." I close and lock the door, and stand staring at Todd. "Come sit down."

I lead him to the couch, and sit on the rocker.

"Where's Nevaeh?"

"My dad hired a nanny to take care of her when I start back to school. We're driving each other crazy, so I had to get out of the house."

"You and your dad are driving each other crazy?"

"Yeah, well, there's that, too. But mostly right now it's Elise. My father actually interviewed five people, and this is the best he could come up with? She's spending a couple of hours a day at our place, so she and Nevaeh can get used to each other. She hates me."

"Why would she hate you?"

"Why not?"

"Todd? Didn't you help your father interview the nannies?"

"Well, Star, that would have made *way* too much sense, don't you think? Me having any input into who spends eight hours a day with my kid?"

"Did you tell him you wanted to help with interviews?"

"Sure, and he told me if I cut my hair, plugged my pierce holes with cement, and burned all my Satan inspired clothes, he'd be proud to have me talk to perspective nannies with him. Said he'd even bankroll a new wardrobe, if he could choose what I wear until I'm eighteen. Why are you looking at me like that, Star?"

"Like what?"

"Like you agree with my dad. I may not look like your jock boyfriend, but at least I haven't blown my own kid off."

My hands burn. Bleach fumes have further depleted brain cells already savaged by pregnancy, and I'm not in the mood for company.

"Look, Todd. First, I told you before that how you look is none of my business, and second, leave Wilson out of this." I wouldn't dump on Maureen for leaving him with Nevaeh, and I don't appreciate him dumping on Wilson. "Why are you here anyway?"

"I called on Monday and left a message on your machine. I wanted you and Wil to meet me and Nevaeh at the park so I could proposition you."

I'm not entirely sure I want to know where this conversation is going, but still, I forge blindly ahead. Has to be the depleted brain cells.

"There was no message on our machine on Monday."

"It's okay that you didn't meet me, Star. You don't have to say that."

"Todd, there *was* no message. I wouldn't lie to you.

My grandmother wouldn't have erased it without telling me. And I couldn't have met you anyway. I only have a stroller on weekends, when I borrow one from the center."

"You don't have a stroller?"

"My grandmother bought Wil a stroller, but I left it on the porch and someone stole it."

"Nevaeh has a couple of strollers. I'll bring one by for you."

"Thanks, but you should keep your strollers. Todd, why are you here?" I mean, *I hate to repeat myself, but we haven't exactly been friends, and my grandmother would freak if she walked in and saw a Goth sitting in her living room. It'd be one more excuse to get rid of me. I know it shouldn't matter how Todd looks, but it would matter to my grandmother.*

"It's about what we talked about at the park. You know, getting a GED, or going back to school. Dad really wants me to go back and finish high school. Star, go back with me, please."

"I can't. I really can't. What would I do with Wil?"

"You could leave him at the center, you know that, or my dad said you can bring him over to my house and Elise can take care of both babies."

"Excuse me?"

"I was telling my dad about you and Wil, and he'll do anything to get me back in school. He even called Elise to ask about it, and is willing to pay the extra money."

"I can't let your father do that, and why would he? I don't get this."

"It would be easier, that's all. To know someone at

school who's going through the same thing as me. I'm not asking you to hang out or anything like that. Honest. Unless you want to."

"Todd, I don't drive. That's one reason I go to the center, because they provide transportation."

"I drive. I can come over and pick you and Wil up, drop him at my house, and drive both of us to school. No big deal. Don't say no—just think about it, okay?"

"You drive? Didn't you walk over here?"

"Yeah, well, I lost driving privileges because of the way I look, but my father let's me have the car for school. Honest, I've checked all this out. Like I said, Dad would do anything to get me back in school. He said he knows that getting a GED is still a diploma, but he doesn't want me to be a dropout. Will you think about it? Listen," he pauses. "Star, is that the door?"

"It is." I bury my head in my hands and take a deep breath before I drag myself off the sofa. I picture Rodney and his giant attitude on the other side of the door. It's a short walk, but it's slow going with these boulder-sized irritations weighing me down.

Todd. Rodney. Goth. Thug. I have my own baggage to contend with and I sure don't need theirs.

"Who is it?" I say through the door.

"Star, it's Miss Grace. I've been trying to call, but the line's been busy. We have a visit planned for this morning, remember?"

Great, this is perfect. The baby's health care nurse is at the door, and the Goth is on my sofa. What should I do? I turn to look at Todd.

"Should I sneak out the back door?" His voice is a whisper—and he looks dead serious.

Yes, yes! Hurry! I want to shout. "Todd, don't be silly." I try to sound convincing.

"Star?" The voice through the door speaks and I put my hand on it—spreading my fingers and hoping to silence it. *No such luck.*

I turn the bolt lock and slowly open the door. The gasp escapes—I can't stop it—and it takes my breath with it. I can't speak; I can only stare at the two women on my porch.

"Star?"

"Miss Grace, Mrs. Fletcher, I'm sorry. Come on in." My voice is tiny, a little-girl voice, inviting dolls to a tea party.

They step over the threshold and stand awkwardly in the doorway. "You have nothing to be sorry for, Star." Miss Grace smiles at me and pats my hand. It's at least 100 degrees out, but her hand is like ice. "Miss Eve said she talked to you about coming along on a visit. I tried to call to make sure today was okay. Should we come back another time?"

Yes, yes! I want to shout, but I chew my lip and try to piece together what's left of my social skills.

"I took the phone off the hook so it wouldn't wake Wil while I was cleaning. I'm sorry I forgot you were coming this morning, Miss Grace. But, please come in and sit down."

As soon as the words are out of my mouth, I remember Todd perched on the sofa, but when I turn to lead them into the living room, he's gone. The relief I feel is mingled with guilt, until he appears in the hallway holding my baby against his stupid black coat. Anger tightens my chest. I rush over to grab Wil from him.

"Star, Wil was crying. I hope it was okay that I picked him up." Todd's voice is soft, and the way he's looking at Wil is so sweet it makes me want to cry. Todd gently puts the baby into my arms.

"Do you want me to get him a bottle while you visit with Miss Grace? Hi, Miss Grace." Todd waves to her, smiling.

Miss Grace swoops over and shakes Todd's hand. "Hi, Todd, it's nice to see you. How's Nevaeh?"

"Doing great, thanks. She's at home with the nanny."

"How's that going?"

"Nevaeh loves Elise. So, I guess it's okay."

"So, you're saying that Elise has won over Nevaeh, but she's still working on her father?" Miss Grace chuckles, pats Todd's arm. "Todd, do you know Miss Eve?"

Todd takes a long look at Mrs. Fletcher. Then he looks at me, and down at Wil. I hold my breath. Sometimes this town feels small enough to fit in a bottle cap.

"Hi, Mrs. Fletcher," he says, finally. "Remember me? I used to play lacrosse with Wil when we were in middle school."

"I do remember, Todd. It's good to see you again." Mrs. Fletcher's words are warm, but she looks confused. She stands straight and rigid as a statue. I see potential in her confusion. Maybe Todd's presence will throw off any thoughts she's having about the parentage of my baby.

"About that bottle," I tell Todd, sweetly, looking up into his eyes. "Would you hold Wil while I warm it?" Todd moves so close to me that my skin feels itchy from the wool of his coat. *Does he know I'm using him as bait?*

"I better just get out of your way, Star," he whispers. His eyes scold me, so I'm pretty certain he's read my mind.

"Oh, okay. I'll talk to you later." It was a stupid idea anyway, and so unlike me.

"May I hold Wil while you get his bottle?" Mrs. Fletcher is beside me now with outstretched arms. Miss Grace looks very uncomfortable, and Todd's already backing away toward the door. I hand Mrs. Fletcher the baby and chase Todd.

"Todd, listen," my hand reaches for his, already wrapped around the doorknob. He apparently doesn't want to hear my apology. He raises his hand to silence me and lowers his head to my ear.

"Mrs. Fletcher is on a serious mission here. Want my advice?" He shrugs me off when I open my mouth to speak. "Just be straight with her. Grandmothers want to be poodles, but they'll be pit bulls if you get between them and their grandchildren." The door opens and closes in one swift motion, and Todd is gone.

I return to the living room to find Mrs. Fletcher in the rocker, chatting nonstop with Wil.

She looks neither like a poodle nor a pit bull. She doesn't look much like a grandmother, either. There's not a wrinkle anywhere on her face. She's petite and well dressed. Her makeup is flawless, and her stylish, short blonde hair is casually tucked behind her ears, exposing gold hoop earrings. I know grandmothers come in all ages, shapes, and sizes, but no one would ever suspect that Mrs. Fletcher has a grandchild.

Miss Grace is draped over the arm of the sofa. She catches my eye and motions for me to go into the kitchen with her. I remember the bottle and go straight to the refrigerator. I prepared several when I first got Wil down for a nap, anticipating that I'd have bleach hands the rest of the day.

"Star, is this uncomfortable for you?" Miss Grace's voice is feeble: a whisper, a quiver. I smile at her—afraid if I speak, the tears that will start won't ever stop.

I hear a siren—it's very close. *Did I lock the door?*

I fill a pan with hot water. The bottle floats, so I pour out some of the water.

Miss Grace has asked me about Wil's father during several of our visits. She's said that he has a legal obligation to support his child financially. I've told her he took me to an abortion clinic and that I didn't want to have one. And even if I did, didn't I need my grandmother's permission?

I mentioned that Wil's father doesn't believe the baby's his, and that he said his parents don't even want to talk about the possibility of him being a father. I've told her everything—except his name.

But what has Mrs. Fletcher said to Miss Grace, and why is she here?

"Wil is probably soaked," I mumble, as Miss Grace follows me back into the living room. I didn't bother to wipe the bottle after grabbing it from the pan, so I'm leaving a trail of water across the floor.

The changing pad is on the dresser in the hall, and both

Miss Grace and Mrs. Fletcher follow behind me. Wil's hungry and wet, so I'm afraid he's going to scream the minute Mrs. Fletcher puts him down.

When he starts to fuss, I move in and put my hand on his stomach so she'll know to back away. I start to recite the *Brown Bear* book. Wil quiets and looks at me. My hands are shaking as I unzip his sleeper and move it out of the way.

I tell him the wipe will feel cool on his skin—just like Miss Ann does at the center. Wil's watching my mouth move. He's being such a good baby it makes me want to cry.

But I always want to cry. I'm exhausted. *Why can't he be quiet and cooperative at two A.M.? Why can't we sleep through the night just once?*

I feel like we're on display and being judged. *If I were a thirty-year-old mother, would I be followed around like this?*

Wil's over my shoulder and we lead the parade back to the living room. I sit on the rocker and take Wil's bottle off the end table. A ring of water remains, and I worry it'll leave a stain. My grandmother's so anal about my using the coaster I put away when I dusted. *I just know my head's going to explode.* And my bleach-burned hand is cracked and bleeding.

The very second Wil starts sucking his bottle, something in me relaxes. He has these gorgeous eyelashes, and such puffy little pink cheeks. He always wraps one little finger around mine when I hold his hand. Sometimes, if the light's right, I think I see red in the peach fuzz starting to cover his head. Wil has this goofy little look on his face; I decide he should be one of the Seven Dwarfs for Halloween.

"Baby boy, I love you," I say, and he smiles around the bottle's nipple and kicks his feet.

Miss Grace clears her throat, and I realize I'd almost forgotten they were here. Maybe it was just wishful thinking. I also realize that I forgot to wash my hands after I changed Wil. I usually try to at least use a wipe.

I look at Miss Grace. She smiles at me. "You're doing a wonderful job with Wil, Star. He looks healthy and happy. How are you?"

If I say how tired I am, will I get a bad report card? That's funny. You can't get much lower than a big, FAT, red 'F,' which I'm sure is my grade so far. I am, after all, an unmarried teen mother/high-school dropout.

"I'm okay, Miss Grace. Thanks for asking." I'm reassured by how positive my voice sounds, and the warm place that Wil has created, cradled here in my arms.

"Well, I brought you some hand cream and rubber gloves. I see you've been cleaning again. The house looks very nice, Star. I'm sure your grandmother appreciates all you do." I brush away the lone tear that sneaks out before I can tighten the floodgates.

"Star, may I ask you something?" Mrs. Fletcher's voice is hesitant. I'm afraid to look at her, so I stare at Miss Grace instead.

"Eve," Miss Grace says, not taking her eyes off me.

"I'm sorry, Grace, maybe this is not the time, but... Star?"

Star in the Middle

I look at the baby in my arms and think about poodles and pit bulls: what my own grandmother has done for me—and what I've done to her in exchange. Mrs. Fletcher *is* Wil's grandmother.

I swallow hard—too hard. I cough and Wil startles. I put the bottle back in the puddle on the table, then put him over my shoulder to burp him.

"It's okay, Miss Grace. Mrs. Fletcher? Did you want to ask me something?"

"What can Mr. Fletcher and I do for you and Wil, Star? Do you need anything?"

My hands are shaking. "I don't understand." I feel my face flush.

"I think you do. Star, I know my own grandchild. He looks just like Wil, except maybe he'll have your hair, and I hope he'll have many of your other wonderful qualities."

She can't be serious. What does this woman want?

Another siren: this one even closer. Mrs. Fletcher sits up tall in her seat, listens to the sounds in the bad neighborhood where her grandson lives. *Does she plan to take Wil away from me? Does she want to rescue him? Is that it?*

"Star, is there anything—anything at all we can do for you?" Mrs. Fletcher's voice sounds desperate now.

"Eve! Star, I'm sorry, honey."

I take a deep breath and hear the little sucking noises Wil makes in this sleep.

"Mrs. Fletcher, what you can do for me is not tell Wil we've had this conversation, please."

"I won't say anything to Wil for now, Star, if that's

what you want. But don't you think he has the right to know he's a father?"

I've been word-slapped. The sting lingers like a cross-hook, and it's knocked the wind out of me. I have less than a minute to be furious with Mrs. Fletcher before thundering footsteps invade the porch and loud pounding assaults the front door, followed by retreating footsteps that batter the steps. *Rodney.*

Wil startles. *Silence.* The baby settles.

Miss Grace's eyes are flooded with sorrow; Mrs. Fletcher's with fear. This is my life, one that I've imposed on this innocent baby. Still, I grew up without a mother—that *will not* happen to Wil. I'll stay with him. I'll protect him. But I'm done protecting Wilson.

"Your son, Mrs. Fletcher, has made the choice to believe this baby isn't his. I'd appreciate it if you and Mr. Fletcher would make the same choice. I have no intention of coming between you and your son. Please don't come between me and mine."

Mrs. Fletcher has *speechless* written all over her face. I'm not even sure she's still breathing. Miss Grace gets to her feet and tells her the visit is over. When I stand up, Miss Grace comes across the room and attempts to hug me. I stiffen.

"I'll lock the door," she whispers. "Go on back to your room, put Wil in his crib, and lie down for a rest."

I stand up and flee the scene, trusting Miss Grace to gather up what's left of Wilson's mother and cart her away.

Wil's eyes open when I lay him in his crib. I pat him

and he falls asleep. I lie down on my bed and pull the blanket over my head. It's probably 85 degrees in this house, but I need to hide.

There's angry shouting on the street out front. Rodney's mother is calling him names. I wonder if he will get a gun and shoot her dead some day. I pull my knees into my body and block everything out: My anger, my tears—the shouting out on the street.

I'm falling, falling through the darkness. I lay naked on the ground. A lone figure stands over me, staring into my dead eyes.

I can see you. Don't you know that? I know who you are. You can't hide behind that mask. I know your scar, your moles. Listen, the dogs are getting closer. Run! Run away, you coward!

Crying? Where am I? Wil? Go back to sleep. Please. I'm so tired. Okay, okay.

My feet are on the floor. My eyes are open.

See, Mommy's coming. I've got you, Wil. I'll never let go.

8
Wilson

Add having sex with Cate Hobart to the list of things I wish I'd waited to do. She called to yell at me about blowing her off at the pool. I asked how I could make it up to her. We went out to play miniature golf on Wednesday, tennis on Thursday, saw a movie on Friday. That's where the serious kissing started. The movie was boring—Cate was not.

We went out to Gap Run on Saturday night and the kissing escalated into messing around. That was apparently enough incentive for Cate. She pulled condoms out of her purse, offering them to me fanned out, like tickets to the circus: Colors. Scents. Flavors. A handful of treats packaged to encourage use, and to protect us from the horrors awaiting those who have unprotected sex.

Sex with Cate wasn't like sex with Star. I knew right away I wanted to be with Star. But with Cate, it was different. I wasn't even thinking about going that far. It was more her than me.

Cate didn't cry like Star. She unzipped my pants, helped me put the condom on. I didn't regret any of it until my cell phone rang later at home, as I was getting into bed.

It was Cate. She called this morning, too. But there's just no connection for me.

And if she was mad that I blew her off at the pool, how's she going to feel if I blow her off after having sex? I'm toast, or I'm stuck seeing her again. Which is it going to be? It's not like I can avoid her—she lives in my neighborhood. She's in my class at school.

I blew off church today. I pulled into the parking lot and Mrs. Peters was there. It was the late Mass, and she never goes to that one. So I pulled right back out again.

It's Sunday morning and now I have nowhere to go. I tried to call Star a couple times last week. I went past her house, too. I still haven't apologized for last Saturday. I guess she doesn't want to see me, because she hasn't returned my calls. I'm toast with her, for sure.

My mother's been acting strange with me, too. I feel someone staring at me and I look up, expecting to see that Mrs. Peters has broken into our house and is coming after me with that huge purse she carries around. I think she's packing heat. I'm serious. She could probably fit an entire arsenal of weapons in that ginormous thing.

Mom is very quiet and still. And that's another thing. My mother never sits still. My mother's never quiet. The other day I caught her in my bedroom, sitting on my bed, clutching one of my long discarded stuffed animals. It used to be a dog, but I hugged it around the neck so much it looks more like a giraffe, a genetic mutant she banished to the attic or cedar chest when I finally outgrew it. *What's she doing? Is she sad about me being a senior or something?*

The more I try to stop thinking about Star, the more I

think about Star. I thought about bringing her flowers, but that won't work with her. I know Star. I'd be eating those flowers for lunch.

So, it's Sunday morning and I'm walking around Towne Shopper, looking at diapers. Diapers! *How could there be this many sizes and brands of something a kid's going to wear for a few hours and crap in? And can you believe the price of these things? Come on, what are they made of, anyway?*

"Wrong size, Fletcher." I jump like I've been caught shoplifting. I somehow manage to drop the box of diapers I'm holding back onto the stack, which sends boxes tumbling to the floor. Elizabeth hands me one box after another, as I rebuild the display.

"Maybe I should get a job here." I'm joking, but the look on Anderson's face makes me believe I should go fill out an application right now.

"Are you biting your tongue, Elizabeth?"

"For months now, Fletcher."

"Go for it. Let me have it. What's on you mind?"

"This size will fit your baby," she tells me, handing me a box of diapers.

"I don't have a..."

"DON'T!" Anderson's index finger is dangerously close to my face. This is a side of Hobbs's girlfriend I've never seen. *Is he afraid of her?* It might explain their enduring relationship.

"I'm not convinced, okay?" I say.

"I never expected this from you, you know that? I thought you really loved Star. You totally had me fooled."

Star in the Middle

"What makes you think I don't love Star?" I don't see the blow coming, and when it lands, I nearly lose my footing, stumbling into the diaper display instead. Elizabeth steadies the pile.

"Lizbeth, did you just hit me?"

"No! I wanted to hit you, but I shoved you instead. What are you doing, Fletcher?"

"How is any of this your business?"

"It's not. Okay, *okay*, OKAY! It's not. I'm sorry. Star would kill me." Elizabeth walks away from me and my stupid make-up gift.

I'm seventeen years old and I'm buying a girl diapers to say I'm sorry for being a jerk. The kid's not even mine. He's not.

I pile on another couple of boxes of diapers and tour the store, looking for Elizabeth. I find her checking out lipstick.

Does she even wear lipstick? Anderson? She's so un-lipstick. Star wears this really cool color that rocks with her hair.

I stand beside Anderson and pretend I'm holding the diapers for her, in case we run into anyone we know. Of course, if they know us, they know Anderson doesn't need the diapers.

The bigger question is, do I?

"What do you mean, Star will kill you?"

"She's so protective of you. She won't tell anyone who the father is."

"Don't hit me again, but, maybe she's not sure herself."

Now I'm sitting on my ass on the floor, amid boxes of

diapers, staring up at my best friend's insane girlfriend. This girl is seriously in need of some anger management classes. Who knew she was capable of shoving over someone twice her size?

"I didn't hit you. I shoved you. And, I'll do it again, Fletcher, if you don't shut up. If you think that baby is not yours—you don't know Star."

Anderson reaches her hand down to help me up, but I ignore her. I drag myself to my feet, pick up the diapers, and walk away from the lunatic.

The checkout line is short. *Thank you, God!* The sales-girl—I've seen her around school—has this smug look as she rings up my purchase. Does everybody in this town think they know more about my sex life than me? *I know when the kid was born, and I know when I started having sex with Star. I can add.*

Anderson is standing at the Jeep. For the first time, I notice she's wearing running clothes. Her car is nowhere in sight.

"Give me a lift, Fletcher."

Can you believe her? Flattens me, and doesn't even say please when she wants a ride.

"Go away, Anderson."

"I'm going to Star's. Give me a lift."

I look at my watch. *Mass is almost over.* Grandma Peters will be home soon. And, like I've said before, the woman could be packing heat in her super-sized purse. My tailbone already hurts from being shoved to the floor—do I need a gunshot wound, too? *God, I know I didn't go to church, but please. Does this punishment really fit the crime?*

"How do I know you won't choke me to death and hi-jack my car?" I ask.

"Don't be so dramatic, you baby. You're a big strong athlete, remember?" She crosses her arms and stares at me.

"You know what, Anderson. Just because you're my best friend's girlfriend, it doesn't mean I have to talk to you, okay?"

"Alex is my best friend."

"Hobbs may be your boyfriend, but he's *my* best friend. Why are we having this conversation anyway? Just get in the car. I'll drop you off at Star's. You can deliver the diapers."

"Where are you going?" she asks.

"Home to hide from you and Mrs. Peters."

"Mrs. Peters is going out of town. Let's call a truce, okay?"

"A truce? You won't shove me to the ground, and I won't what?"

"You're kidding, right?" Her tone of voice is incredulous. *Which ticks me off.*

"Do I look like I'm kidding, Anderson?"

"I won't shove you to the ground, and you won't smear my best friend's name. Come on, let's stop and buy Star some lunch." Anderson latches her seat belt and sits back in the passenger seat, like I'm her private chauffeur. Now she's *really* ticking me off.

"What did I say to smear Hobbs's name?"

"Star's name."

"Oh, I thought you just said that Hobbs was your best friend."

"He is. So is Star."

I want to argue that they're my best friends, too. But the truth is, I'm not sure. Hobbs is different with me now. I'd like to blame it on Anderson bad-mouthing me, but maybe I did it to myself. Star's his friend, too. And Star won't even speak to me.

"You're *so* going the wrong way, Fletcher."

"I think I know the way to Star's"

"Yeah, but we're picking up lunch."

"I heard that. There's a couple of fast-food places on the way to Star's."

"We're going to Steward's."

"Steward's? I just bought four boxes of diapers. What makes you think I have money to buy lunch at Steward's?"

"Because, Fletcher, if you look up spoiled brat kid in the dictionary—your picture would *so* be there."

"Anderson, I thought we called a truce. Why are you busting on me?"

"Did I say I wouldn't bust on you? No, I said I wouldn't *shove* you. Take the next right, and give me your cell phone." Who knew this girl could be so bossy?

I do as I'm told. I take the next right and drive toward Steward's. I listen to Anderson on the phone, getting the number for Steward's from information, calling and placing an order that would easily feed the varsity football team at Hamilton Valley.

Why didn't I know that Star likes crab cakes?

"I've got twenty bucks, Wil, what do you have?" Anderson's smile is so charming, I actually wonder if all that other stuff really happened.

It's nice to be called *Wil* again. I open my wallet and hand her all the money I have left—which is about sixty bucks.

"Thanks. I'll bring you your change." The door slams and Anderson goes marching off with my phone in one hand and all my money in the other.

I sit in the Jeep and watch a bunch of Sunday-dressed people go in and out of Steward's Seafood. I have no patience for sitting still. *None! I'm just like my mother. I have to be moving.* Come to think of it, my father's pretty hyper, too.

My sister, Bridgett, insists that she was adopted. Just give her a book and a spot near the pool, and she won't budge for hours.

Anderson is taking forever. Okay, this is getting stupid. What? All the fishermen on the eastern shore of Maryland slept in? The seafood truck was hijacked before it ever crossed the Chesapeake Bay Bridge? This was just Anderson's ruse to get my money? Where is she?

I crack the window and a cool breeze filters in. *Finally.* Thunderstorms during the night cleared out the heat wave.

I close my eyes to an array of condoms. Lavender, strawberry....*Is it really somebody's job to design condoms? Why is sex such a circus?*

My hands are shaking. *I didn't know this relationship stuff would be so hard.*

The door slams, I bite my lip, squeeze my eyes shut tighter. *Oh, God. Am I ready for another round with Anderson?*

"Wil, are you asleep?" I *wish*. I open my eyes and look at her.

I guess what makes me mad is that I admire her so much. She's the kind of friend who won't dirt me just because she thinks I'm being a jerk. She'll torment me, but she won't dirt me. The problem is, I'm just not up to being Elizabeth's friend right now. *I'm just not good enough.*

"Almost, I'll drop you and the condoms..." I rake my hand across my big mouth. *I can't even believe what I just said.* "I'll drop you, and the food and diapers, off at Star's," I say, slamming the gearshift into reverse.

Elizabeth's quiet. She's angry with me again. Not that she ever stopped being angry, but I was beginning to think the truce might work. Was it the condom slip, or is she mad that I said I was dropping her off?

The food smells good and my stomach growls. We pass City Park and Anderson cranes her neck to look at the lake. This would be a great day for a picnic.

There are three police cars parked in front of a house four doors down from Star's. *Maybe I'm not just dropping Anderson off. I need to make sure she at least gets in safely; Star's safe.* I get out of the Jeep and go to open her door. She has the food. I have the diapers. I slam the door and look back at Anderson as she moves away from the Jeep and into Hobbs's waiting arms.

"Just got here," he tells her. "Mom had all the stuff we needed at home, so I didn't have to stop at the store." *So that's why Anderson needed my phone.* He reaches out and shakes hands with me. "Hi, Fletch."

"Hobbs." I manage to nod my head at him. *I'm feeling a little betrayed here.* I try to hand him the diapers.

"You're coming in, Fletcher." He insists, turning and following Anderson up the steps.

The door flies open before Anderson knocks. *How many phone calls did she make?* Star and Anderson are hugging and spinning around screaming. They stop to exchange greetings, and Star looks up at Hobbs with this wonderful smile on her face. He leans down and kisses her cheek. "You look great, Pete," he tells her. *What's this Pete crap?*

Star looks happy until she sees me. Her smile disappears and she looks pissed off. Maybe she feels as betrayed as I do. Hobbs actually looks sorry for me. Or maybe he looks sorry for Star. Obviously, no one bothered to tell *her* it was a double date, either.

Anderson acts fast—she scoots Star and Hobbs in the door, then swings around and takes me by the arm. "Behave yourself, Wil, promise me."

"Look, Lizbeth, this is a bad idea."

"No, you dating Cate Hobart, the Condom Queen, is a bad idea." I'm so shocked to hear those words come out of Anderson's mouth that I let her lead me through Star's front door without any resistance. Anderson never says anything negative about someone who's not present to mount a defense, so her current snit was over my condom remark. She probably thinks I was lusting over Hobart while I was waiting for her to pick up lunch. But I wasn't.

There is a flurry of activity going on in the kitchen. I stand in the doorway, not knowing where to drop the diapers. Hobbs is unpacking paper plates, napkins, and drinks from the bag he brought. Anderson's dropping wrapped crab-cake sandwiches on plates, taking lids off coleslaw and potato salad containers. Star brings silverware to the table and puts serving spoons out.

I first notice how much weight Star's lost when she stands next to Anderson, who's tiny, too. Star's jeans are hanging on her, her cheekbones are sunken, and she has bags under her eyes. She's so thin, I begin to wonder if she's sick. Then I hear the baby cry, and I freeze.

"I'll get him," Hobbs says. He charges past me, grabbing the diapers. Apparently, he knows where to drop them. Both Star and Anderson look at me.

Am I supposed to go with Hobbs? Fight him to hold the baby? I've never held the baby. When has Hobbs held the baby?

"Wil, come in and sit down," Anderson says, taking me by the arm, leading me to a kitchen chair. Hobbs comes in with the kid. He's getting so big, I don't even recognize him. Not that I ever really look at him. He must be almost three months old by now.

"I'll take him, Alex," Star says, reaching for the baby.

"Pete, sit down and eat. I'll put him in that bouncy seat thing. Where is it?" This baby must be a team sport, because before Star can answer, Anderson comes into the room with some kind of seat contraption that everyone seems to know about—except me.

"Does he need to be fed, Pete?" Anderson asks.

"No, he's good, thanks," Star tells Elizabeth.

Star in the Middle

What's with this *Pete* stuff, already? Is it because Star hates her name? That's why I started calling her *baby girl*.

I slide down in my chair, try to make myself disappear. Hobbs puts the baby in this playpen thing near the table. The kid's lounging in his little seat, looking around at all of us. Then, all of a sudden, everyone's talking to the baby and to each other, and reaching for the food.

It makes sense that Star and Elizabeth have been getting together without me, but Hobbs? I look at him with his mouth full of the food I bought. *Traitor.*

I stick my thumbnail in my mouth and start to chew. *This whole scene is surreal.*

Anderson reaches over and unwraps my crab cake for me. "Eat, Wil. Your stomach was growling the whole way over here."

This is ridiculous. Do I really want Star to see me as a languishing idiot who can't even feed himself? I sit up, pull the chair closer to the table.

"Please pass the potato salad." My voice sounds normal. *Good start.* I spoon potato salad on my plate and take a bite. It's really good. Not as good as my mother's, but I'm hungry and finish it in three bites.

Anderson passes me the coleslaw—I decline, reaching for more potato salad. Coleslaw's nasty and I never eat it. I take a big gulp of the coke Anderson poured in my glass and choke like a four-year-old. I'm the opposite of cool today, and no amount of pretending's going to make me look any better than I do with Coke coming out of my nose.

"Need a straw?" Hobbs says, cracking himself up.

I pick up my crab cake and start to eat. It's huge, but I

notice that Star's is gone and she's looking at mine like it's Prince Charming.

"What?" I ask her.

"Nothing, Wilson, that's okay," she says.

"What's okay?" *I really want to know.*

"I thought maybe you didn't like crab cakes because you were filling up on potato salad."

Filling up on potato salad? I'm starving here. I always only eat one thing at a time, and save the best for last.

"Do you want this, Star?" I ask, handing her my sandwich. "I'm not all that hungry."

"That's so sweet, Fletcher," Anderson coos at me. "But you're such a liar. Eat your sandwich. We have two more left."

"I'm okay," Star says. "You probably got those for the guys. Girls one, guys two."

I reach in the bag and toss Star and Hobbs a crab cake, since Anderson still has a half eaten one on her plate. Star doesn't hesitate for a nanosecond. "Yummy, thanks, guys."

I begin to wonder why Star is so thin. She catches me staring at her and looks away quickly.

Lunch over, the kitchen's cleaned up like none of us have ever been here. We go into the living room. Anderson's holding the kid, and Star's holding the bottle she warmed for him.

I'm secretly hoping that forcing me to feed the baby isn't part of Anderson's master plan. But she sits in the rocker and Star hands her the bottle. I feel a knot in my stomach.

Hobbs grabs some book off the coffee table and sits

on the sofa, looking through it. "This scrapbook is great, Star. Lizbeth was telling me about it."

I stand over Hobbs and look at pictures of the baby. He has rosy, fat cheeks and a lopsided smile framed by dimples. Hobbs starts flipping back through pages and the baby gets smaller and smaller, until he's in some kind of see-through container, hooked up to tubes.

"I remember how scared you were, Pete," Hobbs says, whistling through his teeth. He taps on the picture of fear: Star after giving birth. She looks exhausted, drained, and terrified. Her cheeks are streaked with tears.

"Everything's cool now, though, right?" Hobbs asks. "Baby's okay?"

"He's fine," Star says. "The doctor said she'd never believe Wil was premature if she hadn't seen him when he was born."

"Pete, Wil's asleep. I'll put him in his crib," Anderson whispers.

"I'll go with you." Star jumps up and is gone.

"Did you know, Hobbs? Did you know Star had such a rough time?" My throat aches.

"I knew." Hobbs levels his eyes at me accusingly.

I return his stare. "Why the hell didn't you tell me?"

"Why the hell didn't you ask, Fletcher?"

"Don't be stupid."

"Look, Pete didn't want you to know anything you weren't willing to find out on your own," Hobbs says, quietly.

"Oh, that's fair," I snap.

Hobbs snaps the book shut. "You want to talk about *fair*," he spits, shoving the book at me. "Grow up, Fletcher."

"Hey! What's going on? No one has said a word to me about Star and her kid in all these months, and now every-one's busting on me."

I look up just in time to see Star walk into the room, closely followed by Anderson. The look on Star's face tells me that she's overheard at least part of this conversation.

"Who's busting on you?" Star asks. "Wilson? Who's busting on you? I hope Lizbeth and Alex didn't force you to come over here. What did Alex say to you?"

"I have to go. Can I borrow this?" I ask, clutching the scrapbook.

"No, Fletcher." She sounds determined.

"Star, please? I'll bring it back tomorrow, or later today. You say when."

"Wilson, give it to me, please." My hands are shaking as I hand her the book, then turn to leave the room.

"Wil, stay," Elizabeth says. "We can all talk."

I turn to find Star hugging the scrapbook so tight I think her arms may turn white.

"I have to go," I mumble again. I get as far as the door, when Star catches up with me.

"I'm sorry, Wilson," she whispers. "Here. Take it."

"I promise to be careful with it." Star nods and turns away.

I drive about half a mile from Star's and I can't hold it back any longer. I get out of the car and throw up in the bushes. I'm shivering as I get back in the Jeep and pick up the scrapbook. It's blue and white checked, with a clear pocket on the cover for the baby's picture. Star chose what looks like a newborn picture the hospital takes. The baby's wearing a little blue hat and his eyes are closed.

I open the book to the picture of Star in the hospital bed. *I don't care if this baby is mine or not, I shouldn't have let Star go through this alone.* I prop the book open on the passenger seat as I drive home.

Mom and Dad are out by the pool with Bridgett and her boyfriend. I ask my mom if I can talk to her privately. She puts on her beach robe and we go into the study. She closes the door and looks up at me.

"What do you have there, Wil?" she asks. I hold out the book, and she takes it from my shaking hands.

"Oh, Wil," she says, tears streaming down her cheeks. "Are you showing me pictures of my grandson?"

"Is he your grandson, Mom?"

"Wil, even if you doubted that, you should have come to us."

"Did Star tell you?"

"Last Monday, I taught a class at the center where Star goes to school. She didn't tell me. But I suspected as soon as I saw Wil. The baby's health care nurse and I visited with Star on Friday. When I held Wil, I knew for sure. Star made me promise I wouldn't talk to you. She said she doesn't want anything from us. How can we not help with our own grandchild?"

"Does Dad know?"

"Of course, I told your father. We're heartbroken that you didn't come to us. Why didn't you, Wil?"

I can't make my mother understand something I don't understand myself. I remain silent.

"It's our responsibility to help Star with your baby. I've been in touch with Mrs. Peters, but Star doesn't know that yet."

I bury my head in my hands. I hear my mother gasp, and when I open my eyes, she's looking at the pictures of Star and the baby in the hospital.

I find my shaky voice, "Mom, could Star have died?"

"I'm sure that her heart was broken, seeing her baby like that. But, no, Wil, I don't think she was in danger of dying. Fortunately, the baby's gaining weight and appears to be doing well. He's very alert, and he looks well cared for and loved." She pauses.

"But I just don't understand your behavior, Wilson. Your father and I were so smitten with Star when we met her. You two seemed like such good friends. Why didn't you come to us? We could've supported both of you during this difficult time."

"I'm sorry, Mom." I wipe away tears I hope my mother doesn't see. *How can I possibly be a father? I'm such a crybaby.*

9
Star

Rodney launched major attacks on the porch and front door all evening, so I'm over the top when the phone rings at 11:00 P.M. I answer only because I think it's my grandmother calling.

"Hello." I sound like I've been drugged.

"Star," Wilson says, "I'm sorry for calling so late. I wanted to wait until your grandmother was asleep. I hope I didn't wake...the baby."

"The baby's awake. He slept most of the day. He must be part bat or something else nocturnal." *I don't really know what I'm saying. Why am I talking to Wilson anyway?* "What is it? What do you want?"

"I want to drive you to the center in the morning."

"No."

"Star, please. I have the scrapbook. I want to bring it back to you. Can my mother scan the pictures? She really wants to, but not without your permission."

"Wil, it's too late for all this stuff, okay?"

"I know it's late, Star. I'm sorry. Should I call you back in the morning?"

"No, Wilson, don't call me, okay? It's too late—period. Just break into my house again, and leave the scrapbook on the kitchen table, when I'm not here. Thanks for mowing the lawn, but I don't want your help. Goodbye."

"Don't hang up. Please."

"Look, I can't see you. It's just too hard."

"I promise I won't make it hard, Star. What's that noise?"

"It's Rodney beating on the door again. He does this when he knows my grandmother's away."

"Where's your grandmother?"

"At her friend's, in Baltimore. She has some kind of medical test tomorrow at Hopkins."

"Star, you can't stay there alone overnight. I'm coming over."

I don't want to be in this house alone. I'm scared. But I can't trust Wilson, and I can't trust myself alone with him. "Wilson, no. I won't let you in. I won't."

"I can get in without your help, Star."

"NO! Please. I don't want you here."

"I'll sleep on the couch. I won't even touch you."

My heart hurts. I can hear it beating. *I miss Wilson.* But I can't let myself give in to the loneliness. I look down and find that Wil's fallen asleep on the bed beside me. I'm so grateful he's asleep. Maybe I can fall asleep, too. Maybe I can sleep through Rodney's pounding, the police sirens, and my loneliness for Wilson. *Why did I let this happen to myself?*

"Wil needs me. I have to go. Please don't call again, Wilson." He's still talking when I turn off the phone and put it on the windowsill with a flashlight. I should put the phone back on the cradle. The battery's low, but I'm betting, praying, it'll last through the night.

I shouldn't be this afraid to stay alone. I told my grandmother I'd be okay, but I'm not. My heart's pounding and I hear every little noise.

Rodney would never break in. I know that. I know he wouldn't really hurt me. I don't know how I know; I just know. He's just annoying.

There are other things out there: terrible things, terrible people. I'm drifting, drowsy. The front door is double-locked. The lock's been changed. *He* never had a key to the back door. Never. Grandma promised. I wanted her to have that lock changed anyway. But she said it was an unnecessary expense. I know that if he wanted to get in, he could break any window in the house.

I should put Wil in his crib. But what if he wakes up? I'm sorry, Miss Marcie—just this once, okay? He can sleep with me just this once.

His breathing is so soothing. How can one little body be so perfect? It's quiet now, except for a distant train whistle. I should get up and lock my bedroom door. My heart's going to beat right out of my chest. The sooner I fall asleep, the sooner morning will come. That's what my grandmother used to tell me, when she came into my room and tried to pick up the pieces of my life.

I don't remember falling asleep, but my mouth's dry, and I shake off bits of a dream about footsteps. *How long have I slept?* Wil's so still, I put my hand on his chest to make sure he's breathing. He sighs. *Footsteps.* I take a deep breath, waiting to hear my grandmother click on the bathroom light. I fight drowsiness.

The realization that my grandmother's not home grabs me by the throat. I startle awake and sit up in bed. My throat tightens as I try to swallow. I pick up the phone and listen for a dial tone. The battery's dead. I get out of bed and dash across the floor. I close and lock the bedroom door and put my ear against it. Silence. Did I imagine the footsteps? Echoes of my past, when my grandmother unknowingly invited terror into the house? All my senses tell me that Wil and I are not alone.

I try to look at my watch, but the room is pitch black—except for a patch of hall light that reaches under the door. I'm trapped. I sit on the edge of the bed and wait. *Should I open the window, and make a run for it with Wil?*

I feel my way across the room and move the shade aside. There's so little light from the streetlight or moon, because of the trees in the backyard. I try to open the window. It won't budge.

Wil lets out a little cry. I dive on the bed and pat him. He cries louder and I pick him up, and rock him in my arms. "Shhh! Wil, it's okay," I whisper. The crying continues for a couple of minutes. I'm frantic by the time he quiets. I go to the door and listen hard: pots and pans, water running?

"Maybe Grandma came home," my hushed words fall against Wil's cheek. I'm not confident enough to open the door. I stand with my back against it, holding Wil, praying to God to protect my baby.

There's a gentle tap on the door and I jump halfway across the room. "Star, I heated the bottle the way you did yesterday afternoon, but I don't know if I did it right. How warm should it be exactly?"

Should I laugh or cry? I'm relieved. I'm angry. I open the door and look at Wilson, standing under the hall light. He's wearing a football jersey and jeans, his feet are bare, and his hair looks like he just crawled out of a blender. He hands me the bottle and disappears.

I sit on the bed with Wil and test the formula against my wrist. *Perfect*. Beginner's luck.

I put the bottle in the crib, while I go to the hall to change Wil's diaper. He starts to fuss the minute I lay him down on the changing table, so I recite the *Brown Bear* book until he's in a clean diaper and zipped back in his sleeper. It's amazing how he instantly quiets when he hears the words to a book or a nursery rhyme.

I go back into my room, sit on the bed, and give Wil his bottle. He is so lazy about nighttime feedings that it seems to take forever to feed him. And he keeps falling asleep, but when I try to take the bottle out of his mouth, he wakes up and remembers that he's hungry. By the time I give up on getting any more sleep, he lets the nipple fall out of his mouth and I put him in the crib.

I take the bottle to the kitchen and put what's left back in the refrigerator. Wilson's curled up on the sofa, sound asleep. I get a blanket out of the linen closet and cover him.

His mother promised she wouldn't tell him that she talked to me about the baby. So much for promises. Is she forcing him to do this?

I think I'm too keyed up to sleep, but my bed feels wonderful. I yawn and burrow under the covers. I can hear the refrigerator humming—a reassuring house sound. Wilson heard the baby, so I'm sure he'll hear if someone tries to break in. *Hey, wait. Wilson heard the baby.* The sagging corners of my mouth fight to smile.

Wilson's been true to his word—hasn't touched me. I think about it so much. *What would have happened if we had waited to have sex? Or if I hadn't been freaked about condoms—and not able to tell Wilson why. He would have stopped.* In my heart, I know that.

My hands fly to my head, and I am twisting fists full of hair. *Sometimes you have no control over what happens to you.* No control over the memories either: Bad memories that lay dormant in the pathways of your brain, until one word triggers them. My mind is such a maze of unwanted memories that travel around and around, but never find an escape route.

Wilson's asleep on the couch. He'll listen for danger. He'll call 911. He'll ward off threats lurking in the darkness. If only he'd heard what I couldn't tell him on other nights. If only tears had a voice—had the same power as words. I wish we'd waited to have sex. I wish we'd avoided all the misery we caused ourselves and our families. I wish, I wish, I wish.

I hear Wil stir in his crib. He's a separate entity: No longer physically tied to the sex act that brought him into existence. Regardless of what we wish, or whether or not we want him here, he's a person. He'll occupy his space in time—will grow and gather memories, just as I have. I can put photographs into a scrapbook, but what will he remember of his family when he's my age?

Star in the Middle

In spite of all the insanity, I can't imagine any mother in any circumstances loving her baby more than I love Wil. *Will I be strong enough to show him? Where's my mother? Wil's grandmother?* I've never needed her more than I have the past few months. I must have a father out there somewhere, too, but I don't think about him the way I think about my mother. I guess it's because my mother was around for a while. I remember her. I chose to remember the good times, not the bad ones my grandmother brings up when she's frustrated and wants to prove a point.

I know I shouldn't, but I pretend Wilson's arms are wrapped around me. I imagine we're lying in bed together: warm and safe. While I'm pretending, I pretend my baby has a father who wants him. I try to soak in enough good thoughts to get me through the night. Night is a memory keeper, storing dreams that haunt me. Wilson's arms are around me; he's asleep. For tonight at least, I'm safe.

10
Wilson

The baby woke up a million times during the night. I don't know how Star does this every single night. I don't know *why* she does it either. There *were* other options. I guess it's pretty easy to see why she looks so tired. Between the sirens, the kid, and the damn noisy refrigerator—who could sleep?

I grab my ringing phone off the coffee table before it wakes the baby. "Yeah?"

"Wilson Theodore Fletcher, where are you?"

"Mom, I'm sorry I didn't wake you last night when I left." Lie alert: I purposely waited until my parents were asleep before I made my break for it. How many lies have I told over the past few months? I'm sure it's some kind of a record, even for a high school kid. Maybe I should try to get in the *Guinness Book of World Records*. My parents would be so proud. "I'm at Star's. I found out she was here alone and I was a little freaked about it."

"Wilson, do you think spending the night alone with Star was the best solution? Her grandmother's not going to be happy. And I'm not so thrilled myself."

"Mom, I slept alone on the couch, okay?"

"And, what about driving around alone late at night? What about that?"

"Look, I know you don't want me out late at night by myself and I'm sorry. But you said you wanted me to take some responsibility for what I've done. So, I did."

"If you'd have come to us, Dad could have gone over there with you. Or, Star and the baby could have come here."

"What was Dad going to do, sleep on the sofa with me, Mom? And Star didn't even want me here. In case you haven't noticed, she doesn't want any of us around. I seriously doubt she'd stay at our house for one minute, let alone a whole night."

"Well, that'll have to change. We're Wil's family, too."

Don't say that to Star right now: Maybe a month ago, but not now. "Look, I'll drive Star and, um, the baby, to the center, and then I'll be home. Oh, wait—I bought a chain lock for the back door on my way over here last night, so I have to put it on the door." The words slip out of my sleep-deprived mouth before I can rein them in.

"You got out of your car alone at Towne Shopper, and in Star's neighborhood? In the middle of the night? What were you thinking, Wilson?"

Star, bleary-eyed, sits in the rocker, crosses her arms, and stares at me. *How is it possible for her to look beautiful on so little sleep?* "Can we talk about this later, Mom? Okay, I'll call you if I need you. Goodbye, Mom." I swing my feet to the floor, toss the phone on the coffee table, cross my arms, and stare back at Star. *I definitely don't need two mothers*. I try to sit perfectly still, but my rebellious hands fly to my face and rub my eyes.

"Go home, Wilson."

"I will, Star. I'll go home after I install a lock on the back door and drive you to the center. If you were better at eavesdropping, you'd know my plan for the day."

"Don't be glib, Wilson."

Okay, well, people should at least give you three multiple-choice guesses when they throw out a seldom-used word like *glib*. You know, like, does it mean: (A) Something a fish says; (B) Wil's a jerk; or, (C) Look at me, my Webster's 101 course is paying off? I somehow think 'B' is the correct answer. I'm remembering that 'glub,' not 'glib,' is something a fish says—although, I've never heard a fish say anything. 'A' is out. And, if I answer 'C,' I'll just be accused of being glib again.

Star's still staring at me. I try to sit perfectly still, but my rebellious teeth dig in and bite my lower lip until I'm afraid blood'll spurt all over my glibness. Which, I'm starting to recall, has something to do with careless speech. *Why is the kid quiet now? I could really use some intervention here.* "What time do you have to be at school?" I ask.

"It's too late to call Miss Patty and cancel the van, Wil. You need to go home. I told your mother I didn't want to come between the two of you."

"Interestingly, my mother's taking to finding out she's a grandmother."

"Yeah, well, just wait. You'll soon find out that no matter how well she appears to be handling being a grandmother, she won't be able to handle *you* being a father."

I gulp so loud that there's no way Star doesn't hear.

She doesn't seem to understand that I can't be a father. I don't fit the profile. My life bears no resemblance to any of the fathers I know. I'm an unemployed high school senior who still occasionally slips and calls his mother "mommy." *I mean, sure, I can heat up bottles, but don't ask me to change diapers, or figure out why the kid's crying. I couldn't even pick that kid out of a lineup of two or fewer babies. How can I be his father?*

"Go get ready for school, Star. I'll listen for—for the baby." *I wish she wouldn't stare at me like that.* Honest, I just crossed my eyes to see if I had a pimple on my nose or something, the way she was looking at me. But Star puffed out of here like a locomotive gathering steam, hoping to pulverize anything that gets in her way.

Star's been in the bathroom for a really long time. I tap at the door, "Do you have a hammer? I have this lock..."

"You need a screwdriver for that, Fletcher."

It's Fletcher now, great! I study the lock shrink-wrapped in clear packaging. Now that I'm actually looking, I see that Star's right—I need a screwdriver.

"Okay, Peters, where's the screwdriver?"

"In the closet with the washer and dryer."

"And, that's where?"

"Off the kitchen, Fletcher, on the right."

Okay, so we're using only last names now. "Thanks, Peters."

There's nothing resembling a Phillips screwdriver in the only toolbox I can find, so I decide to go back out to the store after Star leaves. She's fed the baby and is dressing him. I know this because she talks to him all the time;

telling him what she's doing. Like he cares that she's pulling his sleeve over his arm. Does she not get that he doesn't understand word one of what she says to him? I mean, I know nothing about babies, but I'm pretty sure they aren't born understanding any language. I'm pretty sure he doesn't even know his mother smells good, and that he's lucky to have her hold him like that.

There's a pretty persistent horn blowing out front. Star comes flying into the kitchen and out to the mudroom. She has her purse and a bag the size of a Volkswagen over one shoulder, and the baby over the other. She somehow gets the mudroom door open and attempts to turn the stroller around.

"You can ask for help, Star," I tell her, taking the stroller by the handle. "Where are we taking this?"

"You're not taking it any place, Fletcher. There're probably six girls on the van who you don't want to have see you."

"And how many girls are there on the van who I *do* want to have see me, Peters? Go." There's a woman with brown curly hair on the porch when Star swings the door open.

"Miss Patty, I'm sorry. What is it about Mondays? This is Wilson."

The woman smiles at Star, and pats the baby. "It's okay, I'm a little early today. I know this is Wilson, honey."

"No, the baby is Wil. This is Wilson." Star nods in my direction.

I shake Miss Patty's hand. "It's nice to meet you. I'm Wil."

"Well, it's nice to meet you, Wil. Would you mind loading the stroller into the back of the van for us?"

I follow them across the street and try to figure out how to collapse the stroller. I think the engineer who designed it must have had a sick sense of humor. Star's friends are all staring out the back window, watching me. The good news is, I find the latch. The bad news is, I pinch my finger and let out a yelp. At least I didn't swear. I open the back of the van to wolf whistles—how degrading.

"Girls, be nice. You're embarrassing Star."

Star? What about me, Miss Patty?

The van pulls away, and I'm left there in the middle of the street. Maybe I can use a knife as a screwdriver; install the lock and get the hell out of here. My dad pulls up and waves to me. He gets out of his truck and waits for me to cross the street.

"Wilson, do you need tools?"

My parents only call me Wilson when they're mad at me. Maybe I'll be Wilson forever, now. Dad doesn't wait for my reply. Instead, he opens the back of his company truck and pulls out a toolbox.

"Show me where the lock goes, son." Dad's on my heels as we climb the steps and I open the front door.

"What a great floor," he says, tapping his foot against the hardwood in the living room.

I guess I've never thought about Star's house in terms of anything but the bad location. My dad owns the construction company my grandfather started and is into architecture. He walks around, knocking on woodwork, running his hand over windowsills.

"The houses on this street are well built. It's a shame about what's going on outside them."

Dad looks as tired as I feel. I wonder if he's avoiding what he really wants to say to me.

He opens his toolbox, then eyeballs the door and the lock in my hand.

"Did you ask Mrs. Peters's permission to do this?"

"Do what?"

"Install a lock like this. It's going to mark up her door. And the proper response to my question is 'excuse me.' Have you forgotten about basic manners?"

"I'm sorry, Dad. They actually don't lock this door. They lock the one in the mudroom. It's pretty easy to break into with a credit card."

There has to be something going on with my face that I'm not aware of, because my father's staring at me just like Star did. I force myself not to cross my eyes and look at my nose again, especially considering how well that went the first time.

"And you know this how, son?"

"Um, Star locked herself out one day and I helped her get in." It's a lie, but my father looks somewhat relieved. He goes out to the mudroom and stands in front of the door.

"Okay, we can put that lock on this door. I know Mrs. Peters is in Baltimore and can't be reached right now to ask permission."

How, Dad? How do you know that?

"I'll just replace the door and frame if she's unhappy. I'd like to do that anyway. This door isn't going to keep anyone who really wants in out, even with the chain lock.

116

It'll slow them down, though. Encourage Star to keep that kitchen door locked, too, okay? That was the original back door anyway. This enclosed porch was added long after the house was built."

Dad hands me an electric screwdriver and supervises while I put the lock on. I'm not as clueless as Star thinks. I help my father with repairs around the house. I've followed him around construction sites since I was a little kid, and I worked the past two summers with his construction crews.

"Good job, Wil. But tell you what, that refrigerator's driving me crazy. I need to go out to the truck and get a level—and stop that noise." Dad unhooks the chain, and goes out the back door.

I sit on the floor in the kitchen and listen to the refrigerator. I'm pretty sure Mrs. Peters wouldn't want us in her house. Star says she's a very private person. Dad's here because he wants to make the house safer for the kid; I know that.

I'm here because I can't get the picture of Star in the hospital bed out of my brain. Do I think that installing a lock on her door's going to ease my conscience? It won't— no more than mowing the lawn eased my conscience over the way I spoke to her the last night we were together. Okay, I'd been drinking, but that's not an excuse for what I said to her.

My father would never speak to my mother, or anyone else, like that. I look away when he comes through the door—afraid he'll see the guilt in my eyes.

He whistles when he places the level on the refrigerator. We wrestle with it, and put a thin piece of wood under the front left side. He opens the fridge door. Now it does what he wanted, which is close on its own.

Next, he takes two screwdrivers out of the toolbox and asks to see the baby's room. I stand in the doorway and watch him tighten screws on the crib. Star's bed is made. The bear I won for her at the carnival last fall is MIA.

Dad moves toward the doorway. I try to step aside, but he puts his hand on my shoulder. I suspect it's a move more to steady himself than to keep me in place.

"Wilson, we all make mistakes in life, I understand that, but this baby hasn't done anything wrong. Nothing. Do you hear me?"

I nod.

"He deserves the best from all of us, and he's going to get it. Do you understand me?"

I nod.

"Answer me, Wilson, because right now, I'm not sure you've understood one thing your mother and I've tried to teach you for the past seventeen years."

I swallow so hard that I hear an echo in my ears.

"Wilson?"

"I understand, Dad." *The baby gets the best of me, but you probably doubt that's good enough.*

I close my eyes, take a deep breath, and hope he'll disappear. It takes me a while to process stuff, and I do it better without an audience. Unfortunately, Dad's still in my face when I open my eyes.

"I hope and pray we understand each other here, son. I have several work sites to visit today. I trust that you'll lock up here. Then I want you to go home. Put your car keys on my desk in the study, and don't touch the Jeep again until your mother and I talk to you. You are *never* to leave the house again that late at night, alone. Do you hear me?"

I study the floor, "Yes, Dad."

My father squeezes my shoulder and walks away. I hear him in the kitchen, gathering his tools. He stops in the living room and puts his toolbox down briefly. Then the front door opens and closes. I'm surprised he doesn't stop to oil the squeaky hinges.

Star's bed squeaks under my weight. I sit and stare into the empty crib. I knew when I practiced football drills, I'd make some great plays on the field. I knew when I practiced driving, I'd pass my test the first time. I knew when I bounced the lacrosse ball off the brick garage a million times, I'd learn to control the ball. I knew that sooner or later, if I made enough moves on Star, I'd score.

What I didn't know was that I didn't even have to think about making a baby. It took no practice or study, it required no testing. *You shouldn't have made it so easy, God. Didn't you know I'd be a miserable father?* I smack the crib rail and leave the room.

I open one kitchen cabinet drawer after another until I find paper and a pen. I want to tell Star that I love her. I want to tell her that she's beautiful. I want to tell her that she's a good mother. I want to tell her that I am truly, truly sorry for everything. In the end, I scribble—"Peters, I'm sorry. Fletcher." I put the note on her pillow.

My father's folded the blanket on the couch. I don't know where to put it, so I put it on Star's bed. I lock the back door, the kitchen door, and the front door as I leave. Too late, I remember my cell phone on the coffee table. I reach for the credit card in my wallet—another memory lapse.

I sit on the front step and turn the credit card over and over in my hand. Dad said the chain lock on the back door wouldn't keep a person out who's determined to get in. I decide not to test his theory.

I go out to the backyard to check on the little dogwood I planted. It looks a little sad. I have my hand wrapped around it, ready to put it out of its misery.

What would Star do?

I walk away.

11
Star

I almost missed it entirely. Once I start focusing on the SAT study guide on the computer, I'm oblivious to everything else in the room. As soon as I see it, I jump up to erase it—too late.

"Very cute," Miss Marcie announces, standing in front of the board. "I like the way they used a star shape rather than your name, and what does it say? 'Your baby's father is one fine-looking specimen.' I'm guessing Jessica came up with the star idea, and Tanya came up with the message. Any bets, Star?"

I glance around the room, scanning for eavesdroppers, but I'm the only other person in the room with Miss Marcie. Everyone else is in GED class, which is where I want to be. Miss Marcie said I can't start GED classes until I officially drop out of school, which I need my grandmother's permission to do. I pick up the eraser and start erasing—the star first. Miss Marcie sighs.

I know Wilson didn't try to cause me all this hassle today, but he did anyway. If I hear one more time that someone knew it was him all along, I'll scream. No one knows anything. Wilson's an unintentional sperm donor. That doesn't make him a father. I don't know what he's up to, being nice, but it's nothing I can trust. In fact, I don't know who or what I can trust.

There are rumblings that a big meeting went down at the center last Friday when I was home bleaching my skin off, cleaning. I wasn't really eavesdropping, but it's pretty easy to hear things around here. It sounds like a whole lot of people got together to discuss my fate, and Wil's. Funny, but no one bothered to ask me what *I* wanted.

Some days I feel totally invisible to everyone old enough to talk. But right now, I'm very visible to Miss Marcie, and she's still waiting for an answer. The problem is, I can't remember the question. I'm aware that I'm erasing a blank board. Miss Marcie's aware of it, too. She's still looking at me.

"Well, the baby's father is what I want to talk to you about," she says. *Oh yeah, that fine-looking specimen.* "Star, I understand he was at your house this morning. I also know your grandmother was out over night. I know that we've talked about this before, but do you realize that you have so much to lose and so little to gain by not going along with your grandmother's wishes?"

"How do you know my grandmother was out over night?" I want to know.

"Because I spoke with her on Friday, Star. I know she had a medical test scheduled this morning in Baltimore. We need to sit down this week and discuss your options about going back to school. We also need to discuss what your grandmother wants for you. She said she's having a hard time communicating with you, and she's asked me to help. I'm guessing she doesn't know you had a sleepover."

"Just because Wilson was at my house this morning, doesn't mean he spent the night."

"Did he spend the night?"

"Well, yes, but he slept on the couch. I didn't ask him to come over. He called and I told him I was alone."

"Isn't that what got you in trouble the last time?"

"I told him I didn't want him to come over. In fact, I specifically told him *not* to come. He scared me to death in the middle of the night, because I didn't know he was in the house."

"Star, how did he get in?"

"Miss Marcie, you don't want to know. All I really want you to know is that he slept on the sofa, and he bought a chain lock to put on the back door. So he's not getting in again—and I'm feeling safer about it keeping other people out, too."

"Other people? Whom are you referring to?"

"Again, Miss Marcie, you don't want to know." *Hello! Can't she hear the phone ringing?* "Should I answer that? It's probably the nursery, for me."

"Okay, but, we need to get back to this conversation ASAP." I hate ASAP. I really do. Miss Marcie's big on the whole 'don't put off until tomorrow what you can do today' thing.

"Star speaking," I say into the receiver, as Miss Marcie stays perched and ready to pounce. "How high is his fever? Is that serious? Should I take him to the doctor? Okay, I'll be right there." I put down the receiver and look at Miss Marcie. "Our conversation's going to have to wait. Miss Patty's going to drive me and Wil home."

"Does Wil need to see a doctor?"

"Miss Ann said that Grandma and I should make that decision."

"But your grandmother's not home."

"Grandma said she'd be home early this afternoon."

"But she may not be up to it."

"Excuse me?"

"Your grandmother had to be at the hospital very early. She may be tired when she gets home. So, I'll tell you what. You go home and talk to her. If you two feel Wil needs to see a doctor, call me and I'll take you. Actually, call the doctor and see what she recommends. Okay? Come on, I'll walk you to the nursery."

Wil had a rough start, but he's been a healthy baby since then. It's sad to see his little face so flushed. Miss Marcie looks over my shoulder as I sit in the rocker and check him out. His skin's red, like he's embarrassed about something.

"It could just be his coloring, Star," Miss Ann tells me, touching Wil's tiny wisps of red hair. "His temperature isn't that high. You just need to keep an eye on it. Do you have a thermometer at home? Listen, call the doctor and see what she says. Tell her Wil's running a slight fever, but doesn't appear to have other symptoms besides being flushed. Check his temp again right before you call."

I just want Wil fixed. I can't fix him, but a doctor can, right? If Grandma's not home, or is too tired to take us, do

I really have to call Miss Marcie? I can call Elizabeth, or maybe Todd would take me. That would be great, because Nevaeh is older and maybe he's been through this. I can ask him all the questions I'm too embarrassed to admit I'm clueless about to Miss Ann and Miss Marcie.

Miss Patty pops her head in the door to tell me she's ready. I know she has to drop her office work to do this, so I feel guilty. I wish I could drive, but I don't have a car anyway.

The van feels very empty. I don't think I've ever been on it by myself, well, I'm not exactly alone; Miss Patty's driving and Wil's sitting in his seat.

"Honest, Star, honey, Wil will be fine. Babies run elevated temperatures for all sorts of reasons. Maybe he's cutting a tooth."

Cutting teeth doesn't seem too likely to me. I mean, he's not even three months old, and he was early. I've been reading this book called *What to Expect the First Year*, and it tells you when babies do things—usually.

"Well, I guess he is pretty young for teeth," Miss Patty says. I swear she looked at me in the rearview mirror and read my mind.

I glance down at Wil. He's out. Sound asleep. *How sick could he be, right? I have a hard time falling asleep when I'm sick. But, maybe babies are different.*

Rodney's sitting on his front porch steps. Miss Patty walks Wil and me to my door, then gets back in the van and drives off. Wil doesn't even stir as I take him out of his seat and put him in his crib. He feels warm to the touch. I want to call Miss Ann to ask if I should wake him up to take his temperature, but I'm afraid that she'll think I am as clueless as I feel. So I let him sleep. He probably won't sleep long anyway if he's sick.

I take the bottles I'd prepared for this afternoon at the center and put them in the refrigerator. I brown stew meat and onions in a pot; peel and slice carrots and potatoes, dump in frozen beans, corn, and a lot of water, then put the whole mess on simmer for dinner.

Miss Louise served chili for lunch. It was an interesting choice. Grandma never serves chili in the summer. I snuck in the kitchen and Miss Louise let me eat early with her. I was starved. It made me so thirsty, though. All I want to do is drink water. I fill a glass with tap water and drink it down. I try to open the back door leading to the mud-room; it's locked. I unlock it and go out to look at Wilson's handiwork. The chain lock is secure. It's not hung upside down, or crooked. I don't know what I expected. Maybe I wanted Fletcher to be as clueless about something as I feel about being a mother.

I prop my feet up on the coffee table and lay my head back on the couch. There's this weird vibrating noise. I can't figure out where it is coming from, and then it's gone. I remember getting a blanket out for Wilson and want to cover up. The blanket's not on the sofa. I go to the linen closet, but it's not there. I find it folded on my bed. I want it to smell like Wilson, but it doesn't.

Wil is still asleep. His breathing sounds fine. I go back to the living room and lie on the couch. I throw the blanket over me and close my eyes. I decide that this would be a good time to make a plan, in case Wil still has a fever when he wakes up.

I guess if Grandma still isn't home, I better call Miss Marcie first. It would be the responsible thing to do. Maybe, if I at least look responsible, she'll take my side against Grandma when I need her, too. Not likely, but maybe. There's always Todd if Miss Marcie's busy. I take a deep breath; feel good about my decision.

Just as I'm falling asleep, there's loud pounding up and down the steps and on the door. I'm furious. Rodney's a stupid moron and he's going to wake my baby. I jump to my feet and run to the door. Without even thinking, I fling it open. Rodney looks shocked and it gives me courage.

"Knock it off." I want to shout it out, but I keep my voice low for fear of waking Wil. "The baby's sleeping and he's not feeling well. How would you like it if someone did this to you?" Rodney shuffles his big fat feet like he's ten again. I almost feel sorry for him, until I remember this isn't the first time he has done this. He turns and retreats without a word.

I close and lock the door, and slip back to my room to check on Wil. He's turned his little head to the side, and I notice a tear on the corner of his eye. Is he crying in his sleep? It makes me want to cry. Did Rodney scare him?

I pick up my pillow from the bed and a piece of paper falls to the floor. The handwriting looks familiar: "Peters, I'm sorry. Fletcher"

Okay, Fletcher, what are you sorry about? Shall we make a list of possibilities? Fletcher's reasons for being sorry: Not loving Wil; Not telling his parents about Wil; Not loving me. No, wait. Scratch that one. It's not fair.

There's nothing in life that says you have to love me, Fletcher. Nothing. And, you didn't say you loved me, did you? But how about sticking by a person, how about that? I doubt you would have treated anyone else the way you treated me the past few months. I thought we were friends. You said you'd stick by me, remember? But we never really thought I'd get knocked up, did we? I HATE THAT EXPRESSION. I shouldn't even try to guess why you're sorry, because I don't even know you. I thought I did, but I don't. Oh, well, that's not exactly right either. I guess I know you better than I want to admit.

My number-one guess is that you're sorry I got pregnant and decided to keep our baby: little baby = BIG INCONVENIENCE.

I should be working on my own list. There's plenty of blame to go around. Star's reasons for being sorry: Expecting Fletcher to love a baby he didn't even want; Expecting Fletcher to tell his parents about a baby he didn't even want; Expecting Fletcher to change something that happened to me, that no one and nothing could ever change. *This is crazy. Why am I doing this? It's going nowhere. Sorry doesn't change anything.*

I just want Wil to be okay. I should wake him and check his temperature. But what if he just needs to sleep? He looks so peaceful. His little chest is so still. Is he breathing?

I lean over the crib rail and peer at his face just in time

to see him smile the sweetest smile. *What are you dreaming about, Wil?*

I clutch my pillow and the note, and stumble down the hall. This is new behavior for me—holding tight to things like they'll vanish if I'm not completely attentive. I know in my heart that things disappear no matter how hard you cling to them, but still, here I am hanging on to a pillow and a stupid piece of paper.

I'm going to try this again—to rest while the baby's asleep. He was up a lot last night, and may be up all night again. I read the note again, hoping there's more. Another fruitless activity: hoping. I stuff it in the pocket of my jeans instead of in the garbage where it belongs. I pull the blanket up to my chin and close my eyes. More buzzing.

I open my eyes to find a phone dancing across the coffee table. I sit up and pull the blanket around my shoulders. The phone feels cool in my hand as I examine it, and recognize that it's Wil's. It buzzes again, and startled, I drop it on the floor. *Should I answer it? Maybe Wil's calling to tell me he left it here? He'd call me on the house phone, right?*

But checking missed calls to see if it was Fletcher wouldn't really be snooping. I flip open the phone and scan the menu. There are five missed calls from a number I don't recognize. *Should I call Wil to tell him? Maybe it's important.*

I put the phone on the table again, and notice that Wilson has returned the scrapbook I made for Wil. It felt good putting it together. It was like therapy, really. Creating a timeline of Wil's little life. But then I had to go and pick it all apart in my mind: There's not one picture of me pregnant anywhere—not one. Grandma was so ashamed. I guess I was ashamed of myself, too. It's very sad.

But the biggest disappointment is who's missing entirely. It's as though Wil never had a father. *See, things I can't control ruin all my hard work.*

I untangle myself from the blanket, jump to my feet and run to the kitchen to grab the ringing phone. "Hello."

"Star, you're home. I was going to leave you a message. I forgot my phone. Why are you home?"

"Wil's sick. Fletcher, your phone kept buzzing. I thought maybe it was you, so I checked missed calls. I hope that was okay. You have five from the same number."

"Just turn the phone off if it's bothering you, Peters."

"I didn't say it was bothering me. I didn't know what it was at first. I'm used to ringing, not buzzing."

"It's on vibrate."

I'm clueless, but not that clueless. "Okay, well I figured that much out all on my own, Fletcher. Don't you want to know the number?"

"What number?"

"Of the person who called you five times."

"That's okay. What's wrong with the baby? Did you take him to a doctor?"

"I don't have a car. My grandmother's not home yet. Miss Marcie said I could call her, and I thought about calling Todd to take us. But Wil's sleeping, so maybe the fever's gone."

"Peters, does he need to see a doctor or not?"

"I don't know."

"Why don't you know?"

My eye starts to twitch, and I rub at it. "Fletcher, stop, okay? We got sent home from the center because Wil couldn't be around the other babies with a fever. He's sleeping, so I'll check him when he gets up. If he still has a fever, I'll call his doctor."

"And then you'll call Miss Marcie, whoever she is, or the Goth?"

"If my grandmother's not home."

"So how long are you going to act like this?"

"What are you talking about?"

"You'd call Goth-boy instead of me?"

"Todd happens to know something about caring for a baby. Why this sudden interest, Fletcher? Didn't you tell me the kid was *my* problem? Mine and whatever thug I did on the street corner?"

My trembling hand slams the phone down, even before I'm done hurling mean words at Fletcher. It rings again before I can gather up enough energy to leave the room.

"Please, Fletcher, don't call again. I'm not going to answer, and you'll wake the baby."

"Don't hang up, Peters."

"We have nothing to talk about, remember? All we have is sex, and I'm done with that, so I guess I'm done with you."

"Look, Peters, I've made some mistakes, okay? I feel sick about what I said to you. I know you'll never forgive me. But, if the baby needs to see a doctor, I'll drive you."

"Some mistakes?"

"Millions and billions of mistakes, okay? Is that what

you want to hear? I'm coming over. And before you freak, it's the same deal as last night. I won't touch you, Peters."

Before I can answer, Wilson hangs up. I try to call his number, but the phone just rings and rings. He couldn't have gotten out of the house that fast, but he doesn't have to worry about the phone waking a sleeping baby.

Should I be worried that Wil is sleeping this long? He hasn't moved. His head feels hot under my cold hand, and he startles awake. I try to soothe him, but he's having none of that. No amount of rhyming calms him while I change his diaper. I try unsuccessfully to take his temperature, and his whole little body feels hot.

He continues to cry as I call the doctor, and leave a message on my grandmother's cell phone. He's screaming uncontrollably by the time Fletcher knocks. I open the door and turn away before he can see my tears.

I hand him the car seat base, tell him, "Fletcher, buckle this into the car, please." He stands there, looking from me to base, and back again.

"How, Peters? How does it fit?"

"Hold the baby. I'll do it."

"Hold the baby?" Wilson looks truly appalled—like I've asked him to hold a bomb that's triggered to explode the instant he touches it.

My throat tightens and I'm having trouble breathing. Why is he even here?

"Never mind." I grab the seat back, and it falls to the floor. I attempt to soothe Wil as I buckle him into the car seat, and tell Fletcher to bring the diaper bag and base. I pick up the car seat and carry it out to the car. Fletcher hands me the base and stashes the diaper bag on the floor. I adjust the straps and latch as he watches over my shoulder.

"I'm sorry, Peters. I'll know how to do it next time," he says. But his voice sounds far away. Wil continues to scream. I pull my seat belt around me in the back seat, lean down and sing quietly into Wil's ear. He screams louder, which I didn't think was even possible.

"Where are we going, Peters?"

I feel totally confused, disoriented. "What? To the doctor's office."

"Which doctor's office? Where?"

"The medical center on Medical Boulevard." It's hard to talk over Wil's screaming. My head's throbbing as Fletcher pulls out and drives to the first intersection.

"Listen, Peters, I don't know anything about babies, but maybe you should hold him."

Fletcher turns around and looks at us as he stops for a traffic light. His forehead is furrowed, and he's tap-tap-tapping on the steering wheel. It's like a billion needles pricking my skin.

"I can't hold him in the car, Fletcher. It's dangerous, and it's against the law."

"It's a law? Seriously? Well, it can't be good for a kid to scream like that."

"It's better for him to scream in a safety seat than to be thrown through the windshield in an accident. Besides, there's no guarantee that he'll quiet down even if I hold him. Green light, go."

Wil finally settles down with the motion of the car. I take a deep breath, lay my head back against the seat and close my eyes. For the first time since my grandmother left for Baltimore yesterday, I realize that maybe it's not a routine medical test like she told me. If she's gone to Baltimore—to Johns Hopkins—maybe it's serious. And what if Wil's really, really sick?

I pretty much don't want to do anything but sleep. Wil's just so good at conking out, once he's rolling along in any kind of moving vehicle. I want to be just like him— blissfully unconscious. It is quiet except for the hum of the wheels on the road. My hair feels soft as I twist it through my fingers.

Soft hair. Red hair. Star. Freckles. What was my mother thinking? Did she not know I'd have to go to school with three strikes against me?

The red hair and freckles would have been fine, but Star with red hair and freckles? I want to be in a cocoon with my baby. We could sleep safely inside, attached to a high tree branch.

I'm falling, falling. He's so strong, so heavy. I can't breathe. Dogs. Barking dogs. Moving closer.

"Where, Peters? Where should I park?" My body wants to respond, but I'm still pinned under his weight. *He'll never be gone.*

"Star?"

When I open my eyes, the medical center looms to the left, plopped in the middle of open countryside. I pull myself forward. "Make the first right and park in section four."

12
Wilson

My hand fidgets with the button I'm betting will release the car seat from the base. *Star already thinks that I'm dirt; I don't want to completely bottom out with her.* Although I don't know how much lower I can go than worm level.

"I'll carry it," I tell her, holding onto the car seat she tries to grab from me. Star takes the diaper bag and we're off across the parking lot. I learn pretty quickly that there's a trick to holding the seat out away from me so it won't bump against my legs as I walk. That's all I need—to give the kid a concussion while I'm carrying him.

The door into the medical center opens automatically. By the time I put the car seat with the baby on the floor and drop into a chair beside him in the waiting room, my hand's red from gripping the car seat's handle. *How does Star do this anyway?*

Star speaks to the receptionist. She then sits two chairs away from me, with the kid sleeping in the seat between us on the floor. I want to count the tiles on the floor, but I know Star would figure out what I'm doing. It'd remind her that

I counted the tiles on the floor of the abortion clinic, which I was stupid enough to tell her. Then I'd be eating even more dirt.

I'm positive that none of my friends are having this much trouble with girls. Of course, none of them have a girlfriend with a baby. Not that Star's my girlfriend. I think she's made it pretty clear that even Goth-boy is higher on her list than me.

The waiting room is alive with misery. There are screaming twin boys in car seats being hovered over by a dazed-looking grandmother and their frazzled mother. There can't possibly be a law about not holding your baby in the doctor's office. *Pick them up, people!*

The mother's rocking both seats at once, while the grandmother coos to the babies. There's a woman I first thought had two extra arms and legs and a spare head, until I looked closer to find she has a kid the size of a Great Dane draped on her. She's reading a book to him that he's not even looking at. He's twisting his mother's hair, like Star does, and she's doing it right now.

There's this father holding a baby that looks like it just popped into the world two minutes ago. It's that small. The mother's leaning into the father's shoulder, and they are both gazing at this kid like it's a mirage or something.

Then there's a big kid, sitting by himself reading *Sports Illustrated*. He looks like he needs a shave and should have outgrown the pediatrician's office by now. I'm not criticizing. I can sympathize; my mother still makes me see a pediatrician.

This place must be huge. The walls are coughing and

it sounds like a kennel. *How many sick kids could there be in August?*

I'm wondering how long this will take. Not that I have anywhere else to go—except home. That's where I want to be when my parents get home. Technically, I'm driving illegally, which could be big trouble. I left my mother a note and told her where I'd be. Actually, I tried to call both my parents—for fear of death by grounding. I left both of them messages.

It's crazy: no kid who is in danger of being grounded by his parents should be capable of producing a baby. Further proof that the kid sleeping at my feet is *not* mine.

Dad never told me to park the car and put my keys on his desk before. I mean, not even when I accidentally backed into his car in the driveway. It wasn't anything major, but his car got the worst of it.

My mouth feels sore from chewing my nails. Either Star doesn't care anymore about the germs I'm swallowing from this disgusting habit, or she's too busy twisting her hair to notice.

"Wilson Gregory Peters." Huh? I look around the room, confused. A woman with frogs all over her smock is standing in the doorway. Star puts the diaper bag over her shoulder and picks up the car seat. Oh no, I'm not staying out here by myself. I attempt to take the car seat from her. She stares at me for a few seconds, then releases it. Shrugs.

"Whatever, Fletcher."

I follow Star through the door the nurse holds open and into one of many smaller rooms. I put the seat on the examining table, and Star unbuckles the kid and lifts him out.

I expect him to start screaming the minute he opens his eyes, but he's too fascinated with the overhead light. I glance up to see what the big deal is. Obviously the kid's just easily entertained, because as light fixtures go, there's nothing special about this one. Still, I find myself cranking my head back even farther. Maybe it's like a car accident. You slow down and gawk because everyone else does.

I sit in a chair and look around, just like I did when I was a kid. Somehow, it all seems different now. I know what most of the stuff's for. Star goes over stuff about the kid with the nurse, who in turn writes stuff in a folder. The nurse gushes over Star like she's a rock star when she weighs the kid. *Okay, so is it that much of a surprise that babies gain weight?* I try to tune them out, but then I get this picture in my head of Star in the hospital bed. Pick your poison.

The nurse leaves. The room's quiet, except for an occasional thud on the wall from the examining room next door, where some tortured kid's probably trying to escape. There are only two chairs, so Star's forced to sit beside me. It's either that or fall down. She looks exhausted. "How are you?" I really want to know, but Star looks at me like I've committed a felony for asking. "Seriously, Peters. How are you?"

"Scared, Fletcher. How are you?" For a second, I think that she's being a smart ass. Then I see that she's really not doing well. Her hands shake as she holds the baby over her shoulder, and she swallows several times in a row, like she trying to keep something down.

"Why are you scared, Star?" I really want to know, but I get the felony look again.

She starts twisting her hair. I reach over to take her hand, but she pushes me away and almost falls getting past the car seat.

Okay, what am I missing here? The nurse said the kid's temperature is down from whatever Star told her it was at the center, so this doesn't make any sense. *Star is so much stronger than me about a lot of stuff. She is. So why is she scared?*

The doctor comes in and shakes hands with both of us. Dr. Ross takes the kid from Star and lays him on the exam table. They talk about how he's eating, sleeping—and filling up his diapers, which I don't find an acceptable topic for discussion under any circumstances.

Dr. Ross tells us the baby has fluid in his ears. She assures Star that his lungs are clear, which apparently is a big concern for babies who arrive before their due date. She writes out a prescription for an antibiotic and tells Star to call her if the baby's fever goes up or there are any changes she should know about.

"I never know what to ask you," Star says. "I feel like my questions are so stupid."

Dr. Ross puts her hand on Star's arm. "There are no stupid questions when it comes to caring for your baby, Star. How can your concerns about your baby's health be silly? Besides, I'm the baby's doctor. I need to know what's going on, right?" Star nods at her.

"Listen, how are you? You look very thin and tired."

I can hear what's left of the air that's in Star escape in

one short sigh. She's deflated. Her shoulders cave and her chin sinks into her chest.

Dr. Ross goes on high alert. They engage in some kind of talking dance, which revives Star. I can't hear the music, and I don't know the steps—but somehow they're suddenly rocking and rolling. They've left me holding up the wall without a partner. They're talking about gynecologists and pregnancy tests, and birth control and weight loss—and me. I try to close my gaping mouth, but it drops open every time I try to shut it by pushing my chin into my upper lip.

Dr. Ross attempts to hand me the baby but I freeze. My arms won't work; my mouth won't work. The kid's just suspended in her arms between us. Star takes the baby and buckles him into the car seat.

"Fletcher, can you sit with Wil in the waiting room for a few minutes?" Star asks, as she hands me the car seat. The paralysis has passed, and I wrap my hands around the handle of the seat. The door closes behind me with a thud. There's a maze of doors before me. I manage to choose the right one, but behind that door I find not only the waiting room, but also Mrs. Peters and my parents: The jackpot from hell.

The three of them start talking at me with no regard to the "Don't speak while others are speaking rule." It doesn't matter, because my brain has just gotten the message that it should have been paralyzed with the rest of my body a while back, and it takes this opportunity to shutdown completely.

I stare blankly at the tiles on the floor, until my father brings my world back into focus with a loud whistle and the words *time-out*. Now the playing field is at least leveled a bit—I have a teammate.

"Sit down, son," my father says, taking the car seat. He drops into a chair and holds the seat on his lap—bad news for our team. He takes one look at the kid and is rendered stupid. The man is gone. He's staring into the car seat like he's seen a vision.

My mother's staring at my father, and Mrs. Peters is staring at both of them. My mother used to accuse me of needing attention—even negative attention as long as I was center stage. I take a minute to thank God that I've outgrown that self-destructive behavior before I start searching for an escape route. Someone else can take Peters and her kid home. This bus is leaving town. *Uh-oh. Too late!*

"Wilson, what did the doctor say about the baby?" my mother asks. "What was his temp? Does he need medication?" I try to think. Three questions. Focus.

"The ki...baby's temperature is down from this morning. But, I don't know the number—maybe 101 point something. He needs to take medicine, but I don't know the name—some antibiotic, I think."

I appear to be talking to myself, because everyone else is now gazing into the car seat. I look down in time to see a dimple explosion on the kid's face, which is met by an outpouring of gushing noises. *Did my mother just clap?*

I sink into the chair beside my father and chew down the side of my thumbnail. It's a little painful, but the tops of the nails are gone—grazed over—and pickings are slim.

The kid starts to fuss and my father rocks the car seat back and forth. Dad's making this clucking noise that sounds like a cartoon hen on TV just before she lays an egg.

God obviously has decided not to wait until I die to send me to hell. *Don't these people all have jobs?*

"Where's Star?" Mrs. Peters asks. She has this haunted look on her face that's spooking me out.

"Star had a few more questions for the doctor, ma'am." I manage to sputter out, as politely as possible.

"May I hold Wil, Mrs. Peters?" my mother asks.

"Certainly."

Well, Mrs. Peters may be certain, but my father's not. He gives my mother this pained look, then puts the seat on the floor, unbuckles the kid and hangs on to his little body for dear life. My mother crosses her arms and taps her foot on the floor. Mrs. Peters is staring at me now, no doubt wondering how I could have deprived my parents of this sheer joy the past few months.

How are they all so certain this kid is even mine? How? Doesn't he have to take some DNA test or something? He doesn't look a thing like me, not even on my bad days.

Peters stops dead in her tracks when she throws open the waiting room door. No doubt I'm looking good compared to the rest of this entourage.

My father and I both stand up. I'm absolutely positive that Peters is going to close the door and go back the way she came, but then her eyes fall on the baby and she rushes over to my father like a mother bird swooping in on a menacing cat.

My dad, having rescued our cat Roger from many a mother bird attack, turns over the baby without the slightest protest.

"Hi, Star. How are you?" he asks. I want to lean in and tell him it's a dangerous question, but after the way he sold me out for the diapered kid, the man is on his own.

"I'm fine, Mr. Fletcher. How are you? Mrs. Fletcher?" Star waits for their answers and then turns to her grandmother. "Grandma, did things go okay today?"

"Everything's fine, Star."

Well, with all of that out of the way, there's nothing left to do but stand around and wonder what to do. There appears to be a lot of eye fluttering going on. Star kneels down to put the baby in his seat. Her eyes are pleading with me to get her out of here.

"I'll take Star home, if that's okay," I say, looking at Star to make sure I didn't read her wrong.

She nods gratefully. "Can we stop at the pharmacy to pick up Wil's prescription?"

"Sure." I pick up the diaper bag Peters has dumped on the floor and hand it to her before I pick up the car seat.

My father hands me money. I almost decline, but then remember that I'm fresh out of cash after seriously depleting the nation's diaper supply and Maryland's crab population.

"Would you like your mother and me to take the baby, so you can take Star out for an early dinner?" Star gives her head a shake.

"No thanks, Dad. Another time," I say. My parents looked crushed.

Mrs. Peters is stoic. "I'll see you at home, Star." *Oh, fun.*

Star's a runner. Even as a freshman, she managed to

keep up with some of the school's elite upperclassmen during cross-country and track-and-field events. I thought having a baby would slow her down. It didn't. She's gone across the parking lot. I have the baby and the car seat, but it's no excuse for her to be that far ahead of me. She keeps looking back at me, and I keep looking back at my parents and Mrs. Peters, who've stopped to huddle up. *What are they talking about?*

"Peters, will you give a guy a break?" Star's hand is clutched around the Jeep's door handle, and she's jumping up and down.

"Hurry up, Fletcher. Let's get out of here. Your parents are freaking me out." Peters is tugging on the locked door now. I put down the car seat—pull my keys from my pocket and hand them to her. She hits the button and opens the door. She climbs in the seat and covers her eyes.

"My parents are freaking you out? Why are my parents freaking you out?" I'm standing beside her now. *Should I hoist the car seat over her, or go to the other side of the Jeep with this kid?*

I start by pulling her hands away from her face. She looks up at me with those green eyes. I just want to pull her into my arms. I want it to be last summer. I want a chance to do it all over again, and do it right this time. *I don't want to be a father. I want to be a high school football player with this gorgeous green-eyed girlfriend.*

"I don't know. There's just something about the way they're acting."

"Who?"

"Your parents, Fletcher. We *were* talking about your

parents, right?" I'm tempted to bring up her spooky-faced grandmother, but I'm learning that Peters's sensitivity button is stuck in overdrive and I better just step away from the pedal and coast.

"Oh yeah, my parents." I'm never very good at playing things off, and Peters is giving me that look again. I mean there's a wide range of put-downs I associate with "the look," but generally, I'm dirt.

"You don't even know them. They're not acting any different than they normally do. Well, of course, they've had a shock. How do you want them to act?"

"Like they had a shock. They're treating Wil like they've never seen a baby before. Were you and your sister adopted or something?"

"Not that I know of, Peters, but thanks for asking. Jump down and let me put the car seat in."

"I'll take him." Star reaches for the car seat and holds it on her lap, staring at the sleeping kid inside. It makes no sense to me, the way she looks at this baby. I mean, I can see my parents being bug-eyed over a baby—they're old. But Star? How did she go from gym class to motherhood?

"He's asleep, Peters. Sit up front so I don't have to feel like a chauffeur."

The seat clicks into the base and Star turns to me. "I always sit with the baby. What if he wakes up?"

"I'll stop the Jeep and you can get in the back. Come on, I need to talk to you."

"Whoa, we have something to talk about? This is BIG." Star leans over and kisses the kid. "I'll just be up front, Wil." *As opposed to what, Peters? What does the kid*

145

know about front, back, left, right, up, down—inside out? What does the kid know about anything? Star climbs in the front seat and we're off.

The driving pattern in the parking lot brings us right past my parents and Mrs. Peters, still standing at the entrance to the medical center. They wave to us as we pass by.

"See, I should have sat in the back, Fletcher. They all think I'm terrible already. Now they'll think that I'm an unfit mother, leaving Wil alone in the back seat."

"That's insane, Peters. Don't you leave him in his crib alone sometimes? Don't you leave him in that seat thing when you have to answer the phone? You're right here with him."

"You don't get any of this, Fletcher. No one ever expects anything from teenage fathers. Why do I even talk to you?"

"Hey, my parents expect a lot from me, and I don't even..." I clamp my mouth shut tight, but the words back up behind my teeth and I don't know how long I can hold them back.

"And you don't even think you're Wil's father. That's what you were going to say, Fletcher, so say it. It's just so convenient, isn't it? So easy for you to justify the way you've acted. Well, what if I'm pregnant again? What? You had sex with me, and then you walked out the door hurling insults at me. Like I'd go near any of those creeps on the corner. Don't you know me at all, Fletcher? Oh, what do you care? I'm terrified, and you've found yourself a new girlfriend."

"Hey, slow down. What are you talking about, being pregnant again? We had sex one time. I missed you, Star. I missed you. Okay? You're not pregnant."

"Why, because you say so? Well, see, Fletcher, it's like this: The egg and sperm don't care why we had sex. They just know they have a job to do."

I pull off on the side of the road. My hands are shaking, and every inch of my body is shaking as well. "What did the doctor say?"

"I peed in a cup. I'll know tomorrow."

"Can't we get a pregnancy test at the pharmacy and know today?"

"We can. It may be too soon to tell. I don't know."

"What pharmacy?"

"Lane's has all of Wil's information on file. It's on..."

"I know where it is, Peters." I signal and pull out on the highway. *This cannot be happening. Star is the only girl I've ever been with. No wait, there's that thing with Hobart.*

"I don't have a new girlfriend, Peters."

Star pulls my phone out of the diaper bag. "Someone has called you . . . thirteen times from the same number today, Fletcher. Look, it doesn't matter." She puts the phone on the dashboard. "You can do what you want. I know it's over between us. I've accepted that. I know it was all my fault."

"What was your fault?"

"Wanting you to love me, being freaked out over the stupid condoms. I accept the responsibility. I don't care about me, really. I just feel bad about Wil. I never knew my father, and I want him to know his. I'm sorry, that's not your problem."

"Peters, will you slow down. First of all, I don't think it's so unreasonable for me to have doubts. I don't think it's so unreasonable for me to want a test to be sure."

"You're absolutely right, Fletcher. I think you should take a test. I think a simple blood test will answer all your questions. I never once said you shouldn't have a stupid test, did I? Did I, Fletcher?"

"No."

"No. Because you just made up your mind that the baby wasn't yours. No test needed. It was just easier for you to think of me as a slut than yourself as a father."

"Stop it, Peters, okay?"

"Stop what?"

"Stop freaking out over everything. If you're pregnant, we'll take care of it."

"How? At the abortion clinic?"

"Would that be such a bad thing? Look how having a baby's turned out."

"How has it turned out, Fletcher? I will *never* have an abortion."

"Are you kidding me? You'd do this again?"

"What do you want me to do?"

"I want you to think, Peters. That's what I want you to do. If you got pregnant when I was with you last, you're barely pregnant. It's a nothing."

"It's not a nothing. It's a baby."

"It's not a baby. Look, how do I make you understand this? If I'm playing lacrosse and I shoot on goal and the goalie knocks it out—then it's not a goal."

"Great analogy, Fletcher. You're exactly right, the goalie is birth control."

"What are you talking about? The goalie's birth control?"

"If you make a goal and the goalie kicks it out—then what? You're screaming foul play, right? Because once it's in the goal, you've scored."

This is the most annoying girl I have ever met. She is. I need a beer. I need a six-pack. I need an eighteen-pack. I need a keg.

The phone hums and we both look at it. I pick it up and yell, "Don't call me again." Thank God Peters is here and I didn't say what I really wanted to say...

"Sorry, Dad. I thought you were someone else. We're pulling into the pharmacy now. He's been sleeping this whole time. Okay. I'll call you if I need you." I snap the phone shut and look at Star. Instead of the tears I expect to see, I see rage.

"Look, I'll go take the test. If the kid's mine, I'll quit school. I'll get a job with my father. We can get married."

"Are you serious?" I want to duck, Peters is that mad. "First of all, you can't quit school. That would be insane. Second, you hate working for your father, you told me so. And, third, if you were the last man left on earth, I would be looking into intergalactic travel to find a mate." Peters slams the door and gets the whole way to the entrance of Lane's before she turns and comes back. I open the window expecting an apology.

"Don't leave Wil alone in the car." Okay, so now I'm furious, too. I'm not stupid. I may not know a lot about babies, but I wouldn't leave him alone in the car. He could get kidnapped. Or, if it was too hot or too cold, he could die.

Plus, what if he woke up and was alone? He'd be scared. I'm not totally insensitive. In fact, I'm pretty sensitive. I am. The phone hums again. If this is Hobart, I know I'll scream. I flip it open.

"Wil, are you there?"

"I'm here."

"Why haven't you answered my calls?"

"I left my phone at Star's this morning. I just got it back."

"Star's? Are you still messing with Star? Doesn't she have a kid or something? She's such a loser. Is she even coming back to school?"

I can see Peters through the window of Lane's. She is talking to the pharmacist about the prescription. I turn to look at the kid asleep in his car seat. How much has she already given up for him?

"Hobart, if there's one thing Star's not, it's a loser. See you around."

I close my eyes to a night sky filled with a billion stars bumping into each other. They are all so beautiful. It would be hard to pick just one favorite constellation—much easier to pick one favorite Star.

13
Star

"Back up, Fletcher." He's been on my heels since I walked in the door and changed Wil's diaper. How many times can I possibly say that I have to give Wil his medicine and feed him before I can do anything else?

I know what Fletcher wants me to do, but I didn't buy a pregnancy test. I didn't have enough money, and I sure wasn't going to ask him for anything.

"Star, how do you know you're giving the baby the right amount of medicine?"

"Because the dosage is listed on the prescription bottle, and this medicine dispenser measures dosages."

"Show me. How can I help if you don't show me?"

"Am I asking you to help? Go home, Fletcher."

Wil makes a face as his medicine drains slowly from the dispenser. Pink oozes out of both sides of his mouth. "Wil!" I catch it in the dispenser and try again. "That's better. You are such a good boy!" I grab his warmed bottle and head for the rocker.

I expect Fletcher to crash on the sofa, but the house is quiet. Maybe he went out the back. Wil smiles at me around the nipple of his bottle. It's the cutest thing. He's had such a long day, but he's in a good mood. Where does this sweet baby go in the middle of the night, and who is that needy, overbearing baby that takes over his body until morning? I put my lips on Wil's forehead. He still feels warm.

"Star, did you leave the back door unlocked?"

"Good grief, Fletcher, you scared me. Where did you come from?"

"Rushsylvania, Ohio."

"Excuse me?"

"It was a joke. I came from the kitchen, where you last saw me less than five minutes ago."

"I thought you left."

"I wouldn't go without telling you. Listen, did you leave the mudroom door unlocked or not?"

"Not."

"The chain lock held, but the door's pushed open."

"I'm sure it was locked when I left. Maybe someone else used your credit card approach."

"Not funny, Star. Make sure you keep the kitchen door locked, too, okay?"

"I don't get this, Fletcher. What's with you, all of a sudden?"

"There was this guy in the alley."

"Now? There's a guy in the alley?" I jump up out of the rocker.

"Not now. Relax, would you? The day I came over to mow the lawn."

I settle back into the rocker. Wil is still sucking down formula. "What did he look like?"

"He took off when I went back to the shed. I didn't get a real good look at him. Don't worry about it. He could be someone you know."

That doesn't make me feel any safer. Sometimes it's the people you think you know that hurt you most. I put the bottle on the table, and Wil over my shoulder to burp. His little body smells so sweet.

"Who's Gregory?"

"My Uncle Gregory?"

"Oh."

"Oh?"

"So you named your baby after me and your uncle?"

"Oh! That oh. Yes, I had planned to name him Steven Gregory after my two uncles, but that's when I thought he'd have your last name. I named him Wilson Gregory because I wanted him to have something of you, and I'm hoping that Uncle Gregory will someday be stationed close enough to be involved in Wil's life. Uncle Steven died before I was born.

"I'm sorry if it was the wrong thing to do. Using your name. Maybe I should have just named him Wil instead of Wilson."

"Why couldn't he have my last name?"

"If you're asking me if I have doubts about who his father is, I don't. I would never have given him your last name without permission."

"Oh."

"Look, Fletcher, you should just go home."

"I want to wait for your grandmother to come back so you won't be alone with a sick kid."

"I'm okay. Grandma probably went to work. She'll be awhile. I guess I should have checked for messages when we came in."

"Do you want me to check the machine?" Fletcher jumps up from the couch. I know he's dying to get out of here and go on with his life. His parents must be using some major threats to keep him here.

"Message light's blinking, Star."

I get up and go stand in the doorway to the kitchen.

"You have one new message. Beep. Star, this is Cate Hobart. I'm sure you know me from. Beep."

"Fletcher, did you just erase the message? Why would you do that? I don't know Cate Hobart. Who is she?"

"She's nobody you want to know."

"Is she your girlfriend?"

"Knock it off, Star. She's not my girlfriend."

"It's okay. You can have a girlfriend. But why's she calling me? Wait, is she pregnant?"

"No, she's not pregnant, we used..."

"Condoms, you used condoms?"

"I didn't say that, you did. You're making me sound like a monster."

"Fletcher, you just erased a message on my machine. *My* machine. Wait, it was you. You erased the message from Todd, too. Right?"

"You don't need Todd hanging around."

"I what? Get out, Fletcher."

"Star, listen."

"STOP TALKING AND GO!" Wil startles on my shoulder. I grab his bottle on my jog through the living room and go to my room and slam the door. Wil startles again and I want to cry.

This is not what I want for him. Shouting. Slamming. Fighting. He doesn't need it. Who needs it? Why was I so in love with Wilson anyway? He's a jerk.

I'm sorry, but I'm just not in the mood for Wilson Fletcher's hurt little boy look. How often did I fall for that? Did I not take into consideration that he's six foot two and long past his fourth birthday? I'm also not in the mood to imagine him with someone else. I know what I said about not caring about his new girlfriend, but my heart hurts. He was *with* someone else.

I prop my pillows and sit up in my bed. Wil latches on to his bottle like he's never going to let go. All I really want to do is sleep. It's the only thing that comes easily—sleep. Unless, of course, I'm up all night with a screaming baby, or terrified to fall asleep because I'm alone in the house. Those are just a couple little things that keep me awake and sleep-deprived.

For a long time after it happened, I wasn't afraid of anything. I kept thinking that the worst thing that could happen to me had happened—and I lived through it.

Then one day it hit me. I didn't live through it at all. I was numb: incapable of feeling anything for anyone. I was dead inside.

I never knew my father, my mother was gone—my grandmother withdrew after, after her boyfriend ... *Breathe: ten, nine, eight, seven, six, five, four, three, two—one.*

I didn't have to feel anything because I had no one. Then along came Fletcher. He was funny, smart, popular, and so handsome. I didn't even know I was capable of the kinds of feelings he made me feel. What else could it be but love? HA! It had to be something else because there's no such thing as love.

"Why are you looking at me like that, Wil? Mommy didn't forget about you—Mommy's just thinking. Okay, well, I guess I can think out loud. Here's what I know, Wil. Are you ready?" *Deep breath.*

"Wil, love is a myth. So don't you go falling for any of those flirty baby girls at the center. I know Mae is adorable, but she's too old for you. Plus I saw her flirting with Tanner. You're much cuter, of course, but he has some mean skills crawling and pulling up on stuff. Not that you won't be doing all that soon, but some girls are so impatient. You don't have to explain to her that you're developmentally not ready, she should know.

"I will not stand for you getting involved with girls until you're a college graduate with a good job. You need to have a plan.

"Love? No such thing. How long did Snow White have to sleep before that stupid prince kissed her? What took him so long? Did he get lost? Was he too proud to ask for directions?

"And what if Cinderella hadn't lost her glass slipper? Think that clueless prince would have racked his brain to find another way to track her down? Hey, you baby boy of mine, stay away from girls in glass slippers. They're stupid. Glass footwear is totally overrated and dangerous.

"Don't you go flashing those dimples at me, mister! That is so unfair. It's just what your father . . . I'm sorry. I promise you, Wil, that I will never do that to you. Compare you, or accuse your father in front of you. I swear.

"Hey, what's that look about? Oh, you want it in writing? Are you kidding me? You little stinker! Oh! No! Here it comes. What? I can't even say stinker without you taking me literally? Didn't I just change a load when we got home? I don't know what you've heard, but you're not getting overtime pay for this. Poop once a day, or twenty times a day—the pay's the same. No. No negotiations. That's my final word on this. People are not exactly lined up around the block to change your stinky little bottom. Do you see a line, Wilson Gregory Peters? Do you? No, it's just me.

"Up for some potty training? Miss Marcie says somewhere between two and a half and three years old on average. I could be changing your diapers until I'm nineteen! *Nineteen.*

"You are such a beautiful baby, Wil. Mommy loves you so much. But three years of changing diapers? That's longer than I got to go to high school. It's one year shy of a college degree. That's thousands of diapers and wet wipes, Wil.

"I guess it's better to think small here. One diaper at a time, starting with the one you obliterated right now. Come on, Mommy's going to pick you up. Ready? Let's go. You're getting so heavy."

The door squeaks as I open it, and Fletcher is sitting on the floor in the hall.

"Excuse me," I step over him to get to the dresser. "Why are you still here?" I lay Wil on the changing pad and unzip his sleeper.

"I won't leave without telling you I'm leaving."

"You've told me. Go home, or to your girlfriend's—whatever."

"I don't have a girlfriend, Star."

"Oh, you just have sex with random girls, then?"

"I can explain."

"No, Fletcher, you can't. It's not necessary anyway."

"I think it is."

"What if...what if I don't want to know? What if I can't handle knowing one more thing about you? Can't you see that I have my hands full here? Seriously."

Wil has filled his diaper and it has exploded up his back, sleeper, and onesie. The tears escape and I hate myself for letting Fletcher see me cry over a dirty diaper. Wil's a mess, and the changing pad is the latest casualty. I'm trying to clean a squirming baby and dispose of a dirty diaper and a million dirty wipes and Fletcher's just standing there, probably holding his breath, I'm sure.

"Tell me what to do," he says. Which makes me hate him even more. Is he really that clueless? I open the diaper pail and dump everything in with one hand while holding Wil's tummy with the other so he won't roll off the dresser. Not that he's rolling, but Miss Marcie said you can't take a chance no matter how well you think you know your baby. I pull off Wil's dirty sleeper and struggle to get his onesie over his head without getting poop all over him. I put the naked baby over my shoulder and get a clean receiving blanket out of the dresser drawer, lay it over the changing pad, and attempt to diaper and dress Wil.

Then I put Wil in his crib and turn on the mobile. He

quiets as the animals go slowly around to the tune of 'Old MacDonald Had a Farm.' I have about two minutes 'til meltdown. I bump past Fletcher in the doorway and gather the changing pad cover, sleeper, onesie, and receiving blanket—and rinse them in a basin in the bathroom sink. I start the water in the washing machine and dump the wet clothes in. Wil is already cranking up, but I gather his other dirty clothes and add them to the washer along with detergent.

I go into the bathroom and throw cold water on my face, washing away the tears. I will never, ever cry in front of Wilson again. My hands smell like Wil's diaper—I scrub, scrub, and scrub some more. Wil's quieted. I stop in the hallway. Fletcher's standing over the crib.

"I know your mother talks to you all the time, little dude. I don't, because I don't know what to say to you. We don't have much in common except our name. Let's see. Hi, I'm Wil, you're Wil. I'm big; you're small. I have hair on my head; you have fuzz. I've outgrown what you do in your diaper, but big guys crap things up in other ways. My advice, try to limit crapping things up to your diaper years. I mean it's okay to smell like a toxic waste dump when you're wearing diapers. Beyond that, it becomes very unattractive. There's no hiding it. People notice.

"I heard what your mother told you about how lame princes are. First of all, it's hard to even think about Star as your mother. She was my girlfriend first. And that stuff about princes: What she said may or may not be true. She's entitled to her opinion, of course. Maybe guys don't ask for directions, and we may wait too long to come to the rescue, and maybe we don't have much imagination past a glass slipper. I think the Beast was a pretty cool dude, though. Get her to tell you about him sometime.

"Also, little dude, that stuff your mother told you about love isn't true. I don't mean to contradict her, but if love is a myth, what do you call what she does for you? It's got to be some kind of crazy love. Crazy love. Oh wait, no, don't cry. What did I say? I'm sorry. Seriously, I'm sorry. Don't cry. I hate it when you cry.

"Star, the baby's crying—come pick him up! Hurry, Star, he's all red and wet with tears." Wil stands over the crying baby. He lowers his hand into the crib. I think he'll pick him up, but then he jumps back like he's been scorched. When he turns to me, all I see is panic in his eyes. I step into the room and pick up the baby, who continues to scream and cry.

"What's wrong with him? What did I do? I was just talking to him, honest. That's all. I thought I was helping. You were busy. I thought I was buying you some time."

"Babies cry, Fletcher, so don't take it personal." I pick up Wil's bottle on the bed. It's pretty much drained. He's fed. He's dry. He's just mad, or sad, or scared, or sick, or maybe just sick of hearing about love and princes from his two clueless parents.

Fletcher reaches over and turns on the mobile. The animals spring into action, playing follow-the-leader in their circle to nowhere. I sway to the music and the baby quiets. Fletcher takes a gulp of air, and spits it out in short breaths. He closes his eyes and sways with us. We each have our own separate dance. I close my eyes and sway.

Star in the Middle

I am so tired. I wish I could go to sleep and sleep until morning.

I don't hear my grandmother come in, but when I open my eyes she's standing in the doorway smiling. She reaches for the baby and I release him into her arms.

"Mrs. Peters," Fletcher says. "Star, I better go." My grandmother chats with Wilson as she walks him to the door. I feel the gravity of her mood shift—no doubt brought about by Mr. and Mrs. Fletcher's involvement. I stand in place, swaying to the music, still feeling my baby, now in my grandmother's arms.

14
Wilson

I am going nuts. I need to forget I'm going nuts. I need a beer.

Bridgett won't buy us beer, but Boland's sister will. I call her myself, even before I call Boland and Hobbs, even before I make it home from Star's. Meg loves me, always has. It's the dimples. I'm sure of it. Getting out of the house is going to be another story. Meg said she'd drop off the booze at the place. She doesn't want any of us getting caught with it in our cars. She knows where the place is— we've been down this road a few times. Meg is cool. Bridgett's cool, too, but not about my drinking.

We're camping out tonight. I haven't told my parents, but I'll sneak out if I have to. Hobbs is driving. We're meeting Boland out there at 10:00 P.M. Hobbs and I will say we're spending the night at Boland's. Boland's spending the night at my house—at least that's what he'll tell his parents. We've worked this all out. There are some things in my life I can still control. Scratch that. The parent factor is still in place.

Hell, how is it possible that I have to answer to parents when I supposedly have a kid of my own?

Both my parents' vehicles are in the driveway when I pull in. This looks ominous. They were the two "workingest" people alive, prior to their alleged grandparents' status. For a while now, Bridgett and I thought our dog and cat, Stu and Roger, were raising us.

It was hard when Mom went back to work because we were so spoiled having her home. But when she went back to work, she threw herself into that like she does with everything else. And I really missed Bridgett when she went off to college. I never really liked being alone. Mom says Bridgett needs her alone time, but not me. Mom said it's because Bridgett was born first and I always had a sibling.

I'm sitting in the Jeep, contemplating what's going to go down with my parents when Bridgett pulls in. She works for Dad during the summer, and never gets home this early. I get out of the Jeep and she comes over and hugs me. This is not an everyday occurrence, so now I feel confused.

"What's up?" I ask.

"Why didn't you tell me, Wil? Maybe I could have helped."

"Helped with what?"

"You know what. You can't do this. This one's not going away, no matter how you pretend it didn't happen."

Did I say Bridgett was cool? No way. She's exhausting. This whole 'face the truth' thing is too much. "Why are you home so early?"

"Wil, seriously, you can't do this. Mom and Dad called me so we could have a family meeting. They thought you'd want me there. When was the last time we had a family meeting? They knew you were on your way home from Star's."

"How could they know that? I didn't call them."

"Mrs. Peters told them."

"Damn! Are you kidding me? That meddling old..."

"Wil, Mom called her to see if you were still there. Mrs. Peters is not out to ruin your life, you know."

"No? It sure feels that way."

"Why's that? Because she doesn't want her grand-daughter to go through this alone?"

"Don't, Bridgett. I need someone on my side, here."

"I *am* on your side. Just clean up your attitude if you want to survive with Mom and Dad."

"Bridg, I don't even think the kid's mine. Mrs. Peters just needs someone to pin this on."

"You're wrong."

"Oh, you know that because Mrs. Peters said so?"

"No, I know it because I saw Star with you. She was totally in love, and Mrs. Peters said you were her first boyfriend. Mrs. Peters is insisting that you take a paternity test so there won't be any doubt. Does that sound like a woman who is looking for a random guy to pin something on, Wil?

"Come on. The sooner we get in there, the better off you'll be. Just listen to what Mom and Dad have to say. I mean it. Pay attention. Don't just sit there with a blank look on your face—pay attention. And, whatever you do—don't say anything."

"I can't even TALK?"

"Do you trust yourself to say anything helpful, here? Because I don't. I think you're in serious denial about this whole situation and that'll just trigger some tough reactions from Mom and Dad."

"Is this fair? I told Star to have an abortion. It's not fair! She's the one who apparently wanted to keep the stupid kid."

"WIL! This is exactly what I'm trying to tell you— DON'T OPEN YOUR MOUTH. Did Star *want* to keep the baby, or did she *not* want to have an abortion?"

"What's the difference?"

"There's a big difference. A HUGE one. Maybe you two should have had that conversation before you had unprotected sex."

"How do you know we had unprotected sex?"

"Because there's a little guy out there with your name, who Mom and Dad say looks exactly like you."

"That is *so* not true. I'm so much better-looking than that baby."

"WIL! Do you hear yourself? Just keep comments like that to yourself. And, who is that, anyway?"

"Who? What are you talking about?"

"The girl in the car across the street. She drove by twice, and now she's sitting there, staring at you."

I know the car before I see Hobart sitting in it. "Damn. Tell Mom and Dad I'll be right in, will you, Bridgett?"

"*Now* what are you doing? You don't have a new girl-friend, do you?"

"What if I do, Bridg? I'm seventeen years old—I can't have a girlfriend?"

"No way. You cannot *possibly* be this clueless. Now would not be a great time to bring home a new girlfriend. Do you see where I'm going with this? Don't be stupid, Wil." Bridgett covers her face with her hands and her next words come out all muffled. "You have five minutes to get rid of her."

"Or what? I turn into a freakin' pumpkin?" I walk away from my perfect sister. The one who likes to work in Dad's construction office. The one who's on the dean's list every semester. The one who doesn't have a kid out there, named after her.

I trip over my big feet trying to get across the street. Why does Cate's smile infuriate me so much?

"What, Hobart? What do you want?" I didn't mean it to come out so nasty, but she had no right to call Star.

"Nice, Wil. Did I do something to you? You weren't this testy at Gap Run."

"That was a mistake."

"Excuse me?"

"You heard me. It was a mistake. And, hey, don't call Star again. Okay?"

"I'll call Star if I want to, and you can go to hell." The girl almost runs over my foot squealing out. *What happened to sweet girls? What happened to polite girls?*

What do I have waiting for me inside?

I pull a couple of weeds in the flower garden outside the back door. I'm turning into quite the landscape person—mowing grass I'm not forced to mow, and pulling weeds voluntarily. You'd think I had nothing better to do.

We do a lot of things around the kitchen table. We eat.

Star in the Middle

We pray. We throw together food concoctions. Bridgett and I do homework while Dad pays bills, or Mom writes letters, or works on her latest hobby. Sometimes we play games like UNO and 500 Rummy. The kitchen table has also been the scene of family meetings when something important is going on. The most serious so far was when my father found out Bridgett was at a drinking party when she was in high school.

Dad went right over there and picked her up. My sister hadn't been drinking, but she had to blow in my parents' faces so many times I thought she'd pass out. I concluded, from that family meeting, that if I ever get caught at a drinking party, I may as well throw back a few, because the consequences would be just as severe whether or not I drank.

My parents like to include siblings in these events so we can learn from each other's mistakes. Of course, the guilty party can choose not to have the other sibling participate. I chose to have Bridgett stay. It couldn't hurt, right?

I can't even imagine what my consequences would be for allegedly impregnating my girlfriend. Apparently my parents can't decide what they should be, either. This meeting is not about punishment for having sired a kid (allegedly).

This meeting turned out to be about: (1) the care and feeding of the diapered one (i.e., 'How many diapers have you changed, Wilson?'); (2) taking responsibility for one's actions; (3) telling the truth; and, (4) how to treat a friend whose life you've (allegedly) altered forever (at least they didn't say I ruined her life, just altered it, and no pity for me and my ruined life either).

There was a lot more, but I stopped listening after a while. *Sorry, Bridgett.* My mind can only absorb things as long as the part of my anatomy parked in the chair is not completely numbed to it. How does *that* work, exactly?

To be clear, my parents never used the word *allegedly.* As far as they're concerned 'diapers' is my done deal. My mother did make an appointment for a paternity test tomorrow. She said Mrs. Peters was adamant about that, before she'll accept one penny, and she even paid Dad for the lock. As far as I am concerned, the woman thinks she has this one nailed, and she wants to gloat. I can't wait to see her face when I fail the stupid test. Mom scheduled the paternity test on the same day as my high school sports physical. I never thought I'd be using *paternity test* and *high school sports physical* in the same sentence.

I must have a light bulb on my face that goes on before I attempt to talk, because every time I even think about opening my mouth, my sister stomps on my bare foot under the table. I think my sister needs to schedule an appointment for me with a podiatrist on my doctor day-from-hell. *Can I have Bridgett evicted from this meeting for stomping my feet into the floorboards?*

I guess what bothers me most about this meeting is how disappointed my parents look. It's nothing like disappointment over a bad grade, or being caught in a lie, or probably even if I'd robbed a bank.

And they've made it clear it's not as much about the baby itself, as not *telling* them about the baby. They're acting like this kid has royal blood running through his veins or something. It's like there's some kind of contest going on between them, to see who could fit 'helpless baby' into a sentence more often. Helpless baby my ass. That kid hollers and Star has him hoisted over her shoulder. *Damn! Bridgett, knock it off. Can you read my mind now? You said I can't speak. I'm not allowed to think, either?*

Okay, well, looks like I missed something big. Everyone's leaving the table, except my mother. Don't boys get to have sex talks with their fathers anymore? Bridgett's hanging back, staring at me. I give her my 'I can handle this myself' look.

"Do you need something, Bridgett?" my mother asks.

"Maybe I should stay, Mom. I know Dad had to get back to work, but I'm done for the day." Bridgett stands behind my chair.

"Bridgett, I'd really like to speak to Wil alone." I feel Bridgett's hand on my shoulder—then she's gone.

"Wil, I had a nice chat with Cate Hobart today. She'd apparently been trying to reach you on your cell phone. When she couldn't, she called the house. I know that you had a couple of dates with her last week."

I have no idea where my mother is going with this. There's no question in there that I can detect, and yet, Mom looks like she is waiting for an answer.

"Wil?"

"Cate and I went out a couple of times. I talked to her this afternoon after I retrieved my phone from Star's house." My mother's drumming her fingers on the table, waiting for more. I don't know what she's looking for, but I need to do damage control so I can get out of the house tonight.

"The baby was good when I left Star's, Mom. I stayed

until Mrs. Peters got home, because I didn't want to leave Star alone with a sick baby."

"Mrs. Peters sounded very pleased when I spoke to her earlier. Now about Cate—can you tell me what's going on, Wil?"

"There's nothing going on with Cate. It was a couple of dates. I don't get this, Mom. Do you want me to marry Star, because that's not what Star says she wants. Do you *not* want me to date anyone? I don't get what you want."

"What do *you* want, Wil?" *I set myself up for this one. How stupid am I?*

"I guess I want to get the test done and go from there."

"Yes, the test." My mother looks into her hands—then folds them together like she's praying. "I guess I want to make sure that there isn't a repeat performance here. I know we've talked about abstinence—about waiting until you're in a committed relationship to have sex. We've also had the talk about protection. Star is younger than you, Wil. You were her first boyfriend. I'm not saying that this is all on you. But, Wil, do you understand that there's a huge responsibility that comes with getting involved with someone? It's your responsibility, Wil. Yours."

"Are you saying I forced Star into something?"

"No! That's not what I'm saying at all. Why, is that what you heard? Did you force Star into something neither of you were ready for?"

"I didn't force her, okay? But I'm not ready to be a father—if that's what you're asking."

"And it didn't occur to you that it was a real possibility?"

"Mom, I get it. I was stupid, okay? I won't be stupid again. Not with Star. Not with Cate. Not with anyone. I just want to get on with my life, okay?"

"You want to get on with your life? What does that mean, to you?"

"It means I want to get on with my life, Mom. I want to take the stupid test. If the kid is mine, I guess I'll try to figure out what Star wants from me. She's angry. I guess I deserve that. I'm angry, too."

"What are you angry about, Wil?"

Is the woman kidding? Is she? Can I really say this stuff to my mother? Bridgett is not here to stomp on my feet, so I guess I can say whatever I want.

"I'm angry, Mom, because I tried to use protection. I'm angry because if it's my kid, too—how come I didn't get to make any decisions? Why is that?"

"I don't understand. Star didn't want to use protection? Was she trying to get pregnant?"

"No. It was more like she was afraid or something. I don't really know."

"Afraid or something? Did you force her to have sex with you?"

"No, Mom. No! How many times do I have to say that? But then, when she got pregnant, she wouldn't even consider having an abortion. How is that fair, if the kid is both of ours?"

"Abortion? Wil, is that what you wanted?" Now I've really opened a vein. My mother looks like she may give up on me all together. She's clearly disgusted. She bites her lip and takes a deep breath. I know I haven't heard the last of the abortion issue. She smoothes her hair and folds her hands on the table. I see her fingers tremble; my gut trembles, too.

"You asked how this is fair. Look, Wil. It's fair because it's Star's body. That's why it's important to be in a committed relationship. Important to really get to know your partner well—and know that you both want the same things *before* you're intimate with someone. You have to make sure you are both mature enough to accept the responsibility, the consequences of your actions. Your father and I wanted so much for you. Star's grandmother wanted so much for her, too. We still want those things for the two of you. We want to keep your lives as normal as possible. We also want all those good things for your baby."

This is too much. All of it's too much. I don't want to think about it. I don't want to deal with it. I just want to get drunk.

"Mom, can I spend the night at Boland's? Hobbs is going over there, too. It's our annual pre-football 'crash-over.'" My mother looks stunned, but she recovers quickly. Now let's see if she *really* wants my life to be as normal as possible.

"We haven't talked about your driving privileges with your father. We ran out of time."

"That's okay. Hobbs'll pick me up. We do this every year. It's our good luck night before football practice starts. You said you want my life to be as normal as possible."

"I'll call Dad and talk it over with him, Wil. You call Star and make sure the baby is doing better. I want you to know that Mrs. Peters suggested your father and I join her when she meets with the school administrators to discuss the logistics of Star going back to school. That's what her grandmother wants, and maybe you should be there, too, to support Star."

"No way."

"Wil."

"No way, Mom. It's none of my business whether or not Star goes back to school. Why would you and Dad be there anyway? It's none of your business, either."

"Wil."

"I'm sorry, Mom, but it's not."

"It's our business because arrangements have to be made for the baby. He can't stay home alone."

"Isn't it Star's job to figure it out?"

"How is it Star's responsibility more than yours? You *both* have to go back to school." *This is bullshit*. It is. Bridgett is standing behind Mom now, giving me the time-out sign.

"I can't talk about this now, Mom. I just can't."

"Okay, Wil. Just think about coming to the meeting at school. The point of it really is to benefit both you and Star. And let me know what Star says about the baby."

"Huh?"

"You're going to call Star and check on Wil, remember?" I close my eyes and picture Mrs. Peters standing in the doorway with the baby. *My future sucks*.

I take the steps two at a time and slam my bedroom door. I just want to shut out everyone and everything. The problem is, my sister's parked in the middle of my bed, cracking her gum.

"You know what, Bridgett, I've had enough. Go away."

"Okay. Right after you call Star and ask if I can go over there and meet my nephew."

"Why would I do that?"

"Because you need me, little brother. And I'm a great babysitter."

15
Star

My grandmother always told me to be careful what I wish for, because it may not be what I really want. *I finally know what that means now. What was I supposed to say, when Fletcher asked if his sister could come and meet the baby?* I mean, I'd just told him that the medicine appeared to be working, and that Wil was in a good mood. I want Wil to know his father, but his family's overwhelming. My grandmother came home and played with Wil—then she went to bed. She says that she's okay, but she looked exhausted.

Bridgett's knock is so soft, I barely hear it. She looks like she just stepped out of a magazine. She's blonde and thin like her mother, but much taller. She's dressed in white slacks, a blue and white shirt, and a short-sleeved, cropped navy jacket. She's wearing navy sandals, too. And it'd be hard to miss the diamond ring on her left hand. She's carrying a gift wrapped in white paper covered with colorful baby hand- and footprints.

"Thanks for letting me come over, Star. I couldn't wait

to meet Wil," Bridgett says as soon as we're sitting in the living room.

We're both on the couch, and I'm holding a wide-awake baby.

"May I hold him?" she asks.

We do a little dance on the sofa. Bridgett puts the gift on the coffee table and I shift Wil into her arms.

"Wow, what a handsome little guy," she says. "You look like you're going to have your mother's great hair, Wil. I love your smile, are you feeling better? Star, what a beautiful baby! Is he good-natured?"

"He's a really happy baby during the day. Nights get a little rough sometimes—most of the time, actually. But I'm not complaining." I catch myself. *What'll get back to Mr. and Mrs. Fletcher?*

"Well, I'd be complaining! Wil, you and your mommy need your sleep. I know you miss her, but she'll still be there in the morning." Bridgett traces Wil's nose with her finger.

I look up to see my sleepy-eyed grandmother standing in the hallway. Bridgett gets up and shakes her hand as she comes into the room.

"Mrs. Peters, hello, I'm Bridgett Fletcher."

"Of course, Bridgett, I've seen you at church. It's very nice to see you."

"It's nice to see you, too. I'll be going back to school soon and I'm hoping to spend some time with my nephew before I go."

My grandmother swipes at her hair, covers her yawn with her hand. She looks as uncomfortable as I feel as she settles into the rocking chair. The room is very quiet now. I instinctively reach for Wil when he starts to cry, but Bridgett pats his bottom and talks him into smiling.

"Would you like to open Wil's present?" Bridgett asks. I put the box on my lap and pick at the tape until the paper's off the gift: Winnie-the-Pooh stares at me from his cellophane window.

"What a cute toy. Thank you." It feels lame, but it's all I can think of to say.

"Pooh's motion activated," Bridgett tells me. "Wil's not old enough yet to hold that big rattle that sets Pooh in motion, so I got him some rattle socks, too. They're in the box. Wil kicks his feet and the socks rattle, Pooh'll sing and move. My friend's baby loves this toy. I want to get Wil some other things too, of course, but I wanted to find out what he needs first."

"We're good, Bridgett, thanks. This is a great gift. Wil will enjoy it for a long time." My grandmother stands up and reaches for the toy—then retreats back to the rocker with it. I watch as she wrestles with the cellophane and packaging until Pooh's free. She reaches into the box and works on freeing the rattle while I get up to answer the door.

"Who is it?" I ask.

"Star, I brought the stroller over while I had the car. Should I just leave it here on the porch?" I open the door to find Todd holding Nevaeh and a folded stroller.

"Todd, really, you should keep the stroller. We're okay just going for walks on weekends."

"What if I'm selfish and I want you to meet us at the

park? We had fun that day, right?" I recognize Todd's loneliness because I'm lonely, too.

My grandmother comes up behind me. "Star, who do you have standing here on the porch?" I stand there without answering. My grandmother stares at Todd for a moment before she speaks: "Todd Ryan, is that you?"

"Yes, Mrs. Peters. How are you?"

"I'm fine. How are you?"

"Fine, thank you. This is my daughter, Nevaeh."

"Well, you don't *look* fine to me," my grandmother huffs. "Come in here with that sweet baby."

I cringe as my grandmother reaches for Nevaeh.

"You used to be the most handsome little boy in Star's class."

My grandmother's holding Nevaeh now, stroking the rash on her face. Todd looks at me shyly. I just want to die.

"Todd, what would your mother say if she could see you?"

"My mother's dead, Mrs. Peters."

"Well, I know that, and I'm very sorry. But don't you think she is looking down on you and your beautiful baby? Don't any of you kids pay attention to your religion teachers anymore?"

"Grandma!" I'm mortified. "Todd's just dropping off a stroller for Wil and me to use."

"I see that. What a nice gesture. Just don't leave it on the porch. That's another thing. This neighborhood. What a shame. Come in, son." Todd has no choice but to follow my grandmother into the living room, since Nevaeh's still in her arms.

What are the chances that Todd's dropped by my house twice, and both times Fletcher's next of kin are present to witness both his visits?

"Bridgett Fletcher, this is Todd Ryan and his daughter, Nevaeh." My voice is high, nervous.

"Hi, Todd. I think I remember you from Wil's lacrosse team." Bridgett smiles at Todd, and then at Nevaeh in my grandmother's arms.

"Hi, Bridgett." My grandmother's in the rocker, so Todd takes the only other available chair in the room.

"Star got a rash on her face like Nevaeh's one time when she was a baby, Todd." My grandmother says. "It was when I wore a wool jacket to Mass and she fell asleep against it." Todd looks down at his coat.

"Really, you think it's that simple?" he asks.

My grandmother looks him straight in the eye. "Is it worth a try?" Todd takes off his coat.

"Okay, now, that t-shirt is fine for you to wear, but do you really want this sweet, innocent baby to be exposed to that stuff?"

"Okay, well, Mrs. Peters, you used to be the nicest grandmother in Star's class." Todd winks at me.

"Touché!" my grandmother tells him. "But, really. You have to think about this baby. Look at this cute toy Bridgett brought for Wil. This is the kind of image you want Nevaeh to be exposed to—not glow-in-the-dark skulls on a black background."

"Mrs. Peters, I am not wearing a Winnie-the-Pooh shirt—no way, no how—not ever. And I've read that showing babies black and white images is a good thing."

"Oh, sure, snoot your nose at Pooh while you're wearing a skull on your chest. Do you like Winnie?" My grandmother asks Nevaeh. The baby is staring at my grandmother like she's trying to place her face. "And I'm sure, what you've read doesn't include scary black-and-white images that'll give small children nightmares."

Todd slides forward in his chair. I hold my breath, waiting for him to pull his shirt off and expose a hundred tattoos. Instead he tugs his arms through to his chest, shifts the shirt around while he's still wearing it, and shoves his arms into the sleeves again. Todd's now wearing a plain black t-shirt.

"You're looking more like that handsome little boy already." My grandmother's beaming. "Shall we work on those earrings in your nose and eyebrow, or wait for another day? They're called earrings for a reason. Tell that to your daddy. Tell him, Nevaeh."

Todd sits back in his chair and crosses his arms. Grandma has pushed him as far as he's going to go. I'm stunned, both at Grandma and at Todd. What did I expect to happen here? I feel like I don't know anyone anymore.

Bridgett clears her throat and smiles at me. I want to change the subject, fast. "Wil was running a fever today, Todd. We went to the doctor. He's on an antibiotic. He's much better now. No fever this evening."

"No kissing Wil," Todd says to Nevaeh. She smiles at her dad's voice. Grandma jumps up and goes to my bedroom, returning with a blanket. She sits Nevaeh on the blanket on the floor, and puts Pooh down in front of her.

Grandma sits on the floor and shakes the rattle—Pooh Bear wiggles and sings a song.

Wil perks up and is looking toward the sound. Bridgett gets up and sits cross-legged near Nevaeh on the floor.

"Look, Wil, see the baby? She's playing with Pooh Bear. See Pooh? Pooh sings songs. Nevaeh's beautiful," Bridgett tells Todd.

"Thanks. She's a happy baby, despite the fact that her father wears skulls and has her napping on wool." He smiles at my grandmother. "I think she'll be the prettiest girl in Wil's class." Did Todd just wink at my grandmother?

"Does she have a favorite book?" Bridgett asks. She's smiling at Todd.

"*The Da Vinci Code*," Todd laughs. "No, seriously, she likes *The Very Busy Spider*. It's probably because of all the barnyard sounds. I never grew out of making pig and cow noises—I do a really SWEET rooster, too."

Todd's so animated as he talks to Bridgett. He's tolerated my grandmother's prodding and probing. He's stuck it out—hung in there—and answered her criticisms with humor. I want to cry, hearing him talk about reading to Nevaeh. Is it because her mother left her? Does one parent just automatically pick up the slack for the one who's absent? Would he have been this involved if she hadn't disappeared and left him to care for the baby on his own?

Bridgett's been holding on to Wil since she walked in the door. "What books does Wil like, Star?" I almost miss her question. I'm looking right at her, but it's almost like I'm not here.

"He likes *Brown Bear, Brown Bear, What Do You See?* I need to get to the library and borrow it. We don't have a lot of books yet."

"We should go to the library together, Star. Take the kids."

I catch my grandmother looking at me. Todd sees her, too. "Star and I ran into each other at the park one day, Mrs. Peters. We hadn't talked in a long time, maybe not since middle school. I'm hoping the babies can be friends." My grandmother reaches out and touches Nevaeh's back, pats her.

"That would be nice," she says. She looks tired. What's really going on with her? What kind of tests did she have today?

The phone rings and I get up to answer it.

"Hello?" I say into the receiver. It's Miss Marcie, checking on Wil. "He's fine, Miss Marcie. He's on an antibiotic. I'll keep him home tomorrow to make sure the fever's really gone."

She tells me that Nikia had her baby. She's way ahead of her due date. "Nikia? Really?" I say. "Is she okay? Is the baby okay? She's really early. I can try to get in to see her soon . . . I know . . . my experience . . . Sure. Thanks for calling, Miss Marcie."

I hang up and see my grandmother and Bridgett staring up at me from their places on the floor. Todd's standing in front of the chair. Obviously, they've all been eavesdropping.

"Is Nikia okay?" Todd asks.

"She's scared—the baby's in the neonatal intensive

care unit. She had her this afternoon—the baby's really early. I wish I could go over there for a few minutes. Maybe she won't even see me, but I know what she's going through."

"If your grandmother is willing to watch Wil, I can take you," Bridgett offers. "Or your grandmother can take you, and I can watch Wil."

"Bridgett, if you're going to stay a while longer, I can take Star and you can help with Wil. Nevaeh and I'll just hang out in the car."

"That's silly," my grandmother says. "Bridgett's willing to stay. We'll keep both babies here. It's settled, then. Do you have diapers in the car, Todd? Star, I'll give you money. Buy a balloon or flowers for Nikia."

I look down at my clothes. "I look..."

"Beautiful," Todd blurts out. He's blushing. "I'll get the diaper bag." Todd disappears in search of diapers. My grandmother disappears in search of her wallet. Bridgett recites *Brown Bear* to Nevaeh and Wil. I remember that Wilson told me that she wants to be a child psychologist—she volunteers at a child development center near her university.

I go into the bathroom to brush my teeth and avoid looking myself in the eye. I cry so easily. Just the thought of Wil's birth, his little body in the NICU for days. I don't trust myself not to cry. This isn't about me and Wil. This is about Nikia and her baby.

"They'll be okay," Todd reassures me in the car.

"The baby's even earlier than Wil was."

"But the survival rate is very high for premature babies now, Star. Right?" He smiles at me, reaches over and touches my hand.

"I'm sorry about my grandmother."

"What are you sorry about?"

"Are you serious, Todd? She was all over you about your clothes and everything."

"You have nothing to be sorry about."

"Okay, well, I'm embarrassed."

"Embarrassed for me, for your grandmother, or for yourself?"

"I was *really* afraid she embarrassed you, Todd."

"Seriously, Star. It takes more than that to embarrass me. Your grandmother's entitled to her opinion, and you have nothing to be embarrassed about. End of story."

"My grandmother may be entitled to her opinions, but she's not entitled to inflict them on you."

"Star, it's not like she was being mean or nasty about anything. She's concerned about the baby. It's funny; my father lectures me all the time about the way I look, but he's never made me see myself the way Nevaeh may see me, but your grandmother made me think about that."

"Nevaeh sees you as a father who loves her."

"Do I love her enough to stop hiding behind stuff?"

"What do you mean?" I asked.

Todd shakes his head and grips the steering wheel with both hands.

What is Todd hiding behind? His clothes? I lean back in my seat and close my eyes. I try to remember what Maureen looks like. *How could she leave Nevaeh? Does she still love Todd? I'm always so tired.* I feel the road—the forward motion of the car. I imagine darkness gathering in the corners of this town, under trees and in doorways. Sleep's my hiding place. It's dark. No one can see me in the dark. If I'm very still, he'll give up and go away.

"Star?" The voice is soft. I open my eyes to find myself in a parking garage.

"Todd, I'm sorry. I fell asleep!"

"Now, why are you sorry about that? Come on. Let's go see Nikia. I'll just say 'hello' and then let you two talk."

Todd comes around and opens the door I'm pushing at. I feel weak and chilled, like those few minutes of sleep sapped my strength and my body heat. I wrap my arms around myself.

"Star, you're shivering. I wish I had my coat to give you, but it's back at your place," Todd says, as I try to still my chattering teeth.

We get into the elevator in the parking garage, then another inside the hospital that deposits us on the third floor. The nurse at the desk tells us Nikia's in Room 315. Todd puts his hand on my back and directs me into her room. Nikia's alone. The TV's on, but her eyes are closed.

"Nikia?" I whisper.

"Star, girl, you're here!" Nikia says. She smiles through her tears. I think about rainbows during a rainstorm, and color breaking through gray clouds when a bit of sun peers out. I see a flash of hope in her eyes.

"How are you?" I ask. "Can I get you anything?" I remember the money my grandmother gave me for flowers. I glance around the room. There are no flowers, no balloons, or cards.

"You're my first visitors," Nikia says. "I mean, except for Miss Marcie. She drove me over here from the center. Stayed with me the whole time. The doctor did an emergency C-section." Nikia's eyes cloud up: The smile gone, tears flow in a steady stream.

"My mother couldn't take off work. She should be here soon, though. She's excited about being a grandmother."

"We won't stay long," I tell Nikia. "I know you'll be happy to see your mom. I just wanted to check in on you and the baby. I know it can be a scary time, but you're both in a good place, Nikia. This hospital took good care of Wil and me."

"My baby—she's so tiny, Star. You know, like those pictures of Wil in the scrapbook. Is it my fault for smoking? Is that why she came early? What if she dies?"

"Nikia, listen, I didn't smoke and Wil came early. Don't think about all that right now. Do you pray? Praying helped me—and Wil, too, obviously. She's going to be okay. Babies are such great little fighters."

"I need her to be a fighter. I won't smoke around her anymore; I won't. Listen, I didn't even have time to name her yet. What should I name her, Star? What if that's all she ever has—a name? What if she doesn't ever get to do anything?"

"Nikia, really, you'll see. I know it's hard right now, but every minute that passes makes her stronger. I remember how scared I was, but I watched Wil get bigger and stronger every single day. I remember his first smile. You'll have that with your baby. You will!"

"Zion didn't even call. He didn't even call me, Star. Doesn't he care about his baby?"

Okay, that's it for me. I want to cry, sure, but mostly I'm furious: Furious at Zion, and furious at Fletcher. Nikia should *not* be going through this alone. I look around for Todd, but he's gone. It's so convenient that men just turn and leave when things get tough.

I lean over the bed and hug Nikia. I feel her tears against my face. "It'll be okay," I whisper. "Think about how strong you are, Nikia. Think about what a strong little girl you're going to raise. Think about the strong women you look up to—your mother, and Rosa Parks. How many times have I heard you talk about Rosa Parks?"

"Rosa, Rosa Parks. What if I name my baby Rosa, Star? My mother's name is Michelle. What if I name my baby Rosa Michelle?"

"That's a beautiful name. It's a strong name: Rosa Michelle. I love it, Nikia. Does it feel good to be doing things for your baby? Picking a name is a big step."

"It does feel good. It feels real, even. Well, look at that!"

I turn to find Todd in the doorway with a vase of flowers and a pink teddy bear. Nikia's looking at him like he's some kind of superhero.

"From Star," he says, putting the flowers on the window ledge. "From me," he tucks the bear into Nikia's arms. She pulls him down and kisses his cheek.

"You were always the sweetest boy in our class," she tells him. "Girls don't forget that."

Why had I forgotten? Why had I *forgotten* that Todd was the sweetest boy in our class?

"Yeah, well, don't let it get around. I have to be tough

187

now. I'm a dad, you know. Dads have to be tough." Nikia bursts into tears again. "Nikia, I'm sorry for whatever I just did to make you cry." Todd hesitates for just a second, then jumps back in: "Hey you, cry if you want to, but I'd rather you talk to me. Been awhile since we talked."

Nikia giggles. I stand back and watch her go through the highs and lows of being a new mother all alone. I remember the extreme lows—such sorrow. Attempts to rise from the depths—trying to grasp at anyone's attempts to cheer me up.

My grandmother stayed until Wil was born, and then she ran off to work. I had no one to call. I'd left my friends at school. I had new friends at the center, but I was in a different phase from all of them, and in another place. I didn't really fit in anywhere.

Elizabeth was the first friend to come and visit me. She stayed, too. Through it all, she's been there for me. Hobbs, too. Elizabeth insists it's not just for her, because he's her boyfriend. She says he really cares about me, and my and Fletcher's baby.

When I was pregnant, Fletcher disappeared as soon as I started showing. And he didn't reappear until after Wil was several weeks old. I never quite figured out why he even reappeared. I know it had nothing to do with the baby.

It is easy for me to recognize what other mothers go through who are so alone: both the love we feel for our babies, which rips through the sadness and pain we feel for ourselves, and our disappointment in our babies' absent fathers.

Todd has Nikia laughing now. I've missed their whole

conversation. I get lost in my own world a lot these days. But I see that Nikia has found her high. I wonder how long it'll last, before the loneliness and the fear grip her again.

Nikia's mother comes into the room, arms full of gifts. There are flowers and a balloon—and a colorful bag full of clothes for the baby. She hugs and kisses Nikia. Then she hugs and kisses Todd and me. Todd and I say goodnight, telling them to enjoy their visit. I make it to the parking garage before I burst into tears. Todd puts his arms around me, pulling me into the shadows and away from the curious stares of hospital visitors coming and going.

"I'm so sorry, Star," he whispers.

"What are you sorry about, Todd?"

"I'm sorry that you have to relive all this."

"It's not about me. It's about Nikia and her baby."

"It's about you, too. It's okay to be sad. It's okay to cry."

"Wilson hates it when I cry."

Todd pulls back and looks at me. "In all fairness to Fletcher," he says, "what does he know about tears? Before my mother died, the skies were all blue in my world. Grass was green, oceans were for swimming during the summer. Mountains were for skiing in the winter. That's pretty much all I knew."

"Todd, I'm so sorry about your mother."

"I know. Thanks, it's okay. Your card meant a lot—and what you wrote in it. Your grandmother's, too. It was a long time ago, but I remember what you said. You probably don't even remember sending it."

"I do remember writing to you. I remember thinking

about you going to bed at night, thinking about your mother being gone, like I thought about mine. I'm sorry, Todd. There're just too many things. Sad things." Todd pulls me into his arms again. He smells like soap. How can a guy that wears a wool coat in the heat of summer smell so clean? A car alarm goes off and we pull apart.

Todd opens the door and I slide into the front seat. The car alarm goes silent. I think about how often I've heard an alarm like that and just looked away. I've seen other people do it, too. Do we all just assume the car owner hit the wrong button? What if someone was in trouble and needed help?

"False alarm," Todd tells me when he gets in the car. Apparently, Todd didn't just look away. I try to give him money for Nikia's flowers. He starts the motor. "Keep it. You can buy the ice cream," he says.

"Excuse me?"

"I called my father to tell him where I was. He suggested I take you out to dinner. I told him we probably shouldn't leave the babies that long, so he suggested ice cream. I called your grandmother to see if it would be okay with her and Bridgett. She said that you hadn't had dinner yet. She suggested we stop at the store for ice cream. She'll have butter pecan, please, and we could all have the stew you made for dinner. She said she and Bridgett were starved, and they may not wait for us to start eating."

"Todd, are you sorry you ever decided to drop off the stroller?"

"Why would I be sorry, Star? Your grandmother's a pretty funny lady."

"*Funny*'s not a word I usually connect with my grandmother."

"*Entertaining*, then?"

"There have been times in my life that she was funny and entertaining," I say. I guess there've been too many bad things, though. She tells me that the human spirit can only take so much. I guess she's right.

By the time we get back home with the ice cream, both babies are asleep. Wil's in his crib, and Nevaeh is on the blanket on the floor—surrounded by cushions. "Where'd they think she'd go?" Todd asks in a whisper.

My grandmother and Bridgett are going for second helpings. "Hey," Todd says, "I thought you invited me to dinner."

My grandmother smiles at him, "There's plenty, Mr. Ryan," she says. "How are Nikia and the baby?"

"Nikia's okay. I didn't actually see the baby," my voice cracks. *I just couldn't.* Todd reaches over and squeezes my hand. "How were our babies?" I ask, as I put the ice cream in the freezer.

"Angels," Bridgett says. "Your grandmother tried to take over and hold them both at once, but I wasn't having any of that. I need my time with Wil before I go back to school."

"Bridgett's exaggerating. She was the one hogging the babies. I told Bridgett she needs to marry that young man of hers and start her own family." I feel my eyes gravitate to the floor. Todd reaches over and squeezes my hand again. He hands me a plate. We spoon stew out of the pot and take our plates to the table.

My grandmother asks Todd, "How's your father?"

He takes a piece of bread off the plate Bridgett passes him. "Dad's good, thank you. Works long hours, has a ton of patients, reads a ton and a half of books to Nevaeh every day."

"Sounds like a busy life," my grandmother smiles at Todd. "I'm sure he loves his little granddaughter. She really is a sweet girl, Todd."

"Thank you, Mrs. Peters. I'm sure you love your granddaughter. She really is a sweet girl, too."

"That she is," my grandmother agrees.

"And your great-grandson, too," Todd says. My grandmother nods her agreement.

We eat our dinner and dessert. Bridgett and Todd clear the table while I wash dishes and Grandma puts the leftovers away.

Todd says that he needs to get Nevaeh home to bed. She sleeps through being picked up and put over his shoulder. Bridgett picks up the diaper bag and Todd's coat, and tells him she'll walk him to the car. She puts things down long enough to hug me and my grandmother at the front door, and asks if she can come and visit us again. My grandmother is very gracious with Bridgett and Todd, inviting them back whenever they want to come.

I'm drained. I want to go to bed and sleep while Wil's asleep, but my grandmother's in the rocker and I know she wants to talk. I close my eyes and take a deep breath to gather my courage.

16
Wilson

Bridgett pulls in the driveway just as we're pulling out. She tries to flag me down, but I tell Hobbs to keep driving. I don't want to hear about her visit with Star. I don't want to hear her gush over the kid. I already know how she feels about children. She wants seven, just like Sean's mother. Sean is such a dork. He'll do whatever Bridgett wants. He's totally in love with my sister.

We stop at Elizabeth's on the way out of the neighborhood. Hobbs and Anderson stand on the porch, kissing. *Have they no shame? I'm right here, guys.* I look away.

Talk about totally in love. Talk about dorks.

I lay on the horn. Hobbs almost falls down the steps. *Got him. What a moron.* He glares at me. I know what he wants to do—he won't make an obscene gesture in front of Elizabeth, though. She's some kind of princess to him. But I don't know of any castles in Western Maryland, and we have no royalty.

Anderson walks Hobbs to the car. "Are you behaving yourself, Wil?" she asks, jumping in the driver's seat.

"Get out of the car, Elizabeth," I tell her. "You are seriously holding us up here."

"Don't be rude, Fletcher," she tells me. "Besides, I'm not going anywhere until you tell me how Star and Wil are doing."

"They're fine."

"Fine? That's it? Talk to me."

"Wil was running a fever today. We took him to the doctor."

"Who took him to the doctor?"

The look on Lizbeth's face tells me she's not moving until I give her a total recap of the field trip to the doctor's office:

"I drove. Star sat in the back seat with the kid. I managed to carry the baby in the car seat into the medical center without accidentally injuring the kid.

"We both sat with him in the waiting room. We both went into the examining room.

"My parents and Mrs. Peters showed up at the waiting room and grilled us about Wil's illness when we came out.

"I drove to the pharmacy. Star went in and got his prescription. I drove them home.

"Is this making you happy, Anderson? Because I'm not happy. I'm bored and I want to go. Can you please get out of the car?"

"Not until you tell me how Wil's doing. What was wrong with him? Is his fever down?"

"Hey, why don't you call Star and ask her? The last I heard, he was doing fine. No fever. Will you please just let us go?"

"I'm very proud of you, Wil. You're finally showing a little class."

I want to deck her, but number one—she's a girl, and number two–she's a maniac and my sore tailbone is a constant reminder of her mean streak. She slides out of the car and into Hobb's arms for another round of kissing. *I definitely don't need this.* Then Lizbeth stands in the driveway and waves to Hobbs as we drive away.

"So cute," I tell Hobbs. "So tell me, how come you and Elizabeth don't have any kids?" His right foot is steady on the gas pedal, but his left leg is having some kind of spastic attack, bouncing up and down.

"Don't be a smart-ass, Fletcher."

"How am I being a smart-ass? It's a legitimate question. With all that kissing, how did you avoid knocking her up?"

"Wil, are you stupid? Just shut up."

"Don't get sore, I'm trying to talk to you. There's not enough birth control in the world—you've been together forever."

"We're not using birth control. That's not where we are right now. We know what we want. We want to finish high school, go to college. We do a lot of kissing, Fletcher, but we know when to quit, okay?"

"You're serious? It's what she wants, right?"

"Is that bad, Wil, to listen to what your girlfriend wants? Should I pressure Elizabeth like you pressured Star?"

My hands turn into fists. "Is that what Star told you?"

"Star didn't tell us anything. We were *there*. We spent a lot of time with you two, remember?"

"I didn't force her, okay?"

"Did I say you forced her? No, I said you *pressured* her. She loved you."

"Loved me? Does that mean she doesn't love me anymore?"

"You are *such* a jerk, Fletcher. Can we just save this until after I've had a beer or two?"

"Is that what this night is about? Are you and Boland going to give me a hard time about Star?"

"Fletcher, you called us, okay? You deemed this crash-over night. We usually save it for a weekend closer to the actual start of football season. This was your idea, remember?"

Our meeting place isn't far out of town, but it is kind of remote. In the times we've been out here, we've never run into anyone else. Boland's and Meg's cars are there when we arrive.

Meg kisses my cheek and shakes Hobbs's hand. "You guys are not leaving here tonight, right? You are not driving anywhere. If you have to leave for any reason, you call me. Do you hear me? I'll come out here and pick you up any time of the night."

"Why so uptight?" I ask her. "You're usually cool with this."

"Yeah, well, I'm getting older and wiser. I know more about what happens when guys get stupid. I would die if any of you got hurt or sick. You all know about alcohol poisoning, right?"

"Meg, there's not enough beer there for any of us to fall victim to alcohol poisoning. And that's pretty sexist, thinking only guys get stupid," Hobbs responds.

"I didn't say only guys get stupid, Alex, okay? Girls and guys both get stupid, and girls and guys together get *really* stupid."

"Do you see any girls here?" Boland asks, lifting his sister off the ground and spinning around with her. "We're free tonight. Free to be stupid."

"Hey, I'm serious here, Craig. Don't make me sorry I did this, okay? Mom and Dad would kill me. Actually, I'm sorry already, and this is the last time. I'm not doing this again."

"Meg, you say that every time, then pretty boy here calls you and off you go to the liquor store," Hobbs says.

This is on me, too? "Come on! That's not true. Meg would do this for any one of us, right?" I ask.

"My big sister has a special place in her heart just for you, Fletcher," says Boland.

"Meg, you know what? I'm not calling you about booze anymore. I didn't know you were freaked out about it. Take it back if you don't want us to have it," I tell her.

"Are you crazy?" Boland says, grabbing the beer. "Go home, Meg. We'll be fine."

Meg hangs back and looks at me.

I really didn't know it was a problem for her. Apparently, I don't know much. Hobbs thinks I pressured Star.

Does everyone think I'm completely insensitive and clue-less?

"Meg, I'll walk you to the car," I say, putting my arm around her and handing her cash for the beer. As soon as we're out of earshot, I pull her close. "Don't worry about us. We're big boys. We'll be okay."

"Hey, Wil, I shouldn't do this. I guess I'll feel better when you're all home safely tomorrow."

"Really, Meg, I won't ask you again. I had no idea you were so freaked out about it."

"Well," Meg rubs her eyebrows, "for one thing, umm, it's the baby, Wil. You have to be around for that baby. Don't go doing anything stupid."

I fall on the ground and bury my head in my hands. Meg sits beside me and puts her head on my shoulder.

"Is that what this is about? Star's baby?" *I wish I didn't sound so defensive. How many rounds have I gone today? I'm feeling a little battered here.*

Meg's pinching her neck now. "He's your baby, too, right?"

That hasn't been determined yet. "What I don't get is why everyone's talking about it *now*. All this time, people kept their suspicions to themselves—now all of a sudden, everyone knows more about my life than I do."

"We're all your friends, Wil. We were taking our lead from you. You just blew the whole thing off. It's getting harder now for Craig and Alex not to think about it because everyone's pulling for Star to go back to school. It's kind of in everyone's face."

"What's in everyone's face? Whether the kid is mine or not? How is that anybody's business?"

"You *have* to know the answer to that, right?"

"No, I don't."

"Your friends care about you. They care about Star. They care about *both* of you in different ways. It's kind of like picking teams, Wil. You know what that's like. This is picking teams, with Star in the middle of you and the baby."

I puff up my cheeks and let the air escape slowly.

"Listen, I'll get out of your way," Meg whispers. "Have fun, but please stay safe."

I lay on the ground and listen as Meg starts her car, backs out, and drives away. The sky's dark, the moon's white. There's one bright star high above me—it looks lonely—separate from the rest. I shut my eyes and shield myself from that lonely, distant star.

Star and I talked every day before she left school. She was alone so much—so afraid much of the time. Part of it was the neighborhood, but it was something else, too. I asked her once, what she was so afraid of, but she just barreled into my chest and hung on for dear life.

Star trusted me. I trusted her, too. The thing is—I still trust her. So does that mean I really don't believe that kid belongs to someone else?

17
Star

I stand in the kitchen doorway, listening to my grandmother rocking back and forth in her chair in the living room. I know she's waiting to talk to me, and I'm scared of what she'll say.

Is it her health? Does she have cancer like my grandfather and uncle? Or, is this about me moving out? Does she really want Wil and me out of here? She hasn't brought that up again since she found me naked in her bed: my last night with Wil, the last time he touched me.

I feel the tears building, ready to flood my face. I remember Todd's arms around me in the parking garage. I felt so safe with him. His body said nothing about his needs. He was just there for me—no other reason. That's never happened to me before. Never.

I go back to check on Wil. I'm tempted to rouse him so he won't be awake all night, but it usually backfires and then he doesn't get any sleep at all. I back out of the room and head for the living room.

Grandma's still in the rocker. I go and sit on the sofa. "Are you really okay, Grandma?"

"I am, for now," she tells me, looking down at her hands. "Please don't worry, okay?"

I know from experience that this is the end of this conversation. My grandmother will share no more information about her medical condition today.

"Star, you'll remember to give Wil his medicine when he wakes up for a bottle, right?"

"Right." I think this signals she's going to bed, but instead, she continues to rock.

"I enjoyed Bridgett. She's very good with children." My grandmother searches my face like she does sometimes when she wants to know what I think but doesn't want me to know she's all that interested.

"She wants to be a child psychologist," I tell her. "You were different with Todd than I thought you'd be."

My grandmother plays with her watch, twisting it around and around on her arm. Her eyebrows knit together. "How did you think I'd be?"

"I didn't expect you to even let him in the house. I thought you'd freak when you saw his clothes and his piercings."

"All I saw was his sadness, Star."

Well, then, why did you pick on his clothes? Nevaeh's rash? I want to ask but don't.

"I don't see sadness when I look at Todd, Grandma." *What I see is loneliness.*

"Sometimes, when a person's very sad, it's hard for that person to see sadness in someone else."

I lean back on the sofa, exhausted. "Am I that sad, Grandma?"

"Yes, Star, you are. And I'm sad for you. I know that so much of your sadness is my fault. I did it wrong with your mother. I did it wrong with you. I should have taken your sadness over losing her more seriously and gotten help for you. But then I would've had to look at myself."

My grandmother's face drains; she is white, ghostly. Her voice sounds disturbed, haunted. "And when it happened. When I got involved . . . When I brought that man here . . . I should have protected you. When I failed to do that, I should've gone to the police. I was so afraid of you going through a trial, reliving it all again—you were so young."

My grandmother shakes her head, closes her eyes—opens them wide.

"I wanted to protect you from that, from breathing life into ghosts. Maybe I was protecting myself. I didn't want to look at myself. I should've taken you to a counselor."

My grandmother's eyes are darting around the room, avoiding mine.

"He said he was leaving the area, and would never return. Why would I believe anything that man had to say, after what he did to you? Why, Star? Am I really that big a fool?"

I take a deep breath. My grandmother has never been willing to talk about this before. If I speak, will she shut down? What is it that I want her to say?

Do I want to hear her take all the blame? Do I want her to tell me none of it was my fault? Do I want her to say it was okay to fall for his lies? Like the lies he told me, saying he'd tell me where my mother was, but only if I did the disgusting stuff he made me do to him? When I finally re-

alized he was lying, he said he'd kill my grandmother if I told her anything.

"I'm so sorry, Star. I should have gone to the police back then. I did go, right after the doctor told me I needed to go to Hopkins for more tests. I went to the police and showed them his picture. Told them I thought I saw him in the area again and that I was afraid for you."

Grandma wipes her brow, and rests her eyes on mine now. "As it turns out, he was a former policeman, just like he told me," she says, quietly. "All those pictures of him in uniform with his co-workers—that was all real. What he failed to tell me is that he's wanted for questioning in connection to two girls missing in other states. One happened since we knew him . . . Oh, Star, what have I done?"

I can't speak. I feel the terror starting in my heart. It chills my whole body as it pumps ice through my veins.

"Don't you see, Star? Todd's an innocent young man who lost his mother. Maybe that's why he looks like that. Underneath those clothes, he's still that little boy who sat beside you in class. It doesn't matter how he looks; we know who he is." She takes a breath.

"But looks are so deceiving. I trusted a stranger because of how he looked—he lied to me, Star. I thought he was so handsome. So presentable. He told me he was a former detective. He said he felt he accomplished more working as a private investigator, brought families together faster without all that red tape. He told me he'd seen your mother and felt he could locate her and bring her home—if we worked together. He even gave me her watch. He said it slipped off her arm when she waited on him at a restaurant where she worked. When I asked where it was, he said she'd already quit that job and that he was following every lead. He said he got to know about us by gaining her trust, but then she fled. He made it sound so real." Grandma wipes away a tear and then goes on.

"I'd come home from work and he'd say he let the babysitter go a little early. He was happy to stay with you until I got home. I never even suspected, but it wasn't because I was being careless. I really believed he was interested in me, cared about you, and wanted to reunite us with your mother. I was that desperate to believe it could happen."

My grandmother's crying hard now. But I can't go to her. I can't even move. I'm pinned under the weight of what she's told me: she thinks he's back in the area. *Is that who Fletcher saw in the alley?*

It didn't stop with the sexual abuse in my bedroom when I was a child. He raped me, Grandma. I know you didn't want me running in the evening. But you were working. I was training so hard for track. If the search lights, if the dogs hadn't scared him that night—would he have killed me? He's wanted for questioning in connection with missing girls. Did he kill them?

I smell the cigarettes on his breath, the booze. My head stings from him dragging me by my hair, off the trail and into the woods. My whole body aches as I roll down the embankment. Just as I get up to run from him, he slams me into the ground. He's on top of me. I feel the knife blade against my neck. I feel the prick. He tells me he'll cut my throat if I scream. He tries to disguise his voice, hides behind a ski mask, but I know who he is. I want to scream. I have to scream. I open my mouth, but nothing, not a sound, comes out.

"What's wrong with you, Star? Don't you hear that? Who is that?" My grandmother's shaking me. I see her frightened face as I'm pulled from that gully in my mind once again.

"Who is at the door, Star? Do you know?" I hear thundering footsteps on the porch, wild knocking on the door—Wil's piercing screams. I find my voice, finally.

"Rodney," I tell her. "He does this all the time to scare me." My hands are shaking. I reach for the scar on my neck. It's tiny, but he wanted me to know—to remember how sharp his knife was. My grandmother scolds Rodney through the locked door, then goes back to my room and picks up Wil. She moves past me in the living room and heads into the kitchen, holding my crying baby.

She screams into the phone, "Do you hear this baby, Mrs. Dobson? He was asleep until your son started pounding on the door. Does that make you proud? Keep him away from my house. Do you hear me? The next time it happens, I'm calling the police. Well, of course he's not home, he's here, beating down my door." The phone slams. My grandmother moves around the kitchen. My heart is beating so fast, I'm afraid to get up. There's so much information fighting for attention in my head that I'm sure it'll explode.

Can I even speak the words of the question that's forming in my mind?

My grandmother comes back into the room and sits in the rocker with Wil. He quiets when she puts the bottle in his mouth.

"I gave him his medicine. Go to bed, Star. I'll get him back down."

No, she can't do this. She can't. She can't lead me down this road and then tell me to go away.

"Did my mother really leave me, or did he do something to her?"

"The police are going to reopen the investigation into her disappearance. I made a big mistake, Star. I should have gone to them right away. I shouldn't have tipped him off that you told me. I should've just gone to the police. Maybe they could've collected evidence."

I smell the latex on my fingers, taste it in my mouth. He knew how to protect himself. He was a policeman. I never told my grandmother everything. Partly because I was afraid: Partly because she didn't want to know. She knows he touched me, she doesn't know what he made me do to him. She doesn't know the rest.

My fingers are in my hair—twisting, twisting. I go to the kitchen and pick up the phone. I know the number to the police station by heart. I've picked up the phone so many times to call since the rape. I never went through with it. I can't go through with it this time, either. I slam the phone down. I know I can't say the words. *I can't.*

I go to my bedroom and lie on the bed in the dark. My head throbs with the thoughts I've never been able to speak.

It's like my heart pumps blood only to my head. The rest of my body's numb. It's numbed by thoughts bigger than my life. My mind tells my body to block everything out until I'm able to say the words, to rid myself of my horrible secrets. But something else intrudes on those thoughts: scratching.

I hear a scratching sound on my window. I try to block it out, but now my ears go on high alert. Scratch...scratch... scratch...The sound makes me shiver. I get up from the bed and stand in front of my dark window. I am looking into nothingness: the blackness of the backyard.

I put my hand on the glass to steady my trembling body. A light goes on under his chin—flooding and illuminating his face. His teeth gleam white as his evil grin glares through the glass.

I'm screaming, screaming, screaming. I can't make the screams stop even after he's gone, disappearing into the darkness. Even after my grandmother comes into the room, I'm screaming. Even after I shout his name and tell her he was at my window. I hear her on the phone with the 911 Operator. I still can't stop screaming.

I collapse to my knees and hear the thump of my head as I crash all the way down to the floor. I lie there in the dark.

Grandma paces the hall, trying to quiet Wil. I see his face flooded with light, mocking me. I beg God to let me sleep. *Please, please, please, God, make his face go away.*

My grandmother sings to Wil. Her voice is soft, calming him, calming me. I feel my breathing steady as she sings about children under their blankets on a train heading for Morning Town. I reach over and tug on the edge of my bedspread until it falls off the bed and over me.

I cover my head; pull my knees into my chest. When his face appears behind my eyelids, I squeeze my eyes shut tighter and distort his image.

I put myself on the train my grandmother continues to sing about, hold tight to the caboose as it heads out of town, until his face is a speck in the distance. I slip under, away from my head crowded with thoughts.

But my dreams are crowded, too. I'm a ghost that goes to the closet and digs for the shoebox. I take it to my bed and lie down into my sleeping body. Fingers appear from inside the box; lifting the lid ever so slightly. I watch as the fingers slip over the edge of the box, curl around and scratch at the cardboard with sharp nails: *Scratch, scratch, scratch.*

I back away from the box, but hands reach out and pull me in. My screams echo off the walls of the box, blowing off the lid. I'm free. I'm in my grandmother's arms.

Wil screams from the crib where she has lain him. We're all sobbing.

Then sirens engulf the house. Searchlights flood the backyard.

I break free and run to the bathroom. My dinner scratches my throat as it leaves my body and splashes water from the toilet back in my face. So much comes up so fast: I feel myself gagging, choking. I can't catch my breath and clutch at my throat. Blows suddenly strike my back.

"Cough, Star, cough," my grandmother shouts as she pounds on my back. My mouth fills—I lean over and vomit, letting it all go. I cough, feel the air, as I inhale and breathe out.

Grandma takes my hand and leads me out to the couch. I lie down as she goes back and picks up Wil. Police lights flash through the living-room window. My grandmother answers the door and leads two police officers into the room. I sit up, dig my elbows into my knees and support my head in my hands. I twist my hair through my fingers.

My grandmother tries to tell a story that she never knew. I want to speak but I can't. The words are still trapped inside me.

"There was no one in the yard," one officer says.

"I SAW HIM," I shout. "HE WAS WATCHING ME THROUGH MY BEDROOM WINDOW." I attempt to stand on my feet, but my knees give out and I fall back into the couch.

"It's okay," the policeman tells me. His voice is quiet, gentle. "My name is Officer Lance, I know you saw him, Star. He's gone now. The yard's pretty dark. Tell me what you heard and saw."

"I heard scratching on my window. I got up out of bed and looked out. It was so dark. Then his face came out of nowhere. It was like he shone a light on it so I'd see him. He was so close to the window. My hand was on the glass—it was almost like I touched him." I feel the sobs start deep inside. I cover my mouth and try to control my shaking body.

"And you're sure this is the same man who sexually assaulted you when you were eleven? The same man your grandmother gave us a picture of...?" His words stab at my eardrums.

"YES, I'M SURE," I feel wild now. I feel the blood rush to my head, my face. "HE WAS WATCHING ME! DON'T YOU UNDERSTAND?"

"Okay, listen, it's okay, Star. We *do* understand how it must have upset you to see him there like that. We'll do everything we can to keep you and your family safe. We're going to continue searching for him through the night. We know he's in the area. You'll be hearing a search helicopter. There also will be a police presence in the neighborhood. Mrs. Peters, with your permission, Officer Kirby is going to go around the house, inside and out, and make sure everything is secure."

"Yes, please!" my grandmother says, her voice cracking. "Thank you, Officer."

"Star, your grandmother has given us a statement regarding what happened to you in the past, but..." I am shaking my head at him. He stops talking and stares at me. I open my mouth, but no words come out. I bury my head in my hands and rock my body to calm myself.

"She doesn't know," I whisper. "No one knows but me."

"The more we know..." he begins.

"I can't." I get up and go to my bedroom. Turn on the light, look at the window. My grandmother's lowered the blind. My shoulders feel chilled and I wrap my arms around myself as I walk to the closet door. I turn the knob. The door creaks open. I dig deep, casting aside stuffed animals, tossing books and shoes out of my way.

The shoebox is tucked in the back corner and I pull it out of its hiding place. I take the box to the living room and hand it to Officer Lance, who's talking quietly with my grandmother and the other officer. I reach for Wil and my grandmother tucks his sleeping body into my arms. He feels sweaty. I kiss his forehead and pull him close to me.

Officer Lance lets out a long whistle as he picks up ziplock bags from the box and examines them, then hands them to the other officer. They don't know that when I wasn't reading, I was watching *CSI* and police shows on TV. I want to tell him that kids know how a stained dress helped impeach a president. I want to tell them that Curtis Gray may have been a police officer, that he may have known how to protect himself, but everyone makes mistakes, slips up.

Officer Lance takes out a spiral notebook from the box. I may not have been able to speak the words, but I could write them. I know he's looking at my little-girl handwriting. I watch his eyes get bigger as he flips through the pages of recorded dates, and times, and details: details about that man's body, things an eleven-year-old should not know. I can tell when he reaches the pages where my little-girl handwriting turns into that of a high school freshman: he looks at me. His eyes are sad. I shake my head, put my finger to my lips.

This is not how I want my grandmother to find out about the rape.

18

Wilson

Meg is long gone when I open my eyes and find Boland standing over me. I expect him to hand me a beer, but instead he hands me a fudge bar. I sit up, pull off the paper and shove it in my mouth. Brain-freeze. *I will never learn.*

"Eat up, Fletcher," he tells me, putting the huge box between us.

"Are you kidding me?" I ask, staring at the size of the box.

"We can do it," he says. "We *have* to do it! They're already melting. Cooler's worthless."

"Yeah, well, there's a reason frozen food is kept in a freezer and not a refrigerator. See, Bo, the temperature..."

"Shut up, Fletcher."

"No respect. I get no respect."

"You get fudge bars. That's better than respect."

"There's nothing better than respect." The words are out of my mouth. I can't take them back. Boland hands me another fudge bar. I shove it in my mouth. Apparently my brain is a frozen tundra now, because it doesn't even react to the cold.

"Where's Hobbs?"

"On the phone with Elizabeth. There's something going on at Star's. There's a police car there."

"What?"

"At Star's. A police car. Fletcher, do you need your hearing checked?"

"How does Lizbeth know that?"

"She went over there to check on Wil. She didn't go in, obviously."

"Drive me over there, Boland."

"No."

"What do you mean no?"

"No means no. Fletcher, you don't need that girl and her problems. Cut your losses, okay? We've got a football championship to win this year. It's our last chance. We need you to be focused."

I pull another fudge bar out of the box and unwrap it slowly. It takes a while for it to melt in my mouth. Boland just sits there, staring at me.

"Wil, there's trouble at Star's. Come on, I'll drive you," Hobbs is standing over us now. I look up at him—concern all over his face, and then look at Boland—chewing on a Popsicle stick.

"Don't do it, Fletch, don't go," Bo says. "Like I said, it's not your problem."

My mouth drops open. Is this for real? I start to laugh. I can't control it. I can't make it different. I just laugh. I roll on my stomach and bury the sound of laughter in my arm.

"Fletcher, are you crazy? What's wrong with you? Someone could be hurt over there."

"Hobbs, leave him alone, okay? What's wrong with you? Star's not his problem."

I breathe in the smell of earth and grass under my nose. I see Boland and Hobbs, one on each shoulder: Boland, a devil, Hobbs, an angel. Hobbs preaching the high road; Boland, the easy way out. It doesn't matter what either of them say. Star doesn't want me because Star doesn't trust me. I'm a giant part of her problem.

Bo and Hobbs are shouting big time now. I can't think—I can't breathe. I get up and walk toward the river. The grass gets higher around my feet. I pull my cell phone out of my pocket and call Star's house. "Mrs. Peters," I say into the phone. "This is Wil. May I please speak to Star?"

"Wilson, this is not a good time right now. I'm sorry. She's resting. Why not call her in the morning?"

"Okay, thanks, is everything okay? Is she safe? Are you safe? Is little Wil okay? Do you need me to come over there?"

"Wil is doing well. He's asleep. We're all safe now. I don't think Star is up to seeing you right now. Maybe if things were different between you."

Okay, well, I deserve that slap in the face.

"I can make things different."

"I hope that's true, Wilson, for the baby's sake. But it won't happen tonight. Goodnight."

"Mrs. Peters?"

"Yes?"

"Will you call if you need me?"

"Yes. Thank you for that, Wil. Goodnight."

I close my eyes. Blue and red lights flash. Why would the police be over there? Mrs. Peters said that they're safe. I feel Star against my chest. I love the way she fits there. I love the way her hair smells, and the way she laughs. I didn't force her. I would never do that. But did I pressure her?

"What's the story?" Hobbs asks. "Are we going back?"

"Don't you think I'd be there in a minute if I could, Hobbs?"

"No, Fletcher, I don't. And I don't think I have to explain why. The past few months tell that story."

I walk away from him. *Nothing I do will ever make this right. Not with Star. Not with her grandmother. Not with my parents. Not with Hobbs and Elizabeth. They'll always see me as a loser who deserted his girlfriend when she really needed him.*

I go to the cooler and pop open a beer. It tastes like crap mingled with the sweet chocolate taste in my mouth. *Why was it so important for me to score with a girl? Why?* I thought every other guy on the football team was doing it but me. Maybe it's all just talk, a bunch of big shots outdoing each other with stories.

But I never told anyone about Star and me. Never. She was too important to me. It happened so fast, loving her. I finish my beer and take out another. Hobbs and Boland come over and open the cooler. Beer can tabs snap the silence. Then it's quiet again.

"They're all okay, Hobbs. You can call Lizbeth and tell her. Mrs. Peters said they're all safe. She said I should call back in the morning. Thanks for offering me a ride, but they don't want me there."

Hobbs doesn't have to tell me he's relieved. It's written all over his face. "Thanks, Wil." He gets up and walks away to call Anderson. His voice fades into the night.

Boland goes to the cars. He returns with all our sleeping bags and throws mine at me.

I lie on the ground and use it for a pillow.

More stars appear, and burn bright in the dark sky above. I search for the original star: it's there, outshining all the rest.

Will it be that way in my life? Ten years from now, will I look back and realize that Star shone brighter than any of the girls I've known—or will ever know? We're connected forever. We have a baby together.

"Are you in love with her?" Boland's voice comes out of the darkness. When I don't answer, he answers for me. "You are. I'm sorry. I think it's harder, Wil, once you've had sex with a girl. It's harder to forget her."

I let his words sink into my thick skull. It's not the sex. That's not why I can't forget Star. I had sex with Cate, too. I can't forget Star because we fell in love. I *can* forget Cate. It was a mistake. I shouldn't have had sex with either of them, but for different reasons. Star wasn't ready and I wasn't ready. I know that now. Cate had her own agenda. Still, every time I see Cate, that's what I'll remember—that it never should have happened. And every time I see Star, I'll remember that I hurt her.

"Are you okay, Wil?"

"Yeah. You?"

"I'm getting there. But Marly really blew me away when we split. It really hurt. You guys busting on me didn't help much either. The quarterback *gets* the hot senior girl, *loses* the girl. You just don't know."

"Tough break, Bo. I get it. I'm sorry. But at least you didn't produce an elephant."

"Elephant?"

"That's what it feels like, you know? I feel like I've disappeared because of the elephant in the room. I just can't see around it. It's just that big. How is it possible? How can one little baby be so big?"

"If I tell you something....oh, never mind."

"No way. You have to tell me, now. I won't say anything to anyone, Bo, whatever it is."

"Not even to Hobbs?"

"Especially not to Hobbs."

"Babies are big, Fletcher. Even when they don't get to be born."

"What are you talking about? Star's kid slid right into the world for all to see."

"But, my baby didn't, okay? Marly didn't even ask me. She just went off and had an abortion. We fought all the time after that. Our breakup had nothing to do with her going away to school. I was ticked off. Wouldn't you be? It was my choice, too, wasn't it?"

"I don't understand. Did you want to have a kid?"

"No! But I didn't want my first kid aborted before I even knew about him. Hey, man, don't say anything, okay? If it got back to my parents, or to Meg—" Boland's voice breaks. He coughs. "I mean, we used protection. What if it

217

was just *supposed* to happen? What if we were supposed to have that baby?"

"Or maybe it was just an accident, Bo. Don't torture yourself about it."

"Easy for you to say. Your kid didn't end up in a garbage can somewhere." I want to tell Bo that technically an embryo isn't a baby. But before I can say anything I get this image of Wil in a garbage can, with coffee grounds and wilted lettuce leaves on his head.

I'm feeling a little queasy. Maybe it's the beer and fudge bars. I dump the rest of my beer on the ground. I clear my throat. Search for words.

"Boland—Craig, I'm sorry. I had no idea. But I don't understand. If you feel this way, why are you always telling me Star's not my problem?"

"I wish I knew. Maybe it's the only way I can forgive Marly for what she did. I mean, you're my best friend, and you feel the same as Marly, right? Maybe it's okay to feel that way. Maybe Star and I are the ones that are wrong. Are we, Wil?"

What can I say? I don't know. I don't know anything anymore. I'm not as sure as I was about abortion, now that I know my closest friend's kid ended up in a Dumpster. Maybe it's one thing to think it, and something completely different once it actually happens.

"I guess that it's not right that she didn't tell you," I offer. "Why did she even tell you after she did it?"

"Because she felt guilty. She was so upset, Wil. She wanted me to tell her it was okay. She wanted me to say that's exactly what I would have wanted her to do. But it's not, Wil. I feel horrible about it. It was our baby." Bo's hands go to his face, covering his eyes.

There's nothing I *can* say. Absolutely *nothing*.

Hobbs comes back with his arms full of wood. "You guys are worthless," he tells us.

Go ahead, Alex, rub it in. I'm pretty sure I can speak for both Craig and me when I say we're feeling worthless.

Hobbs starts a fire. It glows bright, fills my nostrils with the smell of burning wood.

Where does an embryo's soul go when it's aborted? Does it go to heaven? Does an embryo even have a soul? I mean, it has everything else, right? I mean, does God say to an embryo, "Oh, by the way, you're too little to have a soul. You can have your soul when you're six." I don't think so. Now I really feel sick.

Hobbs produces a garbage bag from his car and starts collecting the beer cans Boland and I have thrown on the ground. He brings us a dripping box of forgotten fudge bars. Boland and I dig in, eating what's left of the melting mess and throwing paper and Popsicle sticks into the fire. "Hey guys, if Coach finds out we're drinking, that's the end of our season," Hobbs says. "Is this or is it not our last chance at a championship?"

My thumbnail goes in my mouth. I'm trying to quit chewing my nails, so I pacify myself with just this one. I spread out my sleeping bag and climb in. River sounds hum in my ears as the waters tumble downstream.

What if I'd known Hobbs wasn't doing it with Elizabeth? Would I have felt so pressured to have sex? What if

Boland had had a kid, too? Would it have made it better for me?

My two best friends are both staring into the fire. I learned something about both of them tonight that I never would have suspected. I guess I learned something about myself, too.

I look up at the sky. Star light, star bright—the first star I see tonight *truly* outshines all the rest.

19
Star

I awaken confused and disoriented to the smell of coffee. Grandma doesn't drink it, so this isn't something that I wake up to, ever. We have a coffeemaker, and keep coffee in the freezer in case we get company.

I squint through bleary eyes at Wil sound asleep in his crib. His little face is turned toward me. I can't see him very well because it's dark with my shade still down, shut tight. But the hall light is on and I'm pretty sure it's morning. I'm also pretty sure that Curtis Gray found a dark place to hide. I'm safe from him, at least for a little while.

My mouth is dry and tastes foul. I wipe sleep from my eyes. Wil slept last night. I did, too. Miss Marcie says that babies can sense tension when you hold them. Maybe Wil senses that I'm afraid at night. Maybe that's why Wil's so different when it's dark out—because I'm different, too.

After it happened the first time, here in this very room, I'd pretend I was asleep when I'd hear his voice with the babysitter. He'd tell her to take the rest of the night off, on him. He'd come into the room and I wouldn't respond— not to his voice, not to him shaking me. He'd pull me out of bed, stand me on my feet, and demand that I look at him or I'd never see my mother again.

Then he'd slam me against the wall and tell me exactly what I was going to do for him. I got good at pretending I was dead until he was finished. Then I'd throw up in my garbage can.

I bury my head under my pillow, not ready to face the day. My room feels different with the box gone.

That box was like an evil force that reached out beyond the closet to grab hold of me, no matter what was happening in my life—good or bad. It contained snatches of a man, gathered by a child who wanted to destroy him. I wanted to destroy him like he destroyed me—or what little was left of me after my mother disappeared.

I thought that when I turned that box over to the police, I'd rid myself of him. My secret's in someone else's hands now. But I'll never forget, not ever.

I had a dream once, that the box was a giant tick attached to my neck, silently gorging itself on my blood. In the morning, I couldn't go to school. I lay in bed and relived so much of what had happened to me.

All those nights, I heard him joking with the babysitter—charming her like he'd charmed my grandmother. Why couldn't they see he was evil?

I know my grandmother wanted to believe. I wanted to believe, too—that he'd find my mother. That he'd bring her home to me. That's what he lured me in with: he said she was in danger, and if I did everything he told me to do, he'd save her. He told me that my grandmother didn't really want to find my mother. And he said that if I told, she'd send him away and I'd never find my mother alive.

I spent a lot of time alone, growing up. The babysitter was there for late nights when Grandma worked, but there were so many hours alone after school and during the summer. It makes you grow up fast, when no one's there to stop you. You shed your little-girl skin and put on armor in its place.

My grandmother always said I was a very mature little girl. Mature maybe, but clueless, definitely. Clueless and naïve. I finally knew he was lying to *me* when I heard him lying to my grandmother, too—when he thought I was asleep. And that's when I started my shoebox.

He was careful. He put everything in plastic bags that he took to his car before my grandmother came home. But once, when my grandmother came home early from work, he buried the bag in my closet. When he came back for it the next day, I told him I'd thrown it in the trash down the street.

"Good girl," he told me, patting my head like I was his pet. And my fear of him turned to hate.

I feel my grandmother sit on the edge of my bed.

"Star," her voice is soft. I flip the pillow off my head and untangle myself from the blankets.

"I want to go to the center. I can't stay here alone," I tell her. "Wil's fever is gone, right? Miss Marcie will let me come in. I know it's too late to call for the van, but maybe you can drive me—or I can call Todd."

My grandmother takes a deep breath. "Star, good morning." Her eyes are so tired and sad, I feel guilty for not acknowledging how she's hurting, too. She looks down at her hands.

"Good morning. I'm sorry, Grandma," I say, touching her hand. She smiles at me and nods.

"You're not alone. We're not alone. There's a police officer here with us. The police found Rodney Dobson unconscious in the alley last night. He'd been beaten and dragged there. When he came to in the hospital, he told police that he saw a man run up and down our porch steps and pounding on the door.

"He said he'd seen him do it before—after you opened the door and yelled at him one day for pounding and waking Wil. He confronted the guy last night. Rodney told him to leave us alone. That's when he got beat up. He identified Curtis Gray from the picture I gave police."

I sit up, pull the blankets up to my chest. "I don't understand, Grandma."

"I don't understand either, Star. Not really. His picture was on the news this morning, with information that he was last seen here on Holly Street, and that he may be armed and dangerous. They're cautioning runners who use the trail that circles back around the old warehouse." I pull my blankets up to my chin, trying to steady myself, to keep my thoughts from plunging down into the gully. "The phone's been ringing all morning. Didn't you hear it?"

"It has? All morning?"

"It's almost noon, Star. Wil's had his medicine, two feedings, and a bath. He played on the floor in the living room for a long time, getting exercise just reaching for his activity gym. He just fell asleep about half an hour ago."

"Grandma, I didn't hear him. I'm sorry."

"It's okay. He slept until almost 7:00 A.M. The poor little guy was probably exhausted after last night. I was already awake. I heard him, Star, so I picked him up quickly so you could sleep."

Now I really feel guilty.

"Star, Mrs. Fletcher called this morning, and I explained a little about what's happening. She suggested we go stay with them. They have a security system. They also have separate living quarters attached to their home for her parents to use when they visit from Florida. The police think it's a good idea, especially since my surgery's scheduled for Monday. I just found out this morning."

"You're having surgery? Grandma, what's wrong?"

"I have a brain aneurysm, Star. It's operable and I should be fine. But I don't want you here alone with the baby, especially not now."

"A brain aneurysm?"

"It's a weakness in the artery that causes a bubble to form. Without surgery it could burst. I wanted to wait until the surgery was scheduled before I told you about it. I'd been working with Miss Marcie to find a place for you and Wil to stay—a foster placement." Grandma smoothes my blankets and goes on.

"I didn't want you here alone with the baby. Now there's no question—you can't stay here—it's not safe. Mrs. Fletcher said that if you're willing, she wants you and Wil there with them, instead of in foster care."

Now Grandma's behavior's making more sense to me—especially her foster-care threats.

I'm scared. Is she scared? Can I ask her?

"I know this is scary, Star, but we'll do the best we can, okay?"

I want to answer, but I am too busy twisting my hair, trying to take in—and sort—all the information she's given me. But there's no room; my head's still filled with last night. I hear a bump outside my window and jump right out of my bed.

"It's okay, Star. Detective Cooper's undercover. She's washing our windows."

My hands fly into my hair again and I sit down on the edge of my bed.

"Listen, I'm sorry, but I have to go to work. I wouldn't go if Detective Cooper hadn't come to stay with you. I need to get things in order at work before the surgery. I'm giving both my employers such short notice that I hope I'll still have these jobs when I'm ready to go back to work."

I want to tell my grandmother that everything will work out. I want to, but I don't know how, and I'm not exactly ready to believe it myself.

"Get up and eat something, okay? Try to do it before Wil gets up."

I nod, but know I can't. It's another one of my secrets. I can't eat when I'm alone. For some reason, it's just physically impossible. I go to the kitchen and stand in front of the window. It looks like any other summer day out there. I look down at yesterday's clothes still sticking to my body. *I should take a shower, but what if Wil wakes up?*

The coffeepot hisses. I get a mug and pour myself a cup. It tastes bitter on my tongue. I spit it in the sink just as this girl comes into the room. I blink at her. She's my size— and her hair is red.

"Hi, Star, I'm Detective Cooper." She goes to the refrigerator and returns with a gallon of milk. "I like it strong," she tells me. She pours a lot of milk and spoons at least an inch of sugar into the mug I've abandoned on the kitchen counter. Then she pours a little coffee into whatever space is left in the mug. "Try this," she says, handing it to me.

I take the coffee to the table and sit down. It feels good to wrap my hands around the hot mug. I take a sip. I can do this. I take a mouthful and drink it down. It's really not so bad.

"Star, I want you to avoid standing in front of any windows, okay?" Detective Cooper says as she sits in a chair across from me. I nod, then stare into my cup. I'm afraid of the dark, not the sunshine.

I suddenly remember a song my mother used to sing to me about not taking my sunshine away. I take another sip of coffee and feel the warm liquid move down my throat.

"Star, whatever are you drinking? You were sick last night, remember?" My grandmother takes my mug and replaces it with a can of ginger ale from the refrigerator.

"Wil's still sleeping. Eat something, please. I'll see you at the Fletchers' this afternoon. Pack enough clothes for a few days. Wilson will call you later today to let you know what time he'll be picking you up."

"Grandma, I've been thinking." I haven't really had time to think about it, and the thought just popped into my head, but oh well. "Maybe I could stay with Elizabeth instead of at the Fletchers'."

"Star, it'll be okay there. You'll see. The Fletchers really want you with them. I'll see you later. Be careful."

They want Wil there, not me.

Grandma kisses the top of my head, touches Detective Cooper's hand, and is gone.

I pop the tab on the ginger ale and take a swallow. It tingles in my mouth and washes the coffee taste away. I shiver.

Detective Cooper stares at me like I'm her long-lost twin. "How are you?" she asks. "Feeling better?" She's sitting back in the chair with her arms folded over her chest. If we had a freckle contest, she'd win.

"I'm okay."

It feels so odd having this stranger in my house. Especially this stranger who looks more like my relative than any of the relatives I've ever known. I get up and put my ginger ale in the sink and move quickly away from the window.

"Good girl!" she says. *I feel Curtis Gray's hand on my head.*

Star in the Middle

Todd knocks on the door just as the phone rings. I open the door and motion for him to come in as I race to get the phone. I sense that it's Wilson even before I pick it up, like I knew it was Todd at the door by his knock. *Mrs. Fletcher wants to know about Wil. I'm sure that's the reason for Wilson's call.*

"Hello?"

"Star." I wait, but he says no more than my name. I close my eyes. He clears his throat: "Star."

"What is it, Wil?" *It feels funny to call him Wil.* I know the name belonged to him first, before the baby. But he's been Wilson and Fletcher for a while now. It's not so much that *Wil* is my baby's name. It's more that Wilson isn't the Wil I used to know. He's not the Wil I trusted, and depended on.

"Star, are you okay?" *Okay* is such a funny word, isn't it? I'm not fine, but I guess I'm okay. You can get punched in the mouth and still be okay.

"I am. I'm okay, and you?"

"I'm good. Well, not good, exactly. But okay."

I love this about Wil, that we speak the same language.

"I was worried about you, Star. Elizabeth told Hobbs…. I talked to your grandmother…. My mother called…"

Wilson can't seem to complete a sentence. How much did my grandmother tell Mrs. Fletcher?

"Anyway, after my doctor's appointment, I'll pick you and the baby up. I'm sure your grandmother told you?"

"Doctor's appointment? The paternity test?"

"No, no. A sports physical. Star, listen, about the paternity test, let's just skip it—I don't need it. I believe you."

229

"No way, Wilson. You have to have the paternity test. Because, Wilson, even if today you say you know Wil's yours, some day when you get mad about something, the whole thing will come up again."

"Star."

"I really have to go."

"Don't you want to talk? I know how you hate to be alone."

"I'm not alone."

"Did your grandmother stay home?"

"No."

"Is Todd there?"

"Yes." Silence. I almost hang up thinking Wilson already has.

"Okay." There's that word again. It's the most over-used word in the English language. "Well, I'll call you later." Wilson's voice is so flat. I hang up and stare at the phone.

All those months, I sat here and worried about Wilson. I probably would've taken him back under any circumstances. It wouldn't have even mattered to me then, that his parents were the reason for his calls.

Todd's lying on the floor, playing with Wil. When he sees me he sits up, and sits Wil up against his chest. "There's Mommy," he says. "Wave to Mommy." Todd waves Wil's hand at me. I wipe away tears and wave back. Everything's so crummy right now—and here's my baby, right in the middle of it. How will I keep him safe?

"Wil, say 'look who's awake, Mommy'."

"Star," Detective Cooper says, pulling me aside. "I noticed you didn't have your visitor identify himself before you opened the door. You really need to be more careful about doing that every time someone's at the door."

I'm careful. Always. I ask before I open the door. "I just knew his knock."

"We have reason to believe that Curtis Gray is watching people who come and go so he can imitate them for the purpose of gaining entrance." I shudder. "I'm not trying to scare you. I just need you to not take any more chances, okay?"

Todd's standing beside me now, cradling Wil.

"Have you met Detective Cooper?" I ask.

"Yes, I have," Todd smiles at her, then looks at me. "Elise is with Nevaeh, Star. I wanted to check on you. I hope it's okay."

"It's fine, Todd," I tell him, taking a squirmy Wil from him.

Todd's hand brushes my arm. "Should I make Wil a bottle while you change him?"

"Your grandmother made the bottles, Star," Detective Cooper says, staring at Todd's piercings.

"I'll just heat a bottle for Wil," Todd says. "Can I get you something, Star?"

"I'm starved," I tell him. My stomach growls—the coffee and ginger ale are churning away.

"What are you hungry for?"

"Bacon and eggs, and toast, and a bucket of orange juice. Scratch the toast—maybe some of those frozen pancakes that my grandmother yells at me for buying."

"Done."

"Are you serious? You'll make breakfast? You'll eat with me, right?" I ask, incredulous.

"Sure. Detective Cooper, are you up for some breakfast?" Todd asks. She smiles for the first time since I met her. Why is it that I like her red hair so much?

"Sounds good. I'm starved, too. Washing windows is hard work."

Todd scrunches up his face at me, "What?" he mouths.

"Other duties as assigned," I tell him.

"You got that right," Detective Cooper smiles again. "I'll make more coffee."

I put Wil on the changing table. His face crumbles and he cries. "You are my sunshine boy," I say, and begin to sing the words that come back to me as if my mother sang them to me just yesterday. As the first verse ends, my eternal pool of tears flows over; remembering my mother and the song she loved does it every time. Wil's quiet now, waiting for more. I keep singing and he rewards me with a smile as warm as sunshine.

20
Wilson

Here I am, sports fans, coming to you live from the pediatrician's office, where I've just had a sports physical—and I'm about to have a paternity test. Get it—a paternity test at the pediatrician's office?

My pediatrician, who used to pull a coin out of my ear on every visit, has also talked to me about sexually transmitted diseases. I have no symptoms, but he wanted my blood anyway.

My mother set this up. I've been coming to Dr. Frazier for as long as I can remember. Long enough for him to have his offices redecorated a few times. We went from farm animals to jungle animals and back again. Right now, I'm staring into the eyes of a *Tyrannosaurus rex* wearing glasses. The bat in the hall is wearing glasses, too.

So, let's recap: farm, jungle, farm, weird. Bats hang upside down, people, and they're blind. And I'm pretty sure T. rex's arms won't reach his nose, so who put his glasses on for him?

"Open, Wil—That's it," Doctor Frazier says after swabbing my mouth with a giant Q-tip. "See, nothing to it."

He's kidding, right? Dr. Frazier's hair has gotten completely white over the years. It's thick and fits him like a helmet. His eyebrows stick out like ledges over his blue eyes that look more gray with his white hair.

"I don't agree that there's nothing to it. This test changes my life forever."

Doctor Frazier looks me square in the eye, "What does your *gut* tell you right now, Wil? Is the baby yours?"

I try to stare him down, but his stare is steady. I blink first. Then I nod.

"Then the test doesn't change anything. Does it?"

I swallow, close my eyes, and try not to see what's been staring me in the face for months now.

"Doesn't the baby have to take the test, too?" I ask.

"We have what we need from the baby. It was done a while ago. Are you okay, son?"

Sure, a person can get rolled under a bus and still be okay.

"Am I happy? No. But, I'll be okay." Dr. Frazier smiles and sits down on the exam table next to me.

"You know, Wil, I've watched you grow into a very determined young man over the years. I see your pictures in the sports pages. Your parents tell me you're a good student. Having a child is an awesome responsibility. I know the timing part of this is difficult. But being a father isn't a bad thing, and I'm pretty sure you're up to it. Give yourself and that baby a chance."

"Do you have a pill for that?" I ask.

"A pill for what, Wil?"

"I don't know—some kind of magic pill that'll make me feel like a father?"

"See, here's the thing. The only way you get to feel like a father is by spending time being one."

"What if I don't want to be a father?"

"Too late, Wil. I'm sorry. Should we talk about birth control?"

"I know about birth control. She didn't want to use it. Isn't that her responsibility?" I expect Dr. Frazier's eyebrows to start doing the jig like the stupid counselor's at the abortion clinic. But he's quiet, and serious.

"Let's think about this whole responsibility thing, okay?"

I nod.

Dr. Frazier takes a deep breath, locks his fingers together in his lap. "If your girlfriend robs a bank and you go along with it, aren't you both going to jail?"

"Dr. Frazier."

"Seriously, Wil. If you're with someone who has AIDS and you know that, would you still have unprotected sex with that person? I know that's an extreme example, but if you partner with someone, Wil, you're in it together. And you're both going to live with the consequences."

What if Star's pregnant again? I wanted to ask if she'd called the doctor when I talked to her earlier, but I couldn't—not with everything that happened over there last night.

"But, Dr. Frazier, you don't get someone pregnant every time you have sex," I argue.

"That's true. But, Wilson, unless you are actively trying to have a baby, you better actively try not to."

"What I say here stays here, right?"

"Right."

"I'm never having sex again."

"Your secret's safe with me. Although I rather doubt that you won't ever have sex again. But be smart, okay? Protect yourself, and make sure you understand that things happen, even if you use protection. If you're not ready for the consequences, it's time to step back and wait until you are before you have sex with anyone.

"I'll call you with test results. Is there anything else I can do for you?" I shake my head and get up to leave. Dr. Frazier follows me out. We shake hands and I hit the parking lot.

I climb into the Jeep, grip the wheel with both hands and slump over.

This can't be happening. I'm going to Star's to drive her and the baby back to my place. Star will be living in my house for a while. How will that work? She hates me. Will she invite Todd over? Cozy.

Back home, my mother has put a giant turkey in the oven. A turkey. What? Are we expecting pilgrims? Mom and Dad went out baby shopping this morning. Dad was setting up a crib when I left the house. There's a baby bathtub, a swing, a changing table, diapers, blankets, clothes, stuffed animals...*There goes the college fund. I don't need it now, anyway.*

Bridgett was filling up a bookshelf in Star's room with books for the baby. Next the kid'll have a library card. Bridgett wants to know if we can call the baby Wils. Suits me, maybe then I can have my name back.

What have I done? I'm an idiot... whack, whack—and WHACK! Take that, you idiot.

"Wil?"

"Jeez! Elizabeth, I'm a little jumpy here. What are you doing?"

"Sitting in the passenger seat, watching you beat your head against the steering wheel."

"Are you following me around town, now?"

"Don't be dumb. I've just had a sports physical, too. I tried to flag you down in Dr. Frazier's office, but you were in some kind of zombie zone. I was hoping I'd catch you out here."

"Okay, you caught me. What's up?"

"First, how's Star and Wil? Do you know anything about last night?"

I close my eyes. Last night seems like it happened a month ago.

"Star and the kid are okay. I know nothing about what happened over there."

What little I do know, I am not allowed to tell anyone, so says my mother. I'm also not allowed to tell anyone that Star will be staying with us.

"Will you give me a ride home? My car's in the shop. My mother dropped me off and said she'd pick me up, but she's going to be a while yet. I'd run, but that crazy man's still out there. Have you seen him on TV? He was a former cop, so the police are pulling cops from all over to help with the search. Now they're saying he may be connected to the disappearance of a young mother here ten years ago. So scary!

Elizabeth went on: "He was seen with two girls that went missing, one in New York and one in Pennsylvania. He's also accused of rape. And you know what else? Do you know Rodney Dobson? He's Star's next-door neighbor. Anyway, this guy beat him up pretty bad."

I've already started to drive, so it's hard to concentrate on the road ahead and take in what Elizabeth just said when all I want to do is get to Star's.

Did this guy hurt Star's mother? Wait, did he hurt Star? Or was he after Rodney all along? That kid's looking for trouble.

But Mrs. Peters told my mother that this Curtis Gray guy was outside Star's bedroom window last night. Elizabeth's words continue to bounce off me as she talks. There's just no more room in my head for any of it.

I slam on my brakes and slide to the right, just missing this car that stopped in front of me.

"Some people still stop for yellow lights," Elizabeth says, pulling her white knuckles away from the dashboard.

Okay, well, I heard that. Girls are so irritating. The scary thing is, I didn't even see the yellow light. This is the longest red light in town. No, maybe it's the one on Center Street—no, it's the—Crap! How stupid am I? No wonder there's zero room for important stuff in my brain.

"I'm sorry, Elizabeth."

"You know what talking to you reminds me of lately, Wil?"

I really don't care what talking to me lately reminds her of, but I jump in anyway. "What's that, Elizabeth?"

"See, it happened again. It's like on TV, when someone gets interviewed by a satellite feed. There's that time delay thing."

"What can I say? I'm just not as quick-witted as I used to be."

"That's not it, Wil." Elizabeth looks out the passenger side window. We're moving again. Her sigh seems to last forever.

"Hey, isn't this where you tell me what I'm doing wrong, now? Or are you waiting for a satellite feed, too?"

"I was waiting for permission. It's just that you are so defensive with all of us. It's like you're always on guard—instead of letting us be your friends."

We ride in silence. It's a twenty-minute drive, but it feels like an hour. When I pull into the Andersons' driveway, Elizabeth unbuckles her seat belt, leans over, and kisses my cheek.

"I used to have a terrible crush on you, Wil."

I knew about the crush, but like I said before, Elizabeth is too good for me.

"Hobbs is a lucky guy," I tell her.

"I'm the lucky one. He's the best."

Elizabeth gets out of the car, runs to the front porch and waves to me. I wait until she gets in the house and then back out of the driveway. I've heard the story so many times: Hobbs was pretending to help her get my attention, and all the while, he was reeling her in.

On my way in and out of the neighborhood I avoid my house, my street—anything to do with what's going on at home. Dad had a lawn service coming in this afternoon. The yard's my job, but it takes most of the day and I had this doctor's appointment. Dad wanted all chores out of the way so everyone could spend time with the baby while Star and her grandmother are with us.

The drive to Star's is a familiar one but feels different today. I never pay attention when I hear about an escaped prisoner or someone on the run. But this sounds personal. I want to grab this guy by the throat if he hurt Star or her family.

It makes me pay attention to what's around me as I drive. It makes me want to stop for yellow lights, instead of trying to beat them. I examine every open space, and peer into doorways and alleys. Is that ape in a tree somewhere?

Both a state police car and a local cop car pass me as I get close to Star's street. I pull in behind Todd's car and get out of the Jeep. A guy gets out of his car across the street and stands on the curb looking at me. I climb the porch steps and knock at the door.

"Who is it?"

"It's Wil, Star."

"Wil who?"

Is Todd putting her up to this? "Come on, open up."

"Seriously, I have to ask. Wil who? And give your middle name."

"Wilson Theodore Fletcher." I sound like I'm barking. The door opens. I'm stunned when I walk inside and find Star with a look-alike standing behind her.

"Freaky, huh?" Todd's voice drifts over from the rocker where he's holding my baby.

"Not as freaky as you," I shoot back.

Star's twin laughs. "I thought he was pretty freaky when I first saw him, but Todd's an okay guy."

"See that, I'm an okay guy, Fletcher." That remains to be seen, Goth-boy.

"Are you ready, Star?"

"I'm packed, but I'm not quite ready. Wilson, this is Detective Cooper."

"Really? I thought maybe she was your cousin, or aunt, or something." Detective Cooper blushes and reminds me even more of Star.

"Sit down, Wil. I'd like to go over a couple of things with you." I sit on the sofa and Detective Cooper slides in beside me.

"Todd's going to leave here with the baby—just like he'd leave with his own baby. The undercover officer across the street will follow him. If the officer doesn't see anything suspicious, no one following him or anything, he'll drop the baby off at your house, where your parents will be waiting for him.

"The officer will then come back here and follow you and Star to your house. Star gave him your cell phone number, so he'll be in touch by cell. Here's his number and mine. Call us if you see anything unusual. Look, we're pretty sure Curtis Gray is hiding out somewhere, but we can't take any chances."

What can I do but stare at the woman? In addition to

having a kid to contend with, I'm now in the middle of some kind of police sting or something.

Star comes out of her room. Her hair's trapped inside the Maryland lacrosse hat that I've been accusing my sister of stealing for months now. She's carrying a duffel bag that she tosses in a pile with the diaper bag. Todd gets up and hands her the baby. She kisses him and puts him in his car seat. Todd grabs the car seat and the bags, and heads for the door. Star attempts to follow, but Detective Cooper stops her.

Star sits in the rocker. She closes her eyes, folds her arms across her chest, and is very still. Detective Cooper leaves with Todd and the baby. Star doesn't open her eyes until the woman returns.

"It'll be okay," she says, patting Star's hand on her way into the kitchen.

I can hear her on the phone. Then it's quiet. We sit in silence. How did I never hear the clock ticking over the mantel? Why don't they ever use the fireplace? There's something else, too. No sirens. Have all other crimes in this neighborhood been suspended until further notice?

"Cooper here..." She's locked in conversation again.

I move across the room and kneel on the floor in front of Star. She shakes her head no before I can say a word.

"Wait," I say. "How can I help you if I don't know what he did?"

Star shakes her head again, harder.

"No one can help me," she whispers. Her eyes cloud over. I've heard that expression before, but now Star's eyes look at me from a deep fog. She reaches out like she's going to touch my cheek but stops herself.

Detective Cooper comes into the room and kneels beside me on the floor. She takes one look at Star's face and puffs a few short breaths from her mouth before she speaks.

"Hey, did you pack that swimming suit like Mrs. Fletcher suggested?" Star smiles and scratches her ear, then nods.

"Good, that's great. You get to swim, and I get to mow your lawn. How's that fair? Okay, we're ready to rock and roll. Let's go."

We move quickly out of the house and toward the Jeep. I open the door and Star slides in the passenger side. I go to the driver's side and open the door. Detective Cooper waves to me from the porch. She could be Star from this distance.

Star's staring straight ahead, crying quietly.

"May I use your phone?" she asks.

"Sure." I dig it out of my pocket and hand it to her. She presses in numbers and waits.

"Todd, was Wil okay when you dropped him off?" Star listens, wipes away tears.

Todd has made her smile.

21
Star

It was hard watching Todd walk out of my house with my baby. It's not that I don't trust him. It's just that I've never left Wil with anyone but my grandmother before. Wil rode in a car alone with Todd, and then stayed with the Fletchers until I could get here. I know they're his grandparents, but they don't know him.

It felt so weird driving into the Fletchers' driveway and then into their garage. Elizabeth told me once that some people think Mr. Fletcher built his house on this hill so he could look down on all the people in the houses he built below. She said that it's not true, that Mr. Fletcher's not like that. She said none of the Fletchers are like that. She said Mr. Fletcher is really proud of his work and is very involved in the community.

Wilson went right to his room when we came in. Mr. Fletcher was on the floor in the family room, playing with Wil. Mrs. Fletcher came into the room and hugged me. The whole house smells like Thanksgiving. Bridgett said her mother's been cooking and baking all day, then showed me around.

Star in the Middle

She said that her parents thought Grandma, Wil, and I would be more comfortable staying in her grandparents' addition to the house. The bedroom I'm using has a sitting area attached. Mr. Fletcher put a crib in there for Wil, and a fully stocked changing table.

Grandma's staying in the master bedroom. I know this is hard for her. She looked really uncomfortable when she first came in from work, but Mrs. Fletcher picked Grandma a big bouquet of flowers from her garden for her room. They've been talking about flowers and seeds and bulbs ever since.

Dinner was really good. I hope no one noticed I finished the mashed potatoes. They were all eating dessert, but I didn't want pie or cheesecake. I just wanted those mashed potatoes.

Mrs. Fletcher held Wil all during dinner. He was asleep. She asked if it was okay. Grandma said sure, but Mrs. Fletcher looked right at me. She's been doing that a lot—checking with me about Wil. Wilson's been so quiet. I feel so anxious, and so out of place here.

After dinner Mrs. Fletcher's cleaning lady arrived to take care of the dishes, so we all moved into the living room. Mrs. Fletcher thanked her again and again for coming.

Wil's awake and happy. Everyone keeps messing with him.

It's like they're trying to show Fletcher how much fun it is to have a baby around. He's not buying any of it. It's like trying to convince someone who doesn't like to get his hair wet that swimming is fun. I'm feeling pretty sorry for

Fletcher. He looks like he'd rather be trampled by a herd of elephants than spend one more minute here with all of us. Maybe he's ticked because he had to cancel a date with Cate or something.

I take Wil and sit on the rocker to feed him, but he's not interested in his bottle—he wants to look around. Bridgett's fiancé, Sean, is here, too. Mrs. Fletcher actually called my grandmother at work to ask if it would be okay to invite him. Grandma told her she was looking forward to meeting him. I guess we're supposed to be some big happy family or something.

Sean's sitting on a love seat with my grandmother. They're laughing pretty loud with Mr. and Mrs. Fletcher and Bridgett, who are all sitting together on the sofa. Wilson's sitting on a love seat by himself.

I think they may have just bought this overstuffed rocker I'm sitting in. It looks brand new. It smells new, too.

Stu, the Fletcher's black lab, is sitting at my feet, staring up at Wil and me, smiling his dog smile. Even the dog's baby crazy. At least Roger the cat's ignoring us. He's stretched out across a windowsill.

I close my eyes and try to push out the thoughts that lurk in my brain. It's like there's a seed in my head that takes over, just like a noxious weed that chokes anything good that comes into my life. Why can't I just be peaceful for a little while?

"Is Wil going to sleep now?" Bridgett asks, leaving her spot on the couch.

"Probably not," I tell her.

"May I take him?" she asks.

I smile at her, kiss Wil, and stand up to give him to her. She takes him to the love seat and sits beside her brother. Now I see where this is going. So does Wilson. He gets up to go.

"Come on, Wil, sit down—please." Bridgett admonishes him. "You're going to hold Wils."

Wils? She called my baby Wils? It's kind of cute.

"Bridgett, don't," he pleads.

"Come on, just hold your arms like a cradle—like you did when Stu got knocked out by a lacrosse ball and you had to carry him to the car."

"I can't."

"Yes, you can, Wil. This baby doesn't have a tail. And there's nothing to break." Bridgett smiles at him, then puts Wil in his arms. He stares down at the baby.

"How does that feel?"

"He's heavier than I thought. Sturdier, maybe."

"He's a pretty tough little guy—like his daddy." Wil begins to squirm and fuss. Wilson has a look of terror in his eyes.

"I can't do this, Bridg, take him," he begs.

"Just pat his bottom, Wil. See, like this." Bridgett pats Wil until Wilson takes over. "See, now talk to him. He needs to get to know your voice."

"I tried that once. He was okay for a little while, then he totally lost it."

"So, babies lose it sometimes. You can't take it personally."

"Hey, that's what Star said," he says.

"See that. And she knows him better than anybody."

"Okay, well, he's staring at me. What's that about?"

"He wants to know if you can talk," she replies.

"Very funny."

"Seriously."

Wilson looks around the room. We're all staring at him now. He looks down at the baby.

"I think I want to try walking with him, okay?"

"Why are you asking me? You're his father. Try putting him over your shoulder, okay?" she suggests.

"Would that be okay, Wils? Can I put you over my shoulder? Star talks to him like that," he tells his sister, and Bridgett winks at me.

"Look, Bridg, he smiled at me! Baby, you do have a cute smile. I think we need to work on some teeth, though. Okay, little dude?

"Look, he smiled again. Okay, here goes." Wilson lifts Wil over his shoulder and pats his back. He stands and moves away from all the curious stares, goes through the entranceway and into the family room.

Every now and then, he passes the doorway with the baby over his shoulder. Stu paces beside him. Fletcher's singing some song about a monkey and an engineer.

My grandmother catches my eye and smiles at me. I want to drop my head into my hands and twist my hair, but Grandma hates that—especially when there are other people around.

I try to take a quick look at Wil's parents without them seeing, but they're both looking at me. They're even holding hands.

If I didn't know there was a lunatic on the loose...if I

didn't know my grandmother was scheduled for surgery on Monday...if I didn't know that I would eventually have to be alone with my thoughts...if I didn't know about all these bad things, I'd think I was in a movie with a happy ending.

But what I do know is that bad things happen. That sometimes you have no control over what happens to you. And that real life goes on—long past the movie credits.

Bridgett asks if I want to come sit with her, so I move to the love seat.

"How did you know?" I ask. "How did you know Wil was afraid to hold the baby?"

"He's always been afraid of small things—like puppies and kittens. Stu cried for his mother for weeks when we first got him. Wil was so upset that he wanted to take him back. He wanted a dog so bad, Star, but he couldn't stand that Stu was unhappy. Plus, he was afraid that he'd never be able to make him happy. The same thing happened with Roger as a kitten. Wil is miserable when anyone cries. He takes it all so personally."

I swallow hard. My throat feels tight.

"What did you mean when you told him that Wil doesn't have a tail?"

"That's a story that maybe he should tell you, Star. It's a pretty silly thing to the rest of us, but serious to him. I would never bring it up to be mean—just to reassure him."

"Will he tell me?"

"I don't know. Maybe if you share something about yourself. At least that's how it works with Sean and me."

"How does what work with us?" Sean asks as he sits

down beside Bridgett and reaches for her hand. Bridgett and I slide over, giving him more room.

"That I have to tell you something serious about me before you'll tell me something serious about you and vice versa."

"Star, don't let her fool you. Bridgett tells me everything. Even stuff I'd rather not hear. Then there's Wil: He tells me things about Bridgett that would drive any sane man away from here. Fortunately, I'm not a sane man when it comes to Bridgett. Am I, babe?" He squeezes her hand.

"Sanity's just not all that important to me," Bridgett tells him.

"We know that about you, Bridg," Wilson says, standing above us. "Star, may I try to put Wil down in the crib? He's asleep."

"Sure, you don't have to ask me."

"Well, I didn't want to go into your room without asking. And what if he wakes up and cries? Do I put him on his back or his tummy?"

"On his back." My voice is like part of a chorus. Fletcher looks questioningly at Sean.

"We've had a lot of babies at our house," Sean tells him. "It's the SIDS thing: putting babies to sleep on their backs decreases the chance of them dying in their sleep."

"Oh my God. Babies die in their sleep?" Wil asks. His eyes are wide and his face goes white.

"Nice one, Sean," Bridgett says.

"Well, he has to know that stuff, right? We can't keep things like that from him."

"Come on, Fletcher. I'll go with you," I say, trying to get out of the love seat.

Fletcher gives me his free hand and helps me up.

"Could Wils really die in his sleep, Star?"

"It happens sometimes. It's pretty scary. Not as much as it used to, before people started putting babies on their backs to sleep—with no blankets, no bumper pads, no pillows, and no stuffed animals."

"He has to sleep on his back without a blanket? That sounds awful. Won't he be cold? I couldn't sleep like that. Could you sleep like that?"

I'm too tired to answer. I take a deep breath—remembering all the nights Wil didn't sleep at all, and how I paced the floor with him to keep him quiet so Grandma could sleep.

Fletcher puts the baby down in the crib; he doesn't make a sound.

"I'm sorry, Star. I guess I should know this stuff," Wilson whispers. "How do you know all this stuff?" We walk into the living room and sit on the sofa.

"I wish I knew more, but I don't. I take this parenting class at the center."

"There are classes to teach you how to be a parent?"

"Miss Marcie says all new parents should take parenting classes. And she says that all babies are different."

"Bridgett and I are so different: You'd think one of us was raised by a chicken, and the other by an egg. I'll leave the rest up to your imagination."

I try not to laugh at him, but I can't stop myself. Wil shakes his head and smiles at me.

"I was afraid you'd never laugh again," he tells me.

"You make me laugh."

Wil looks sad. "I also make you cry. I'm sorry. I'll make it up to you."

I take a deep breath and rub my eyes. I feel weary.

"Don't, Wil, because then I'll have to make it up to you."

Wil looks confused. "What do you have to make up to me?"

"I can't talk about it, okay?"

"Will you at least try? Because I'm really in the dark here."

"I'll try—if you tell me what Bridgett meant about Wil not having a tail."

"It's a really embarrassing story, Star. I mean *really* embarrassing."

"You can tell me."

"It happened when I was in kindergarten, okay? It was that long ago, so how important could it be?"

"Some things stay with you forever, Wil."

"Is that what happened, Star? Did something happen that will stay with you forever? Did I do it to you?"

"No, Wil, no. Is that what you think?"

I turn away from him. I don't even want to hear his answer. He's quiet. Faint laughter filters through the walls from the other part of the house. Stu lies across the doorway, guarding it. Wilson rubs his eyes, and clears his throat. "One of the kids brought this lamb into kindergarten for a visit. We were all sitting in a circle taking turns holding it. I was so excited when my turn came. It was the sweetest little animal, Star. It nuzzled into me. All of a sudden, the lamb's tail fell off and rolled onto the floor. The kids all laughed. The lamb started to *baa*, and struggled to get away from me. I cried in front of everyone, Star."

He took a breath. "The teacher tried to explain to me that the farmer banded the tail so it would fall off, but I didn't believe a word of it. It wasn't until a long time later that I understood farmers really do that for health purposes—and that the lamb didn't cry because I hurt it. It cried because the kids' laughing scared it. So now you can laugh at me, too. How stupid am I?"

"Wil, I'm not five years old. Only five-year-olds would laugh about that."

"Not true. Kids teased me forever, until I started fighting back."

"I'm sorry that happened to you, Wil."

"Yeah, well, now that I'm a big boy, I should understand that there are a lot of worse things in the world. I need to get over it, don't you think?"

"It doesn't matter what I think. It only matters what you think. It happened to you, Wil. It's part of you."

"What happened to you, Star? What's part of you that you can't let go?"

I feel my whole body fold. I curl my feet under me; wrap my arms in a tight hug. I lean into the sofa with my face near Wil's shoulder. He rests his face against the sofa and looks at me.

"Don't, Wil. Don't look at me, okay?" He closes his eyes. I try to swallow the fear that is lodged in my throat.

"I was eleven. He made me do things to him. He wore a condom—and he—grabbed my head. And he..." My throat is so tight, I'm afraid I'll choke if I say another word.

Wil's eyes open wide. I feel his warm breath on my face as he exhales.

"Star, I'm so sorry."

"The baby is my fault. I couldn't—because—"

"Don't. Star. Don't. I should have known. I shouldn't have pressured you."

"Wil, you would have stopped. I know you would have stopped. But I couldn't find the words—only tears. And now you have this baby that you don't want."

"Don't you do this, Star. Do you understand me? Don't do it. What he did to you was not your fault. And what we did together was not your fault. Okay? I knew you were upset about something. I should have stopped. How am I any better than him?"

Wil sits up and leans forward. I put my hand on his back. I can feel his whole body shake.

"You're nothing like him. Nothing. I thought you could fix me, Wil. I loved you. I thought you could fill up the places he'd been." Wil is looking at me now. "But Star, we never—you never—."

"I was running. It was getting dark, but I wasn't afraid. Not on the trail. That was my safe place. Don't you see, Wil? That's where I was free. I heard all the stories about the old warehouse, but I'm not afraid of ghosts. I'm not. I was more afraid in my own bedroom—where he—he—do you understand? The trail felt safe to me. My grandmother told me not to run close to dark. She told me. But I was training for track. Always training. I wanted to be good at something. I was good at running. But then he found me. Where did he come from? He pulled me off the trail into the gully. I tried to fight him. He was so strong. It was the night those prisoners escaped. The search dogs and helicopter scared him—or he would have killed me. I know he would have killed me. He kept telling me he wouldn't hurt me if I cooperated. But, Wil, he did hurt me. He knew he was hurting me, but he wouldn't stop. He held the knife to my throat. He ripped my clothes, and he— he—" I take a deep breath so I can go on.

"I... I... I couldn't tell my grandmother, not after she warned me not to run at night. She never reported the abuse anyway. So what good would it have done for her to know? It would have just hurt her to know. All I ever do is hurt people, Wil. I'm sorry. Don't you know how sorry I am?"

I feel Wil's arms around me. I want his arms around me, but I push him away because I'm so ashamed. I don't want to see his eyes. I get up and run into the bedroom and lock the door. I hear his footsteps get closer and closer.

"Star, please unlock the door. Come on, I won't touch you. I'm sorry I touched you. I just wanted to hold you, nothing else. Star, please."

But I can't speak. I just can't. I lie in the dark until he goes away. It's so quiet. I can't even hear the baby's breathing from this bed. There's so much space between us. There are no sirens. Closing the bedroom door put one more buffer up to drown out sounds from the part of the house where people are still laughing and talking.

I didn't even say goodnight. I didn't thank the Fletchers. When Wil tells them what happened, will they ask us to leave? I don't really care. I'll go back to the house where Grandma raised me. We'll have to go back there anyway, after the surgery. When Grandma's better. She will get better. She has to. She's all I have—well, Grandma and Wil and Uncle Gregory. Grandma will get better; Uncle Gregory will come home from Iraq. The baby and I will be okay.

Wilson knows now. He knows why he wasn't the first. I know he suspected. I had to tell him the truth. It wasn't my choice.

The baby's his, but it's not his fault.

This baby—that he doesn't want—was *never* his fault.

22
Wilson

I want to kill him a thousand times in a thousand different ways. But I can't get past wanting to choke the life out of him. I'm going to find him, and I'm going to choke him to death—and then I'm going to wrap this Jeep around a tree. That way Star can be rid of both of us.

She needs us both gone. She needs us both exterminated.

Why didn't she tell me? Oh my god! She did tell me, in a hundred different ways. I just wasn't listening. But she did want to be held. She wanted to be kissed. She wanted to be close. She did tell me that in a hundred different ways, too.

When she cried afterwards, I just thought I wasn't man enough. I wanted to make it right. I wanted to make her happy.

It was a bad decision to bring this dog. Stu never did anything to anyone. He's not going down with me. He'll find his way home.

That bastard's out there, hiding somewhere. I'm betting I know where. Every minute that passes squeezes a little more light out of this day, just like I'm going to squeeze the life out of him. What kind of a man does that to a child?

I am grinding my teeth so hard that I've probably cracked every tooth in my head. If I had any fingernails left, my face would be bloody from digging my claws into it. I'm going mad driving. It's taking too long.

I need to be there. I need to be running on the trail. I need to find the freedom Star felt out there. I need to feel him threaten to take my freedom away, the way he took it from her. Then I'll know how she felt. Then I'll be able to do what I need to do to him. I know that rape is so much more. I know that, but if I let myself think about how much more she lost—I'll wrap myself around the nearest tree before I do what I have to do. He's out there somewhere, and I'm going to find him.

Traffic thins. Roads narrow. Street lights get further and further apart. The lights on my dash seem to grow brighter the darker it gets. Maybe it's my imagination.

The Jeep bounces over the rough surface of the neglected parking lot. I grab Stu's collar to keep him from hitting the roof. He sighs as the Jeep comes to a stop facing the abandoned warehouse. I check my ringing phone to see my home phone number.

"Hello."

"Wil, where are you?"

"Dad, I just needed time to think. I'm driving around. I'll be home soon, okay? I would have told you, but I didn't want to interrupt your conversations."

"Wil, that's hardly an acceptable excuse."

"I'll be home before curfew, okay? Hey, I'm losing

you." I hang up and sit back against the seat. I hate lying. Especially when I'm sitting in a creepy place.

Most of the moon is still tucked behind the warehouse. I leave the motor running as I take in this place for the first time alone. It's so eerie here. The windows look like black holes. Wild vines climb trees that tower above the ground. I'm out here alone. How crazy is that?

My friends and I only come here at night in groups, puffed up on each other's bravado. How did Star come here alone?

If I close my eyes I can see her leave her house, running fast under the streetlights toward the park. My parents wouldn't want me to run that route alone at night, through her neighborhood to the park.

The trails around the park are pretty busy, though— even in the evening. They circle around the lake in different directions—a maze of paths that end at the starting point, all except the trail that snakes toward the river past the warehouse. It skirts the gully, crosses a wooden bridge, and then zigzags back to the park.

Stu's eager to get out. His nose is pressed against the passenger side window, and he's panting. I cut the motor and the headlights go out and the interior lights fade. It takes me a minute to adjust my eyes to the darkness. The faint sound of crickets turns into a roar when I open the car door even a crack.

Stu squeezes between the steering wheel and me, and pushes the door open as he jumps to the ground. The dog is gone. I get out and call to him. I listen to my voice in the hollow darkness and hear Stu running through weeds. He stops—then moves on.

I open the back of the Jeep to look for Stu's leash—and for something to use for a weapon. Star didn't have a weapon that night. I stab at the tears threatening behind my eyelids. I find the flashlight and turn it on. No leash. No weapons.

I start off in the direction of the gully. I find what I think is a path and follow it. Eyes peer out through the underbrush and disappear. I feel my hands shake, think about going back, and then remember Star curled in a ball, whispering her secrets into my shoulder.

My feet take off almost without me and I run; then stumble on a branch and fall forward onto the path. Eating dirt reminds me of whining to Star about a stupid lamb's tail falling off and kids laughing at me. Some guy held a knife to her throat, shoved his—

I pound my fist into the ground, jump to my feet and take off. The flashlight casts a shaky glow out ahead of me on the path. *How can I ever face her again?*

The moon is climbing higher. I can make out shapes of trees, rock formations, and a white church clothed in light on a distant hill. Then I see it—the wooden bridge that crosses the gully. Stu is sitting right in the middle of the bridge. He stands and wags his tail when he sees me. I pat his back and try to move past him, but he blocks my way.

He retraces my path back over the bridge, and runs down over the slope into the gully. I chase after him as he heads toward a light that appears to be coming out of the rocky embankment. Stu is excited now, jumping up and down, ears flying. He barks and the light goes out.

I stop cold. Did I see what I think I saw? I turn off the flashlight, grab Stu's collar and pull him back up over the hill toward the bridge. He's tugging against his collar, trying to get away from me. But I tell him to come as sternly as a whisper allows.

I need a plan.

The light went out, so whoever is there doesn't want me to know he's there. Plus, he knows I'm here. Maybe it's not Curtis Gray, but why would anybody else be out here? Stu decides that he's not going to fight me anymore. We take cover in a clump of trees where I can observe the area where I saw the light. I sit down and listen hard. I can't hear anything except crickets, Stu's panting, and an occasional car passing on the street beyond the trees and the clearing.

Then my stupid phone rings and I jump four feet off the ground. I flip it open fast, expecting to see my home number, but instead, I find Star's grandmother's number. I put the phone to my ear.

"Wil." I know this voice—but who is it? I can't think. "Wil, it's Detective Cooper, get out of there right now!"

"How do you know where I am?" I look around me. Who else knows I'm here?

"Star told me what she told you. She's so freaked out that you left the house. Sergeant Shockey saw your car parked at the old warehouse. Get out of there right now."

"I can't. I think he's here."

"He's dangerous."

"I don't care."

"Sure, give Star something else in her life to feel guilty about."

My throat tightens—Star's sorrow—her apology.

"None of it's her fault."

"I know that, but she doesn't. Where are you?"

"I thought you knew."

"Wil, you're wasting time." I hear fear in her voice; my hands start to shake. Is it my fear that's keeping me here, under the cover of darkness and overgrown brush?

"I think there might be some kind of cave in the hillside, just beyond the wooden bridge. I'm okay. I'll see him if he comes out."

"There could be more than one way out. He could be sneaking up on you right now."

"Stu will hear him."

"Listen to me, Wil. Start moving toward your car. Don't hang up. Talk to me like you're talking to your girlfriend."

"I don't have a girlfriend."

"Wil, would you focus, please?"

"If I walk out of here, I'll never find this place in daylight."

"Didn't you say it was near the bridge? We'll find it."

"Listen, I'm looking directly across the gully to the spot where I saw the light. Why would I leave?"

"Because I told you to leave. This is not a request, Wil. It's an order."

"There's no law against my sitting in the woods—. Wait...Stu hears something. Stu, what do you hear, buddy?" Stu has stopped panting. He stands up tall and still. I grab his collar as he takes off. He drags me nearly ten feet before I have to let go.

I drop my phone—search for it through the weeds. Got it!

"Are you still there?" My voice sounds excited, wild. "Stu's gone. I need to find him."

"Stay there. Don't move."

"What if he hurts my dog?"

"Wil, do you hear yourself? Stay...!" *Is she talking to me or the dog? Seriously. What is wrong with this woman? Stu dragged me out into an open area. How safe can this be?*

"Good work." I hear her voice, but she's not talking into the phone.

"Excuse me? Hey, Detective Cooper, are you there?"

"I'm back. Sergeant Shockey has Stu. They're headed your way. Stay put."

"Stu doesn't make friends with strangers. He'd be barking and growling if he found someone out there."

"Sergeant Shockey has a way with animals."

I want to argue, but what can I say? I hear someone moving toward me fast. Stu breaks through the weeds and nuzzles my leg. I get down, rub his ears, and tell him not to go to strangers. I smell beef jerky on his breath. *Yeah, this guy has a way with animals all right.*

"Wil, I'm Sergeant Shockey," the policeman shakes my hand. "Let's get you and Stu out of here."

Oh, so Detective Cooper also told him my dog's name. It's all making sense now. I can just hear this guy: "Stu, old buddy, we're on a first-name basis here, and do I have some beef jerky for you!" Very Clever. I stand staring at this cop, hoping he'll go away.

"Wil, did you hear me?"

"Yes, sir, but I don't think we should leave. There's a cave entrance or something over there. That guy's here." I'm trying to sound tough, but my voice is all shaky and weird.

"My partner's in the area, Wil, and we have backup on the way. We'll make a sweep of the gully as soon as we get you guys out of here. Come on, let's get you and Stu back to your car and on your way home."

This guy is really starting to irritate me a lot. But he's a policeman—a big one so I'll make him happy. I'll go back to the car, drive away—and come right back.

I'm feeling a little braver now. The man has a gun and he's one of us. We play follow-the-leader with Sergeant Shockey in the lead.

But Stu decides he wants to take off toward the opposite bank of the gully—where we saw the light. The moon's climbed high and floods the area with a soft glow. I call to Stu as he disappears into the embankment right before our eyes. His bark echoes like it's coming from inside a cave.

"Well, I'll be damned," Sergeant Shockey mutters. "Stay back, Wil," he whispers, like whispering is going to do any good, with Stu going nuts barking, and me shouting his name. Before we even reach the area where we saw Stu disappear, we hear him in the gully about a hundred yards back toward the warehouse.

"Well, I'll be damned," Sergeant Shockey shouts back at me, as we both run toward the cars.

I know something's not right as soon as I see the Jeep. It is sitting low. Stu is circling around it, his nose to the ground—on the trail of whoever did this. All four tires have been slashed. I run toward it, but Sergeant Shockey grabs my arm.

"Stay away from the vehicle, Wil. He may have wired it. He targeted your Jeep. He hasn't touched mine. Call the dog. This guy isn't playing!"

"Stu, come... STU, COME!" I shout. The dog, with nose low and tail high, races toward the warehouse. He's not turning back.

Sergeant Shockey is on his phone. "Wil, stay close." His voice tells me that we're now the 'the hunted' instead of the hunters. We follow Stu's path toward the towering walls of the warehouse.

Stu is growling. Sergeant Shockey shines his light in the direction of the commotion. Stu's teeth are bared. I see the flash of silver.

"Dodge ball, Stu," I shout. "DODGE BALL." Stu moves to the right, and then left—as the knife blade lunges forward. "DODGE BALL," my voice is wild. Sergeant Shockey is holding me back as I struggle to get free.

"Wil, stay back." He draws his gun. "Drop the weapon," he yells. "Drop it now."

Stu is making wide circles around the guy, closing in. The madman actually has a smile on his face. He's watching the dog, knife raised—. The sound of sirens grows louder—moves closer. A light comes in from the far side of us. The guy startles and Stu jumps him, knocking him to the ground. The knife comes up—Stu yelps.

"Drop the weapon," Sergeant Shockey commands. I'm breathless, running to keep up with him.

Stu has the psycho pinned on the ground. His mouth wrapped around the guy's arm that holds the knife, shaking it violently until the knife falls to the ground. The maniac is pulling the dog's ear, trying to break free.

Sergeant Shockey runs in and grabs the knife off the ground. "Freeze," he tells the freak. "Okay, Stu, steady," he says, in a calm voice. "Come on, boy, I've got him now. Steady, Stu. You're a good dog. It's okay." Stu backs off.

"Don't move!" he tells the psycho. "Roll over and put your hands behind your back." A second cop appears, and both police officers are on the crazy person now.

"Stu, come," I shout. Stu runs toward me. Sirens are close. Police cars line the parking lot, lights flashing. The area is flooded with light.

I drop down to hug Stu as he sits near my feet. His fur is wet. I lift my arm and stare into my bloody hand. "Stu's hurt," I shout. I press my hand against the wound on Stu's neck. Detective Cooper is on the ground with me now.

"He'll be okay, Wil. I've called for help." Stu flops on his side now. Detective Cooper puts her hand on mine as we try to stop the bleeding.

23
Star

Sometimes it is hard to believe what you see with your very own eyes, but the images are right there on the Fletchers' big, flat screen TV. The room's darkened, and light from the TV decorates the walls with moving shadows.

Mrs. Fletcher holds tight to Wils. Grandma's head is bowed, and if I watch closely, I can see her lips moving. I know that she's praying.

Bridgett is pacing in circles. I'm almost dizzy watching her from my place on the window seat. Mr. Fletcher and Sean left the house as soon as images of the old warehouse filled the screen, its windows reflecting the lights of the dozen police cars called to the scene. Wil's Jeep, tires slashed, is parked in the old parking lot, its wrecked pavement heaving out of the ground in places.

The newscaster is clearly excited, pumped up on details of a big story that never happens in a place like this. He describes every bit of action like it's part of a sports event:

"The suspect, Curtis Gray—you see him there in handcuffs—is being taken to a local hospital to be treated for multiple dog-bite wounds.

"Rick, can you get us a picture of the young man who hasn't yet been identified by police? Here he is, being led to a police cruiser. The dog in his arms looks almost lifeless. We have no word on what happened to the animal, or its condition. We have not been told what part, if any, this young man had in the apprehension of this suspect, a man who has been eluding police for months, possibly even years.

"This crime scene is extensive. You can see how much of the area around the gully has been roped off with police tape.

"We're told that the police are investigating a hidden cave they were led to by the dog you just saw being rushed away in the police cruiser. It appears to be a cave that local officials closed off years ago to keep children out of danger."

I know the words by heart. We've been watching the same footage over and over, as the newsperson breaks from live, on-the-scene coverage that's producing no new information. And yet, they stay right there on the scene, hoping for an even bigger scoop.

I guess it's true that a person can become desensitized. I feel numb as I watch, twisting my hair like a security blanket. I know this is real, but it's not what's happening now. I know that Wil is safe with Detective Cooper. I talked to Detective Cooper myself.

I know that Wil's father and Sean are on their way to the veterinarian clinic to be with Wil. Stu has been stitched and is being held for observation. Detective Cooper said that the knife wound was superficial, and although Stu lost a lot of blood, he's expected to make a full recovery.

"Star," Mrs. Fletcher's whispers, standing over me, "Wils has finished his bottle and is asleep. I'm going to put him down in his crib. I've encouraged your grandmother to get some sleep. How about you? Are you ready for bed?"

The guilty tears I've been holding back break loose, and I cover my face with my hands. This woman, holding my child, knows that her child put himself in danger because of me.

"I'm sorry, Mrs. Fletcher."

Mrs. Fletcher sits down and slips her arm around me.

"Star, honey, none of this is your fault. It'll be okay. That horrible man's been caught. He's in police custody now. He can't hurt you anymore."

"But Wil."

"Wil is safe. Detective Cooper has been wonderful about keeping us informed. Why not try to get some rest?"

"I want to watch for a little while longer. But I won't be able to hear Wil from here."

"You're okay out here. I'll turn the monitor on for you."

My grandmother gets up from the sofa and comes toward us. I see sadness and guilt in her eyes. *How much did you know, Grandma? How much have you kept from me over the years? What secrets are you still keeping?* Her lips brush my cheek; she squeezes my hand.

"You'll be okay now," my grandmother tells me. She follows Mrs. Fletcher into our wing of the house built for

Wil's grandparents. This addition to the Fletchers' house is bigger than the whole house I grew up in.

"Are you okay, Star?" Bridgett asks. She's sitting on the floor now—her upper body folded over her legs, her hands stretching out over her toes.

"Exercise helps. Take a swim with me."

"But what if Wils wakes up?"

"Believe me when I tell you that my mother will not go to bed until Wil is back in this house. She'll hear the baby if he cries. Really, Star. Go get into your suit."

"But I should take care of my own baby."

"Star, you've been taking care of your baby by yourself for months now. My parents are trying to make that up to you. Your grandmother's told them how attentive and loving you are with Wils. Come on, we need to get out of here for a little while. It'll make us both feel better." Bridgett gets up. "I'm going to put my suit on. I hope you'll join me."

It's my *job* to be attentive and loving to Wils. He's my baby. I stare out the window. Moonlight floats on the pool water, paints the patio chairs bright white.

Wil told me that his mother plants a moon garden every summer. I see it out in the middle of the backyard. The planted circle of white flowers is as round as the moon, and it reflects the moon's light.

I get up and walk through the house, toward the bedroom where my baby sleeps. Curtis Gray has never been in this house. He never sat on the sofa in the living room, or drank coffee out of a mug in the kitchen. He's never stood over a bed in this house, eager to inflict his evil on an un-suspecting child. This house is safe.

I've spent so much time bleaching dishes and cups and sheets—trying so hard to get that man out of the house that I shared with Grandma and Wil.

I dug a deep hole in the backyard behind the shed, the morning after he came into my room the first time. I had to stand my skinny eleven-year-old body on the shovel and force it to rip through the sod. I still clamp my teeth to-gether every time I think of tearing through the grass and dirt and rocks and pebbles. I unearthed earthworms and ants and other creatures hard at work in the soil. I locked rocks into my fists and pounded them together until my arms ached and my fingers were raw. I smeared dirt on my face and on my arms and legs.

When I refilled the hole, the dirt didn't fit the same way. There was just too much of it. I stood on top of that spot and jumped up and down, trying to force the dirt back in the space it had fit in so well before being disturbed.

Every time it happened, I went back to that hole and dug. Each time it got a little easier to manipulate the dirt. Soon I was digging with just my bare hands. And each time, depending on the phase of the moon, the dirt fit differently when I refilled the hole. Sometimes there was too much dirt, and sometimes not enough to fill that same space.

After my grandmother threw him out, I planted my feet in the soil and closed my eyes. The sun was on my face, and the breeze blew through my hair. I held my arms out and swayed back and forth. When I looked up, all I saw were blue skies, but when I looked down I saw the scar I had created on an otherwise green lawn.

Over the years I tried to plant flowers and tree seedlings there, but nothing grew—it remains a scarred piece of earth: A constant reminder that I will never heal.

Mrs. Fletcher is on the living room sofa. "I'm sorry, Star. I just lay down for a few minutes."

"No, stay there. This is your house."

"Well, it's your space right now. I just wanted to be close to the baby."

"Really, please stay. Bridgett wants me to take a swim with her. Do you think it would be okay? Are you too tired? Are you going to bed? Are you...?"

"Star, go swim with Bridgett—unless you don't really want to and my daughter has pressured you into it. Not everyone wants to swim at this hour of the morning. But if you do, there are beach towels in the hall linen closet."

"Are you sure it's okay?"

"Absolutely. Go put your suit on."

I tiptoe into my room and check on Wils. He has his little hand under his chin. I dig my swimsuit out of the suitcase, tug off my clothes and slip into my green one-piece.

When I come out, Mrs. Fletcher's eyes are closed, so I slip past her and peek in on my grandmother. She's fallen asleep on her back with her rosary beads in her hands. I take the rosary and put it on the nightstand. She rolls over on her side.

Bridgett's already swimming laps in the pool. Pool lights shine through the water. I wait until she's on the shallow end and dive in. I feel her swim by me, mid-pool, as we swim laps in opposite directions. My body adjusts to the coolness of the water and the night air.

The smell of chlorine mingles with the strong scent of honeysuckle. I use every inch of my body: I reach and stretch my arms and kick my legs. Long before I found running, I wanted to be an Olympic swimmer, standing on the podium with medals around my neck.

I continue to swim long after I'm no longer meeting Bridgett halfway through laps. I pull myself out of the water by holding the handrail over the steps in the shallow end of the pool. I feel exhausted but strong, as I sit on the top step.

I look up just in time to see Wil and Sean dive in off the deep end and swim toward me. Sean makes the turn and swims toward the other end. Wil sits on the top step on the other side of the handrail. Bridgett has wrapped herself in a beach towel and is huddled in a lounge chair.

"Star."

My name hangs out there in the darkness. Wil looks up at the sky. I follow his gaze, away from the moon and into the stars. I make a wish that my voice will work.

"Wil, I was so scared. Are you okay? How's Stu?"

"Stu's okay. He can come home tomorrow. I'm okay, too. They wouldn't let me stay any longer at the clinic tonight. Stu's sedated, so maybe he's not so scared."

"I am so sorry. I shouldn't have told you anything. I never thought you'd go out there by yourself."

"I wish you'd told me a long time ago. I wish I'd told you some stuff, too, Star. I should have asked more questions. I should never have let my stupid pride get in the way. I acted like a jerk. I'm really sorry. Maybe we should promise to tell each other stuff from now on."

"I'm not sure I understand, Wil."

"When the baby came in May, I convinced myself he wasn't mine. I knew you'd been with someone else, and I thought you cheated. I should have trusted you, Star. And I'm sorry about the abortion clinic. It was so wrong. If you're pregnant now, I won't ask you to do that again. I promise."

I turn away from his words. From the memory of Curtis Gray ripping my clothes. I wasn't *with* that man. He had a knife. He used my body, but I floated high above him. I floated high above my bedroom—and high above that gully.

My teeth are chattering. I wade out into water deep enough so I can stand with my body submerged and out of the cool night air.

Hearing the words from Wil's mouth—just knowing he knows what that man did—but he doesn't know. Not really. How could he know how violent the man was? But he does know. He saw Curtis Gray stab his dog.

What have I done to Wil?

Now Wil wades out and whispers in my ear. "I'm sorry, Star. I'm making this worse, I know. I don't know how to talk to you about any of it."

"I'm not pregnant, Wil." It's all I can think of to say. Something about us—something he wants to hear.

His eyes close. "Are you sure?"

I'm sure, but I can't tell him about my period starting, or about the cramps. Here I've had a baby with this boy, but I can't talk about my period—I'm just too embarrassed.

"Wil, I'm sure."

I reach up and touch his shoulder. Wil wraps his arms around me. The water moves around us, still in motion from swimmers doing laps. We stand strong together—unmoved by the waves. Quiet with our own thoughts.

I feel his body against mine, but it's not real. It won't last. My mother is gone. My father never had a face. My grandmother is ill. My Uncle Gregory left here and never looked back—not really.

My baby would be better off with the Fletchers. I love him, but they can give him a good life. They can keep him safe from the Curtis Grays of the world. He was led away in handcuffs, but how many more pedophiles are still out there? How many rapists?

I slip out of Wil's arms and under the water. It would be so easy, just to let my lungs fill with water and float away.

I watch my arms move through the water as I sink to the bottom of the pool. It's like I'm conducting an orchestra. Diamonds of light move through the water as I look up toward the surface.

All the nightmares I've had about falling, floating. Maybe this is where the nightmare ends. I'm dizzy, but have no desire to breathe. It's too hard—all of it. Besides, how many times can a person start over? And, how can I start over when I don't even know where to start?

Wil is beside me underwater now, fear in his eyes. I try to breathe air, but all there is is water. I gulp—the water chokes me. Then I feel water rush by my face as we surface together. I'm coughing and choking up water as Wil carries me out of the pool. Bridgett brings towels and Wil wraps them around me.

"Wil, what happened? What was Star doing?"

"Go, Bridgett. Sean, can you get her out of here?"

Wil lies on the ground next to me and pulls me close. His hand moves in a circular movement over the towel on my back, warming me.

"I know what you were trying to do, Star. I know. I wanted to plow my Jeep into a tree. That fool wanted me dead, but he slashed my tires and stopped me from killing myself.

"But, Star, don't you see? We're nothing like him. I saw the evil in his eyes. I saw the violence spill out of him. We're nothing like him.

"We're in this together. I'm not going to leave you. Whatever you want from me—that's what I'll be. We have to make this right for Wils. But I can't do it alone, Star. And I'm so sorry that I let you do it alone for so long. I know you're tired, but it will get better."

I turn away from Wil and curl into a ball. He curls around me and holds on tight. I can see the very tops of the flowers in the moon garden as they reach for the stars.

24
Wilson

Star's grandmother freaked out when she found us asleep together, out near the pool this morning—despite the fact Star was wrapped like a mummy in beach towels. Besides, the last thing either of us had on our minds was sex. But there's no way Mrs. Peters would ever believe that. It's just one more strike against me in that woman's mind.

She must have apologized to my parents fifty times for Star's behavior. That's what freaks me out. Does the woman not know how fragile Star is right now? Even I know, and I'm a stupid, clueless idiot—a big dumb kid.

My parents took it all really well—all of it. I think they're just grateful that the car tires got slashed and not me.

I'm going to pick Stu up this afternoon. Mom said I could drive her car. She's taken a leave of absence from work. Apparently Bridgett and Sean talked to my parents about what they think happened in the pool, but there hasn't been much time to dwell on any of it.

There was quite an assortment of people at the breakfast table. Dad and Sean cooked. Sean spent the night on the couch. We have this abstinence rule at our house—unless your married, you're not sleeping together, engaged or not.

Dad insisted that Detective Cooper spend the night, so she had the guest room. Dad didn't want her to go back to Star's place so late alone. The woman has a gun, but she doesn't seem all that intimidating. I'm not sure she could shoot someone if her life depended on it. Maybe if someone else's life depended on it. But, hey, who am I to judge people? I am clueless about how people feel.

Phones have been ringing all morning long: house phones, office phones, cell phones. Everyone wants to know about Stu. He's famous. *Hey, people, the dog didn't drive himself to that creep's hideout. Give me a little credit here.*

My mother got Star away from Mrs. Peters—and into a hot shower pretty early on. Mom sat and talked to Star for a long time on the patio before they came in to breakfast. I watched them from the family room window. They passed Wils back and forth. Star twisted her hair. Mom talked with her hands.

My parents are both pretty cool with Star. It's funny. They haven't always been cool with the girls I've brought home. Not that there's been that many girls. None serious.

I felt better after a hot shower, too. Sleeping on cement can't be good for your body. But I slept. I was exhausted, I know, but still. There was just no place else I wanted to be but with Star—even on cement. I was so afraid for her.

I sat next to her at breakfast, but she wouldn't look at me. I don't know what will ever make it right between us.

Mrs. Peters and Detective Cooper took Star into Dad's office after breakfast and closed the door.

They've been in there a long time. I hope they know what they're doing. I don't think Star can take much more.

I grabbed up the baby after breakfast. I changed his diaper. It was no big deal. Of course, it was only wet. I can see how it could be potentially lethal, though. I mean, there could be serious consequences if that kid takes a whiz while I'm trying to figure out where to fasten those sticky tabs on his diaper.

Dad bought this snuggly carrier thing that I can wear to carry Wils on my chest. It's pretty cool. Then my hands are free to play lacrosse, or sack a quarterback. *Just kidding.*

Wils fell asleep about two minutes into our walk in the yard. He sleeps a lot now. My mother said that's a sign of a contented baby. My father says he's just trying to get out of mowing the lawn. It's a family joke that I don't find especially amusing.

I pull my fingernail out of my mouth and rub the baby's back instead. The pool water is crystal clear. Okay, I know it's a cliché, but sometimes only a cliché will do. It's funny how something that is so beautiful can also be so dangerous. I've spent my childhood in this pool. I feel so safe swimming. My parents preach safety. I never once thought about drowning. But it happens. Parents turn their backs; kids wander away and later they're found face down.

I can't get the image out of my mind of Star's eyes when we were underwater. She looked so totally lost.

Right now, this minute, I'm okay with being a father.

I am. But then, when I think about the next twenty years, I'm scared. It's kind of like taking a test, you know? You have to give up TV for the evening to study. Maybe you don't answer your phone because you don't have time to talk and study at the same time. Sometimes you even miss some sleep studying. The thing is, you take the test and it's over with. You get to go on with your life until the next test. Well, having a baby is like prepping for a never-ending test.

"Wil, Star needs you." Bridgett dabs at her nose with a tissue. Her eyes are red and puffy.

"Bridgett, have you been crying?" I hate it when Bridgett cries. It makes me feel all out of control.

"No. Yes. I'm so mad. Star needs you. Take her out, Wil, take her away from here."

"Did Star say she needs me?"

"No, but trust me she does. I know you've done some stupid stuff, but the rest of those people—you're her best bet."

"Hey, way to flatter a guy."

"Sorry. Here, give me Wils. I'm not going to work. What's Dad going to do, fire me?"

"Yeah, he can fire you. He's the boss."

"Who cares? I'm going back to school soon."

Is this really my sister? Did she forget Dad also pays her tuition?

Bridgett pulls Wils out of the snuggly thing and puts him over her shoulder. "I love this little guy," she says.

"Where's Star?"

"The last time I saw her, she was walking toward Elizabeth's house." *Oh, that's just great! I need to find her be-*

fore she gets to the Andersons' and I have both of them to deal with. My mother's waiting inside the patio doors with her car keys.

"Wil, take your phone. If you need anything, call me. Where's my baby?"

"Wils is not your baby, Mom, and Bridgett has him."

"Well, he's more my baby than Bridgett's baby." *Is there not one sane person left on this planet?*

I get into my mother's car and push the seat back from the steering wheel. *How can the woman drive like that?* I also lower it to get my head away from the ceiling. *Why does this car always smell like cinnamon? It's gross.*

Detective Cooper said she has no idea when the police will let me have my Jeep back. It's evidence. I am so ticked-off.

I pull up beside Star. She takes one look at the car and starts to run. *What the hell?*

I get out of the car and call to her. She stops when she hears my voice. She turns around and comes charging at me. I think that she's going to attack, but she throws herself in my arms. Then, before I can hold onto her, she pushes me away.

"You scared me. I didn't know the car. I thought it was him."

"Star, he's in jail. Remember?"

"He's smart. He'll get out."

"He's not getting out. Come on. Get in the car."

"Where are we going, Wil?"

"Does it matter?"

"Where's my baby?"

"Being stalked by his grandmother."

"Wil, that's not funny."

"I'm sorry. Bridgett had him, but my mother was in hot pursuit. He's in good hands either way, Star." I open the car door. Star crawls in and curls into a ball on the front seat. I get in and put my seat belt on. I tell Star to do the same.

"No," she tells me.

"Star, come on. I can get fined if you don't have your seat belt on."

"So I'll give you the money. Just drive, Wil." Star's twisting her hair. I take her hand and chew on her nail.

"Okay, I'll stop," she says. She locks her hands between her knees. Her eyes are closed.

"Guess what, Wil."

"What?" I wait, but Star doesn't say anything.

"Star?" I put my hand on her shoulder and she laces her fingers through mine. We drive in silence. The tires hum on the road. Star cries quietly. I'm sure to go mad listening. *How can I help? She won't let me help?*

I pull into the parking lot at City Park and open a window. Star sits up when she hears the geese on the lake. She gets out of the car. I put the window up and turn off the motor. I climb out of the car and go to Star.

"Tell me," I say, taking her hand again. "You can tell me, remember? We're telling each other stuff now."

Star has this question-mark look on her face. "Who decided that?"

"We did. Last night. Don't try to pretend you don't remember." She looks suspicious, but face it, I'm good.

"I have a—," she says, pulling me toward the lake and onto the path that leads to our bench. I almost trip over her when she stops suddenly and turns to me. "A father. I have a father."

"Everyone has a father." I get whiplash as Star takes off again, gripping my hand.

"Well, not me. Not according to my grandmother. The story was that he was a no-good, worthless man who left my mother and me and never looked back. Having a father like that is like having no father at all. That was the old story." She takes a breath.

"The new story is that he never knew about me, and still doesn't. His family moved to New York, and my mother never told him she was pregnant. He went off to college, then joined the service, and he's a decorated officer in the Navy. He's stationed in Norfolk, Virginia." She shrugs.

"Oh, and Wil, get this—he's married and has three sons. Doesn't that sound like the good life?"

I step closer and reach for her.

"Don't!" she says. "Don't put your arms around me. Don't try to comfort me when all I need is to be furious and cry."

I take a deep breath and hold it. I want to tell Star that it's okay if she cries, but it's not. I hate it. I'm having trouble with my mouth: It won't work. So I just stand there and suck in air, like I don't have a brain in my head.

Star stares at me—holds out her upturned palms in front of her, like she's holding cantaloupes.

"We're telling each other stuff, right?" she asks, bunching her hands into fists.

Technically, yeah, but please stop crying.

She wipes her nose with the back of her hand. Now would definitely be a good time to be carrying a handkerchief.

"And listen to this. It's no coincidence that Detective Cooper was assigned to this case." Star takes a deep breath. "She's been interested in my mother's disappearance since she first heard about it in one of her law classes. She's been following the case since she joined the police force in Baltimore. She was so interested in the case because she grew up here, and her brother dated my mother."

"Star."

"No, wait! I know you already figured out that she's my aunt, but you have to hear this—"

She's your aunt? Are you kidding me? No wonder she looks like your twin.

"My grandmother has talked to her several times on the phone over the years about my mother's disappearance. But, her name is Cooper not Clancy, because she's married. Grandma never figured it out." She huffs out a breath.

"Detective Cooper knew that my mother had a child. But she didn't figure out that I was her niece until she was assigned to the case undercover. Officer Lance called her in as soon as he saw me. He thought they could use her resemblance to me to lure Curtis Gray in. She was in the area because they were closing in on him."

I sit down on the bench I've been dragged to at approximately forty miles an hour. I cover my eyes with my hands. Why not? I'm not allowed to hold and comfort Star while she's furious and needs to cry, and I need to do something with my hands.

Why is she not exhausted? I'm exhausted, and this story isn't even about me. I've also had enough exercise for one day, but apparently Star's just getting started.

She kicks at a tree stump and paces in circles around the bench. I know this because I'm peeking between my fingers. That's how I also know that Goth-boy has come to the rescue and has his arms around Star. Well, one arm at least. The other is holding his baby.

And he doesn't look like Goth-boy, either. He's wearing a blue shirt and khaki shorts. I haven't seen Todd's knees for years. Not that I care about Todd's knees. It's just that he went Goth after his mother died, and that's when he stopped playing sports. Or maybe he went Goth when he met the Goth-girl.

So what's with the new look? Is it Star?

Now I'm really ticked-off. Star has yet to push him away like she did with me. I stand up to deck the guy.

"Give me the baby." Did I say that? "Seriously, Todd, Star seems to need you more than she needs me. Let me hold Nevaeh."

See, I even remembered the kid's name. She comes right to me. She smells like such a girl, too. All sweet, like lilacs or something.

"Come on, Nevaeh. Let's let your creepy father work his magic on Star. Do you like it when I whisper? Hey, if he can make her stop crying, I'm all for it. We'll give them some privacy. Well, at least we'll make it look like we're giving them some privacy. You are such an agreeable baby! I like you. Do you know that?" I smiled and went on.

"Look, she may be letting Goth-boy hold her, but she's not talking to him. She talked to me. I'm not bragging or anything, but she did. *No way, did he just pull out a hand-kerchief? Come on*. Hey, don't you and your dad have anything better to do than hang in the park all day and rescue damsels in distress?"

"Da Da."

"Huh?"

"Dada."

"Did you just say Dada? How old are you? Is Wils talking yet? Have you heard him say anything like Dada?"

"Dada."

"I'm not your Dada—Todd, I hate to interrupt, but Nevaeh's calling you. Hey, look, Nevaeh, they're coming our way."

"Can I hold you, Nevaeh?" Star takes the baby from me and buries her head in her neck. "Come on, we'll go for a little walk. Okay, Todd?"

"Sure. Take your time."

I expect Todd to go after them, but he stands there staring into space.

I take a step.

"Give her a minute, Wil, " he says.

"How much did she tell you?" I ask.

"Nothing," Todd says.

"What's with the two of you?"

"We're friends, Fletcher."

Todd's earrings are gone. His hair is cut and combed.

"What's with the new look, Ryan?"

Todd looks down at his clothes like he can't quite believe it's his body. "Someone convinced me it was better for my baby."

"Star?"

"Her grandmother."

"Really?" I'm curious, but it can wait. "So what's with you and Star?"

"Didn't you just ask me this question? The answer hasn't changed. We're friends."

"I see the way she looks at you. It would take her five minutes to fall in love with you."

"Really, Fletcher? And, how long will it take her to fall out of love with you?"

My throat closes up. *Is there really still a chance?*

"Correct me if I'm wrong, but wasn't she just in your arms?"

"Look, we're friends, Fletcher. And this is yours to blow—or not."

"Haven't I already blown it?"

"Yes, Fletcher, you have. Big time. And you better figure it out fast. Because if I see my chance I'm taking it. Fair enough?"

At this point, I just want Star to be happy. I don't want her to feel desperate enough to sink to the bottom of the pool and have to wonder if she wants to come up for air.

"Fair enough." *It's probably more than I deserve.*

25
Star

Wil was really quiet driving over here. I know he doesn't understand why I have to do this. I'm not sure I understand myself.

Rodney's on his front porch. I open the door and force myself out of the car. I know that Wil is right behind me as I walk up the steps. Rodney's eyes have not left mine. I'm afraid to blink. Is he trying to communicate something to me? His jaw is wired shut, and his right arm is in a sling. This is so much worse than I ever imagined.

"Rodney, I'm so sorry," my voice is shaky. I reach out and touch the cast on his hand.

He nods at me. He picks up a dry whiteboard and writes a message in purple marker with his left hand.

"Im OK. Dont cry." *What's with boys not wanting me to cry? Todd's the only one who gets that tears help.*

"Thank you for what you did. It was very brave."

The marker squeaks across the board. I take the board from Rodney. "That jerk hangin' 'round here. I didn't knock again after u said bout baby wakin up. It was him. Sorry."

"It's okay." I hand Rodney his board, a card, and two CDs that Wil helped me pick out.

Some 'hip hop' that I really don't listen to much.

Rodney writes, "For me to keep? Really?" He tears off the clear wrap on one of the CDs, and fiddles with his CD player.

Music blares. Mrs. Dobson comes out onto the porch and lowers the volume. She looks surprised to see me. She pulls me into a bear hug and holds on tight.

"Star, are you okay?"

"I'm fine, thank you."

"Your grandma, that beautiful baby?"

"Everyone's good."

"Is this that young man that was on the news?" She rushes over and shakes Wil's hand. "You're a hero. The police said that without your persistence, they wouldn't have found that Gray guy's hideout."

Wil looks down at the floor and shuffles his feet. "It wasn't like that. It was my dog, actually."

"They said that, too—the dog. Both of you are heroes."

"Well, Rodney's a hero himself, Mrs. Dobson," I say.

"He can be a good boy when he wants to be," she says, with a giant smile on her face. "Time for your medicine, Rodney."

"We'll just go. But we'll stop in again," I say. Rodney is lost in his music. His cheek feels warm and sweaty as I kiss him. He smiles, gives me a thumbs up.

Wil's hand's on my back as I walk down the Dobsons' steps and up the steps to my front porch. I slip the key out of my pocket and into the lock, then step inside. The house is all closed up and it still smells like bacon. It seems like I haven't been here for a very long time.

"Wil, are you coming in?"

"You said you needed some time alone. I'll be in the backyard."

"I'll just be a few minutes. Is it time to pick up Stu?"

"Almost. I'll call and check on Wils again. Take your time."

I walk back to my bedroom. Curtis Gray has always been here, ever since that first night—the night my world changed.

When I started dating Wil, I'd come home so happy. But there was Curtis Gray—standing over my bed, mocking me the minute I closed my eyes. Sometimes in my dreams, I'd hear him in the closet, laughing. He'd find the shoebox of evidence and set it on fire—right before my eyes, the flames blazing through the darkness.

I open the closet door, kick off my sandals, and lie on the bed. I stare into the closet—at my clothes, my books. I get up and reach for the bear Wil won for me at the carnival. I stuffed it head first into a basket in the closet one night after arguing with Wil on the phone. The bear is big and brown and soft, and he's wearing a green bow. I hug him tight. "It wasn't your fault, Willy Bear."

I twist the bear's silky bow through my fingers as I lie on the bed. After Wils was born, I refused to let thoughts of Curtis Gray into this room. It was the only place I had for my baby to sleep. I had to make it a happy place for him.

But I couldn't control what happened in my dreams. I

close my eyes. Somehow I thought it would be different now, with him locked up. But it's not. He's still here in my head. I can taste the latex in my mouth, smell the cigarette smoke on his clothes. I can feel a pain so much worse than labor as he rips my clothes off and tears my insides apart.

I roll over and try to make the pain go away, and the never-ending tears stop. Wil hates my tears. How can I be with someone who hates what I spend my life doing? I pull Todd's handkerchief out of my pocket. It feels cool on my face, soaks up my tears.

Todd knows. He lost his mother. Maureen deserted him and Nevaeh. Todd understands me more than anyone. Of course, he can't understand about the abuse, the rape. He's so gentle.

Wil knew. He knew he wasn't the first. Did that make it okay for him to pressure me? He was gentle and sweet, but that pressured me even more.

I thought he could fix what happened to me by wanting me so much.

"Star? I don't want to bother you. I just wanted you to know that Wils is fine. He's in the pool with my mother. Dad picked up Stu, so there's no hurry. Take as long as you need, okay?"

I want to sit up and look at Wil, but I don't want him to see my tears. I know it's rude to talk to the wall.

"I'm sorry, Wil. I know you wanted to be the one to bring Stu home. You can go home, really. I'll be okay here. Can you send my grandmother back for me later?"

"I'll see Stu later, Star. I'm fine being here with you. I'll go back in the yard and leave you alone."

I close my eyes and picture Wil, not under the shade of the oak tree or sitting at the picnic table, but standing on the bare earth that I dug up over and over.

"What were you doing out there, Wil?"

"Watering a little tree I planted behind the shed."

I shoot up, still hugging my bear. "You planted a tree? When? Are you sure it's still alive?"

"Yes, it's alive. I planted it when I mowed the lawn that day, Star. I was going to mow it again, but Detective Cooper must have done it. The tree looks great. It was thirsty, but very much alive. Actually, it's a weird time for it to bloom, but maybe it got confused when I transplanted it from its place in the alley."

I slide out of bed, dragging my bear with me. I slip on my sandals. "Show me, Wil."

I follow him out the door, through the backyard. There's a robin sitting on the fence post, singing. A toad takes cover in the wet grass clippings piled around a little tree that stands no more than three feet tall. The tree's covered with white blossoms that appear bigger than they should be, considering the size of the tree.

My knees feel weak and I sit on the grass. Wil sits beside me, pulls at the grass.

"This is crazy! Nothing ever grows here. Every time that man touched me, I came out here and dug up the dirt. I thought that if I dug deep enough, I could bury what happened to me and no one would ever know.

"The problem was that I still knew, Wil. I made my grandmother buy flowers and trees from the nursery, but nothing ever grew in this spot. I followed every planting and care instruction for anything I planted. But everything wilted and died. It was the hate, Wil. The hate I buried in the dirt. It sucked the life out of everything.

"How could this little tree grow in this toxic soil?" I watch Wil's face. His eyes are so clear. He looks so sure.

"It's not so much the soil as the plant. This is not some hothouse tree, Star. This tree grew wild just a few feet from where it's planted now. Some bird probably dropped a seed and it grew, or maybe the wind planted it. It didn't wait for someone to water or fertilize it. It took to the soil the bird or wind chose for it. It took whatever rain fell on it." He takes a breath.

"When I transplanted it, it already knew how to survive. It put out roots that are willing to grow around pebbles and rocks, and maybe even around hate. The tree just wants to live. Dogwoods don't look very tough, but they are.

"It's just like you, Star. You look so fragile, but I've always known that you're stronger than me. What I didn't know is what you had to go through, to become such a strong person. It's not fair for anyone to have to go through all the things that you've had to put up with. I'm so sorry for what I've done. I'm really, really sorry, Star."

I lay on the grass using Willy Bear as my pillow. The robin is now dancing around in the spray of mist created by a small hole in the garden hose. Wil stretches out beside me. He rolls over on his side and props his head on his hand.

"Most of all, Star, I'm sorry that I resented how strong you are, instead of appreciating it."

"How could you think I'm strong when I cry all the time? You hate my crying."

"I don't hate your crying. I hate that I can't make it better. It makes me feel so weak. The times that you cried when we'd been together, I just thought I did it wrong, or that maybe you were missing someone else. I had no idea what had happened to you. All I wanted was to get it right, and I was just making it worse."

"This is a really weird place to hide out, you two." Detective Cooper is standing over us. "I didn't want to leave town without saying goodbye. Can you come inside for a few minutes?"

Wil is already on his feet and pulls me to mine.

"It's kind of nice out here right now, Detective Cooper. It almost feels like it did when I was little. No sirens. No one shouting obscenities."

"Well, that's what a heavy police presence will do for a place. Hopefully, it'll last for a while." Detective Cooper waits for Wil in the mudroom as he turns off the hose and rolls it up. She locks the back door as soon as he's inside.

"Wil, can Star and I talk privately? I'll drop her back at your house in a little while."

"That's okay. I've told Wil most everything," I say.

"Here or the living room," she asks, pointing to the kitchen table.

"Living room," I lead them through the kitchen doorway and sit on the sofa. Wil sits beside me and Detective Cooper sits in the rocker. She leans back in the chair and takes a deep breath.

"Okay, first of all, Wil, thank you. Stu is doing great and you were both amazing, leading us to Curtis Gray. Having said that, please don't put yourself or your dog in danger like that again. Neither of you might survive next time."

I think that I'm all cried out, but I'm not. I haven't even thanked Wil for what he's done because I feel guilty and angry with myself for putting him in danger. The tears flow and my whole body shakes with sobs. I gesture at both of them to stay away.

"Detective Cooper, she just stopped crying and you had to go bring it all up again."

"I'm sorry, Wil. Listen, Star. It's over. You both helped put that man behind bars. Star, your detailed evidence will keep him there for a very long time. And Wil, the evidence we're gathering from the cave will keep him in jail until the day he dies."

I drag out Todd's handkerchief and wipe away my tears. I cradle Willy Bear in my arms as if I'm holding Wils.

"Do you know anything about my mother?" I ask her.

"Star, I really believe that your mother would have come back to you if she could have. I believe your grandmother knows that, too. Evidence from the cave may support that theory. We'll know very soon."

"Then why did my grandmother think it'd be easier for me to believe that my mother didn't love me enough to stay here and be my mother? Why did she keep telling me my parents left me?"

"Maybe your grandmother thought it would be easier for you to believe that your mother would come back someday than think about the alternative. She's seeing things so differently now that she's facing this surgery. Star, she's going to a wonderful hospital. I really believe that she'll be fine. Are you okay?"

"You tell me. Do I have a choice? Everything else has been decided for me, so why should I get to decide if I'll be okay or not?"

"I guess I had that coming."

"But it's not just you. It's my grandmother and it's Mr. and Mrs. Fletcher. You all made it sound like my life had been decided for me. No one bothered to ask me what *I* wanted. And, why should my father not know about me until I'm ready to meet him—haven't there been enough secrets already?"

"We were wrong, Star. We thought it would be easier for you not to face too many more decisions right now. As for my part of it, for suggesting we not tell your father about you until you were ready to meet him, I'm sorry. I just had a two-hour conversation on the phone with Ted—your father.

"He let me know that it would have been an unfair burden on you—knowing you were keeping something from him. Your grandmother has his phone number now and he's coming in this weekend to speak with her and to meet you. He'll stay through the surgery if you'd like. He also said that you and Wils always would have a home with him if you need it." She paused and took a deep breath.

"And I'm hoping that you and I can have a relationship as well. You're my only niece, and I'd like to get to know you. May I call you?"

"I'd like that, Detective Cooper."

"Please call me Jen."

"Is that your real name, or just one you like?" Wil asks, rubbing his hands together.

"Wil, you're such a goof-ball."

"Well, someone has to lighten up this conversation."

"You two should head home soon. And I have to get on the road, too."

"I *am* home, Aunt Jen."

Detective Cooper—my aunt—crosses the room and sits beside me on the sofa. She hugs me.

"You and the baby can't stay here alone. Your grandmother doesn't even want to come back here, after knowing more about what happened to you here. That's why she's going to stay with her sister in Pennsylvania after the surgery. She needs that time to recuperate. The Fletchers want you and Wils with them. Your grandmother didn't ask them—they offered. They're good people, Star."

"I know they're good people, but I can't stay there." Wil gets up and stands in the kitchen doorway. He is looking around the room like he's lost.

"Do you want to stay with Richard and me, or with your father and his family?"

"No offense, but you're all strangers. I know my great aunt in Pennsylvania is older, but Wils and I wouldn't be any trouble."

"But Star, she just doesn't have room for all of you. And you have a wonderful option in the Fletchers. Besides, you'll be going back to school soon. Right? I'll call you this evening, okay?"

I nod my head and walk Aunt Jen to the door. She hugs

me again. Willy Bear is squeezed between us. I put him over my shoulder and pat him. I'm missing Wils.

"What's so bad about my parents?" Wil asks. He's leaning against the kitchen doorway.

I close my eyes, but he's still there, in his blue-and-white Valley football t-shirt and denim cut-offs.

I open my eyes and look at him. His brown hair is almost blonde from the sun. His dark eyes are very sad. "Your parents are wonderful, Wil."

"But?"

"But, Wils doesn't need me there. Maybe that's what they want me to see, so I'll just leave him with them and go away."

"Oh no, don't put that on my parents. They know how important you are to Wils."

"And why is that, Wil? Why am I so important to Wils?"

"Because you loved him first, Star. You're his mother and you kept him safe. When I wanted him to be part of some Dumpster tossed salad, you turned your back on me and walked away. Don't ever say you're not important to Wils. Nobody else believes that. Hey, I understand if you don't want me around. I can come and stay here, in this house."

I grab a fist full of hair and twist it through my fingers. It makes my words come easier.

"I can't put you out of your own house. You have every right to be there. To bring your girlfriend there."

"Oh—that's what this is about?" Wil rubs his eyes and drags his hands through his hair. "Star, I went out with Cate a couple of times. The only time I'm ever going to see her again is to apologize. She initiated it, but I did something that probably led her to believe I was interested. I'm not.

"Listen, if there is one thing I figured out through all this, it's that I love you. I kept coming back, Star. It wasn't about sex, and it wasn't because I wanted to prove that I'm a man. It was because I couldn't stay away from you, even if I wanted to.

"So if you're worried about me bringing girls home while you're there, forget it. I know I've blown it with you probably forever, but I have a lot of things to figure out about myself before I can get involved with anyone.

"I want you and Wils at our place, Star. I know it is the best place for both of you right now. Hey, it won't be so peachy for me to see you with Todd, but, I'll suck it up."

"Todd's my friend."

"So I've heard."

"You sound angry."

"I'm not angry, I'm jealous. He has a clean slate and I'm not even on the board."

"Wil, I'm sorry."

"What are you sorry about? I did this to myself. I'll figure it out. Let's go home. You need to show me some stuff about Wils. Like, can't we use the power washer when he smells like a toxic waste dump? And isn't a swim in the pool as good as a bath? Hey, when can he just start eating fast food?"

"The power washer idea has merit, but we both know it's out of the question. Wils loves his bath. And no teeth, no fast food. I'll put Willy Bear back in the closet and we can go."

My closet door is still wide open. I go right for the shelf with books and pull out a worn copy of *This Room is Mine*. I know the book by heart. It's about two sisters named Chris and Mary who use a jump rope to divide their room in half because they're not so great at sharing. One problem that seems insurmountable is that one sister no longer has access to the door, so she can't leave her room. She decides to pretend her closet is an elevator that transports them both away from the boundaries she's set. And even though they're in the very same place when they emerge from the elevator, their problems seem to have vanished.

When I was a little kid, I believed I could step into my closet, close the door, and like these clever sisters—step out into a problem-free world. But that was before Curtis Gray. Now my life's divided into the before and after of him. I process everything differently now. Everything. Nothing feels new. Nothing feels safe. I'll always be on this side of what happened with Curtis Gray.

I want so much to believe that it can be different for me now. I look at the familiar, whimsical cover of this little book. I step inside my closet and close the door. It's dark, hot, and stuffy. I take a deep breath and stand perfectly still.

I'm alone. I have my hand on the doorknob. I can choose who I want to let into my life. I can decide whether I want to move forward, or stand still and let the past continue to drive me. I decide that not even Willy Bear should have to spend another minute in here. I brace myself, hesitate as I turn the knob—and then fling open the door.

I expect to find everything the way I left it. But things have changed. Stu is sitting on my bed smiling at me. His hair is shaved from his back at the mid-collar line down around his neck and under his chin. There are more stitches than I even want to think about.

Wil's standing in the doorway, grinning at me.

"I don't even want to know what you were doing in there, Star," he says, with this smirk on his face. I bite my lip.

"I was looking for a book, and the door accidentally closed."

"You are such a bad liar," he says.

I hold up the book as proof and lay Willy Bear on my bed.

"Chris and Mary are such dorks," he tells me. We're both petting Stu, who has rolled on his back with his feet in the air. His eyes are closed and he has that look of doggie ecstasy.

"You know this book?"

"If you tell anyone, I'll just deny it. My mother read that book to Bridgett and me every time we wouldn't share. How'd the closet trick work out for you this time?"

"Very funny, Wil. Where did Stu come from, anyway?"

"Dad said Stu couldn't wait to see me, but he ran right past me and came in here looking for you. He found you, too, didn't he? Reliving your glory days with Chris and Mary."

I try to ram Wil with my shoulder, but he puts his arms around me.

"Mom's here, too," he whispers in my ear. I take a deep breath, toss the book on the bed and slip my arms around his neck. He holds me tighter.

"The baby missed you, too. Mom and Dad said no one could console him, so they put him in the car and came over. Star, you loved him first, and he loved *you* first, too. Don't ever forget that, okay?"

I lean into Wil and pluck at his t-shirt. "I would have come up on my own, Wil. You know. In the pool." I take a long, calming breath.

"And thank you for rescuing me from Curtis Gray. I can't ever repay you for what you did, for helping the police find him." I look into his eyes now

"But—about the pool, I wouldn't do it. I'd never leave Wils."

Wil kisses my cheek, saying, "I won't ever leave him, either. Whatever else happens, I'll try to be a good father." Wil lowers his head, looks at me, "Do you think we can be friends?"

I swallow, nod, "Friends."

Wil holds my hand as we walk into the living room. Wils's in his car seat. I feel shaky inside as I look at Mr. and Mrs. Fletcher, but they're smiling at me. "Sorry, Star," Mrs. Fletcher says. "There are times when only Mommy will do."

I sit beside the car seat on the floor. Wils is still making little gasping noises that babies make in their sleep after they cried for a long time. He's dressed in a new blue-and-white outfit with a red boat sailing across his chest.

I unbuckle him and lift him from the car seat. His clothing feels soft as I snuggle my face into him. He smells like lavender. I get up and go to the rocker. Stu sits at my feet as I settle in with my baby.

"Hey, Mom and Dad, come see this little volunteer dogwood I planted in the backyard. It's blooming now. Crazy, huh?" Wil winks at me and ushers his parents out the back door.

I lean back in the rocker, and pat the baby's back. I close my eyes.

I'm back in the closet and it's a moving elevator.

Wherever it stops, I'll emerge holding my baby.

Author's Note

Star and Wil are fictional characters. But, all too often the heartbreak that they experienced within the pages of *Star in the Middle* plays out in real life. If you find that you are experiencing a difficult situation, there are people and resources available to help you.

While Star never called the police, it doesn't mean you can't. If you have been the victim of abuse, telling someone places the blame where it should be, on the predator. If you feel uncomfortable telling someone in your home, tell your school counselor, school nurse, or family doctor.

Acknowledgments

There are so many family members and friends that I would like to acknowledge, but have so little space in which to do that. You know who you are, please know that I love you and appreciate your support.

Many thanks to—
Evelyn Fazio, my publisher, for being so accessible, for sharing her talents, and for giving me this wonderful opportunity to work with her and West-Side Books.

My husband, Joe, for *believing with me*—and for understanding my need to tell this story.

My daughter, Cara, for *sharing my passion* for reading and writing, and for always being eager to read "my next chapter"—and to share her thoughtful insights.

My son, Bryan, for *believing in me*, and for inspiring me with his wonderful sense of humor.

My daughter-in-law, Stephanie, and son-in-law, Bob, for their support, interest, and enthusiasm.

My sister, Nancy, for always being willing to answer the question, "What would Mom think?" and for supporting me unconditionally.

Many thanks most especially to—

My grandchildren, from youngest to oldest: Carol, Bryan, Julie, Alyssa, Olivia, and Trevor, for adding a wonderful dimension to my life that I didn't know was even possible!